INEVITABLE

THE CURSED DUET

LOREN LEE

Author Loren Lee, LLC

Inevitable: Book 1 of the Cursed Duet

Copyright 2025 Author Loren Lee, LLC

Line and Copy Edits: Caroline Palmier (Love and Edits)

Developmental Edits: Stacey LP

Publisher: Author Loren Lee, LLC

Cover Design: Turning Pages Designs

TRIGGER WARNINGS

A full list of trigger warnings for this book are available on my website www.authorlorenlee.com/trigger-warnings for any who are interested. Please protect your mental health.

TRIGGER WARNINGS

A full list of trigger warnings for this book are available on my website www.authorlorenlee.com/trigger-warnings for any who are interested. Please protect your mental health.

DEDICATION

To every woman who has ever tried to redeem a fuckboy.

Don't try this at home.

CONTENTS

PLAYLIST

1. Devil Like Me - Akine
2. The Thief & The Heartbreaker - Alberta Cross, Band of Skulls
3. I Stay Away - Alice in Chains
4. To Let Myself Go - Ane Brun
5. You're So Dark - Arctic Monkeys
6. HUSHH - AViVA
7. Awaken - League of Legends, Valerie Broussard
8. Too Close - AWAY, Midoca, Dark Waves
9. ANYTHING>HUMAN - Bad Omens, ERRA

63. Smells Like Teen Spirit - Tommee Profitt, Fleurie
64. In The End - Mellen Gi Remix - Tommee Profitt, Flueurie, Mellen G
65. A Little Wicked - Valerie Broussard
66. Figure You Out - VOILÁ
67. Apple Blossom - The White Stripes
68. Keep You - Wild Belle
69. Sacrilege - Yeah Yeah Yeahs

SERAFINA - THEN

"*Does he have wings?*"

"Why does he have wings?" I rounded on my companion with an accusatory look.

She shrugged, unconcerned. "I don't know, love. When Dave did this, the guy ended up with a tail. Hey, mate? Do you have a tail?" Felicity cocked a brow in his direction.

We both looked at the newly minted demon-kind in front of us, who was staring back at us balefully.

"What the fuck have you done to me?" he growled before turning in circles in an attempt to determine if we had, in fact, granted him a tail.

"No tail, then," Felicity stated with a wave of her hands in the direction of his backside.

I turned to look at her with wide eyes. "This was supposed to curse him! Why does he have wings?"

She shrugged, rolling her eyes at me. "Not sure, but if I had to give it my best guess, I'd say…balance?"

PART I

THEN

*"Believe nothing that you hear,
and only one half that you see."*

-Edgar Allen Poe

Chapter One

FELIX

The hidden door at the end of the alleyway swung open as I shoved it, the sounds of laughter and the live ragtime music spilling into the crisp air, before it swung closed again with a clang, cloaking us in darkness as I pushed her against the stone side of the building.

Both of us were panting and half-drunk from moonshine, and I caught a glimpse of her smile as she looked up at me. For just a moment, I swore I could see twin images of a candle's flame reflected in her eyes. But before I could focus on them, the illusion faded, and they returned to the sparkling blue orbs I'd been gazing into all night. I shook it off, certain the moonshine was playing tricks on me.

"Mmm, you smell amazing." I buried my nose in her neck, inhaling the musky scent of the sweat she'd worked up as we danced and an underlying scent of lavender. "I'm not ready for the night to end. Come with me?"

She tilted her head back against the wall, a wanton expression on her face as she considered my offer. "Yes."

I grinned and reached down to grab her by the hand, tugging her to the mouth of the alleyway and looking both ways quickly as she yanked the hood of her cloak up to cover the moonlit shade of her hair, wisps of it glinting silver in the light as they framed her face.

When I was assured no one was observing our stealthy exit from the alleyway, I pulled her across the street while she held fast to her skirts with the other hand, matching my pace. "I have a room at the boarding house just down the way, but I'll have to sneak you in." I shot her a conspiratorial look. "Are you up for a bit of tomfoolery?"

She grinned and pulled the hood of her cloak further down, effectively shielding the top half of her face, leaving only the crook of her mouth visible. "I could go for some tomfoolery."

When we'd reached the doorway to the boarding house, I relayed my plan to her in a whisper as she nodded and giggled behind her hand. When I was sure she had the gist of it, I gave her a quick salute and pulled the door open, ensuring it didn't latch behind me as I stepped closer to the tall counter.

I looked around for the attendant and was about to declare the coast clear when a birdlike wheeze erupted from behind the counter.

I leaned over it and found the old chap quite cozily laying on the floor behind his station with his head propped on what appeared to be his waistcoat wadded into a makeshift pillow. A bottle of the absolute lowest form of rum was clutched lovingly in one of his hands, even in his slumber.

While his condition rendered the rest of my plan unnecessary, I couldn't resist the opportunity to rag her a bit, so I whistled softly to signal her, and she carefully edged through the small gap I'd left in the door, quickly hunching down to sneak by.

"It's okay, love. He won't be giving us any trouble tonight. You don't need to give yourself a spasm to crawl past."

"What did you do?" she whisper-shouted from her position, still bent at the waist.

"I told him I was having a gal in for a shag, and he tried to be tough, telling me it was against the rules and he'd have me evicted and I took this here"—I scanned the counter for a likely weapon—"ledger and whacked him in the head. I may have hit him a bit harder than I realized. I don't think he's dead, but we'd best get upstairs before anyone notices."

"Dead?!" she gasped and rounded her eyes at me before they narrowed again. "You're full of absolute shit, Felix. What's actually happened to him?"

I tossed my head back with a laugh. "My guess is one of the fine muckers here wanted him out of their hair for the night. He's been well and truly dosed. He'll wake with an aching head, but wake he will. And none the wiser to your visit this fair evening." I winked and took her by the hand again, tugging her toward the stairs that led up to the third floor where my rooms were. "Chop, chop, the night is already waning and I've yet to debauch you properly."

I gathered her long silver-blonde hair in my hand, tightening my hold until her neck was pulled taught. I leaned in to lick a drop of sweat that had appeared at her temple, catching it on my tongue before it rolled down her cheek.

"Just like that, you naughty girl. Push back against me. You're desperate for it, aren't you, love?" I pulled my hand away from where I gripped her hip and smacked her ass hard enough that it left a perfect pink imprint of my hand when I looked down.

Her moans reached a fever pitch, and I landed another smack, loving the way she clenched around me with each strike. Her expression in the silvered glass in front of us was glorious. Eyes rolled back in her head, pink lips parted on a pant, and her cheeks flushed exertion.

"Let me hear it. Tell me how bad you want it," I growled at her and then smirked when her eyes opened, a glare reflected back at me.

She bared her teeth. "I'm not begging you for something you're obviously so eager to give me." She squeaked when I thrust against her harder. "Yes, do that again so I can come apart all over that gifted cock of yours."

"Ah, ah, ah, darling, get it right. It's not my cock that's gifted. Give credit where credit is due, the skill is *all me.*" I dragged out the last two words as I grinned at her, figuring she was moments away from turning me into a toad if I wasn't careful. I didn't know for sure she was a witch, but I'd seen enough mysterious behavior over the course of our night together that I had a pretty good hunch.

"If you don't shut up and…oh. Oh my goddess. Yes," she hissed as I interrupted her tirade by pulling out of her and slamming back in.

I leaned back, releasing my hold on her hair, and used both hands to part her delectably pert ass cheeks, baring all of her to my view.

She mewled when I spit, and I paused my movements momentarily to watch it drip down her crease in fascination.

"Is this what you need, love? Need me to slide my thumb into your tight little hole while I ruin your cunt for any man after me?" I returned my gaze to meet hers in the mirror and her eyes had glazed over, lashes fluttering. She was close to coming apart just from the thought of it.

"Yesss," she moaned. "Please."

"There it is." I grinned, vindicated. "Begging sounds so sweet rolling off that sharp tongue of yours."

I ran my thumb around the edges of her hole teasingly, using my saliva to ease the way. When I could feel her walls start to flutter around me, I dipped my thumb in, working it past the tight ring of muscle, gently at first, until it was fully seated. My satisfied groan was accompanied by her exclamation.

"Ohmygoddessyespleasemore!" Her words came out

on a rushed pant, running together into one long exclamation of pleasure.

I began to slide my thumb in and out of her while I
snapped my hips harder, faster. The filthy sound of our
flesh slapping together was music to my ears. I was
getting close to my own finish, but I wouldn't allow it
until she was mindless and absolutely ruined for all
other men. That was what I was after; that was the high
I chased without ceasing.

"I'm close," she groaned between clenched teeth.

"I know," I replied smugly as I increased my pace;
my thumb and my cock working in synchrony.

I returned my gaze to the scene in the mirror just in
time to see her gasp and throw her head back, rocking
against me as she exploded in a glorious rush, muscles
locked, rapture personified.

"That's a good girl, gushing all over my dick. I love
it," I grunted and thrust against her while her muscles
clamped around me, trying to drag me over the edge
with her. "I'm going to fill you up now. Where do you
want it?" I panted as I cocked a brow at her in the
mirror, out of breath myself.

She opened her eyes and blinked back at me, before
a wicked look came over her face. "Back there." She
ducked her head shyly for moment before she met my
gaze again in the mirror. "I've heard...I want to know
what it feels like."

I put my fist up to my face, biting my knuckle.

"I do aim to please, love."

I eased out of her dripping cunt and scooped up
some of her juices, sliding my hand up and over her ass,

getting her nice and slick. She was already writhing and moaning again, and I knew she would reach her peak again. *Greedy girl.*

"Are you ready?" My stare was fixed on the way her tight little hole was gaping just from the size of my thumb.

"Do it," she gasped.

I wrapped my hand around the fat head of my cock, sliding my hand down until I was gripping it at the base before I pressed forward an inch, watching the glorious sight of her stretching to accommodate me. I pulled back, watching her face for any signs of pain, but when there was none, I pushed forward again, sinking another couple of inches into her.

"Push out, love. Let me in," I coaxed.

Her muscles pushed against me before she slowly relaxed so I could slide the rest of the way in, firmly seated with my hips pressed against her backside.

She let out a guttural moan that I felt down to my bones.

"Ah, fuck, you love having my cock here where no man is supposed to be, don't you?" I gritted out, nearly mindless with pleasure. I threw my head back, rocking my hips against her. "So tight..." I grunted. "You're choking my cock. I can't wait to see my cum spilling out of you."

Her only response was a keening moan, and I reached around her hip, putting the heel of my hand against her nub.

"Relax, love." I began a slow circular motion over that bundle of nerves and slid three fingers into her fluttering pussy, hearing her gasp just before she bucked against me. "There you go. Ride my fingers and come for me again."

I increased the pace with my hand and hips, as pleasure worked its way from the base of my spine, making my balls draw up until I was on the verge of exploding into her.

She writhed against me, the noises coming from deep in her throat almost animalistic in nature.

"I'm about to come, love. I'm going to give you every single drop I have, until it's leaking out of you with each step you take when you leave here. You'll climb in your bed tonight like a good little girl with my cum leaking from you, and you'll love it, won't you?"

I gave my hips one last snap and unloaded every drop I had into her while she rode my hand, making herself explode again and soaking my fingers while I languidly slid them in and out of her, drawing out her pleasure.

I leaned over, panting and sated, trying to catch my breath before I eased out of her. The sight of my cum leaking out of her ass and dripping down was almost enough to make me sorry I wouldn't be seeing her again.

Almost.

I laid back on the bed in my rented room with my arms folded behind my head. I watched as she tried to comb her hair back into a semblance of order with her fingers, occasionally glancing at me in the mirror.

"That was pleasurable," she offered, her eyes darting away from mine as she adjusted her dress.

"Indeed." I smiled at her warmly.

"Can I ask you a question, Felix?" She bent down, tightening the laces on her boots.

"I've just had my dick in nearly every hole in your body, love, I think you're entitled to a question or two."

She laughed, but when her gaze met mine again the amusement was gone from her expression. "Is it true what they say about you?"

I raised a brow at her. "I suppose that depends on who 'they' are. Lots of people say lots of things about me."

She turned away from the mirror to face me directly. "They say you never invite the same woman to your bed twice. That you derive some kind of hedonistic satisfaction from pleasing women so well that they're cursed to pine for you, even knowing they'll never experience such pleasure again." Her gaze didn't waver as she asked her question and I had to admire her candor.

"I suppose that's one way of putting it, and there's no need to argue the incidentals, as the end result is the same," I replied.

She just stared at me, like she was attempting to decipher the real truth behind my words, before she nodded.

"Well, I suppose that's that then." She gathered her cloak and draped it over her shoulders. "I should have known better."

"Did I mislead you, love?" I called at her back as she strode toward the door to my room.

She paused, but didn't turn around. "Don't call me 'love.' My name is Serafina. If you must address me, please use that."

Ahh. So the little witch fancied herself jilted now the fun was over with.

"All right. Did I mislead you, *Serafina*?" I put emphasis on her name.

She turned and addressed me over her shoulder as she put her hand on the doorknob. "Maybe," she declared. "But not with your words."

I pondered her meaning for a moment, but my interpretation, whether right or wrong, wouldn't change the outcome, so I just nodded.

"I can walk you home..." I offered, knowing she wouldn't accept.

She just shook her head. "Thank you, but I can take care of myself, Felix."

A FEW WEEKS LATER...

"Mmm. You smell amazing." I buried my nose in her neck, feeling the shiver my breath against her skin caused. I allowed myself a grin and she smacked my arm.

"I've heard about you, Felix Vincent." She placed a hand on my chest and pushed back a little, creating space between our bodies.

"Is that so? And what is it that you've heard, sweet Delilah?" I leaned back in, but she doubled her efforts to keep me in place. I'd never forced my attentions on a woman, so I acquiesced and took a step back, cocking my head to the side.

"That you ruin women for all other men and then disappear, never to be seen again. That you never grace the same bed twice. That you're a slut." She blinked up at me with a quirk in her smile.

I gasped. "Who dares to besmirch my character thusly!"

Her giggles filled the nighttime air and she smacked my arm again. Violent little thing. "You know as well as I do that you've done everything to earn such a reputation."

I bowed, tipping my hat at her. "I fear I must concede, fair lady. I've been accused, but not falsely. Does this mean I'll be returning to my rooms alone this evening?" I offered her a sad face.

"I didn't say that." She batted her lashes at me. "But I don't want to be the talk of the town. So we'll need to go somewhere very private. Somewhere no one can catch us." She leaned in close, speaking into my ear for the next bit. "I want to see what all the talk is about, but my father will kill me if he knows I willingly allowed you to have your filthy way with me."

I grinned at her, leaning in and pressing my body against hers. "Ah, but you *are* willingly going to let me have my filthy way with you, aren't you?"

She shivered and nodded, her silky hair sliding against my throat as she tilted her face up to mine.

I leaned back just a bit and rubbed my chin thoughtfully. "Somewhere no one will catch us. Somewhere private, hmm?"

She nodded eagerly.

"I think I have just the spot. But cover your head just in case, and we'll have to be quick so we're not spotted." I tugged on her hand and took off toward the center of town, my head on a swivel making sure we weren't being observed.

"This is what you call private, Felix?" she whisper-yelled as she looked around the room with comically large eyes.

"What? Do you see anyone around?" I gestured at the large empty space.

"Well…no. But this is the theatre! It's a public building!" Her voice had risen an octave, and I couldn't help the smirk from spreading across my face.

"Ah, yes, it is. But there's nothing on the bill tonight or for several nights following. No reason for anyone to be here." I stepped closer to her, lowering my voice. "Plus, I've always wanted to fuck someone here. Just picture me laying you down in the center of the stage, with the open sky above our heads. Can't you just imagine a theatre full of spectators watching me fuck you senseless, their knickers soaked while they watch our bodies moving together up there. And how amazing your moans and screams will sound echoing throughout? It'll be the performance of a lifetime, Delilah."

I reached a hand out to her and she took it gingerly, despite her reservations, as she continued looking around like she expected an audience to appear at any moment.

When we stepped onto the stage I released her hand. "Trust me. We're all alone." I reassured her. "But you can pretend when I shove my cock deep inside your perfect little cunt that every..." I started circling her, running my finger along her collar bone. "Single..." I stopped when I was behind her, leaning in to whisper into her ear. "Person in this town is watching. The women, jealously wishing they were you, and the men, wishing they could fuck you half as well as I'm about to."

She shuddered and let her head fall back against my shoulder, baring her neck to me and giving me a lovely view down the front of her dress. I slid a hand up and cupped one of her breasts, loving the tiny gasp she let out when I pinched her nipple through the material.

"Do you want me to stop?" I breathed against her neck.

Her response was another full-body shudder before she vehemently shook her head no. "Please, don't stop."

"Good girl." I smiled against her neck. "Now, I'm going to kneel down in front of you and I want you to place one of these gloriously long legs on my shoulder." I gently spun her around before I sunk to my knees in front of her, grasping the bottom of her dress and sliding it slowly toward her waist until her thighs were bared to me.

"Oh, I do like these," I murmured as I pressed my mouth against the skin of one of her thighs, just above the tops of her silky stockings. I nipped the skin before I continued lifting her dress until her cunt was bared to me.

"Delilah! I am scandalized. Where *are* your knickers?" I leered up at her from my position and she gave me a saucy wink.

"I was hoping I'd run into you tonight." She giggled into her hand.

"Oh, you naughty, naughty girl." I leaned forward and pressed my face to the juncture of her thighs, breathing her in. "You were hoping I'd eat this perfect cunt until you couldn't stand anymore, weren't you?"

"God. Yes. No one has ever...I've heard tales... please, Felix. I want to know." She wound her fingers into my hair and stared desperately into my eyes.

"You poor, neglected girl. I'm going to take such good care of you." I crooned against her skin, nipping and pressing kisses everywhere except where she wanted me.

"Now, put this leg over my shoulder and let me taste you. I can't wait to slide my tongue inside your tight channel and make your eyes roll back in your head out of sheer pleasure." I lifted her leg and draped it over my shoulder.

"What if I fall? Or smother you?" she squeaked out.

"I won't let you fall, and if you smother me, I'll die a happy man. Now open for me, Delilah. Let me in." I breathed against her. When she leaned into me, sliding her leg further to the side and baring her core to me, I groaned.

And then...I feasted.

"Oh my. Felix. Oh my. God. What..." Her words stuttered and her grip in my hair tightened to the point of pain.

I loved every minute of it. "You taste fucking amazing, Delilah."

I wrapped one of my hands around her thigh to keep

her steady and slid the other between her legs, getting my fingers slick from her juices, before swirling my thumb around the sensitive bundle of nerves at the top of her slit.

"This spot right here"—I moved my thumb over it in a circular motion, applying just a little pressure—"is magical. And I'm going to use it to make you come all over my face before I lay you out on this stage and fuck you for the moon and the stars and all the deities in the sky to see."

I fitted my mouth over her, flattening my tongue and laving the entirety of her cunt with it before I rolled it and teased her hole with the tip.

She gasped and moaned again, and I tightened my hand on her thigh, knowing I was probably leaving a bruise, but the likelihood she was about to lose control of her limbs was high, and I didn't want the poor girl to hurt herself.

I ducked my head at the same time I tilted her toward me more fully, spearing my tongue inside her, feeling the muscles grabbing as I thrust it inside her with increasing speed, all the while my fingers worked that bundle of nerves relentlessly. My efforts were accompanied by the sounds of her moans and cries that were growing louder by the second.

"God, yes, Felix. Oh my god, what's happening to me, I..." Her words failed her, and I doubled my efforts, thrusting my tongue in and out of her, pausing between each thrust and making sure to stimulate all the areas I knew would give her pleasure.

She gasped one last time and I heard her catch her

breath and hold it just before the gush of her juices flooded my tongue, the taste divine, and I lapped at her until her legs would no longer hold her.

I helped her to the stage floor, crawling up her body until I hovered over her, pressing a kiss to the corner of her mouth, then the sensitive spot just beneath her ear, then the indention in her breast bone.

"Oh my god, Felix. That was…unnatural. I've never…" She let her sentence drift off, and I offered her a smug grin.

"Why do you think they've all been talking, love? But I'm far from done with you. If you didn't summon an audience with that performance, then I think I need to try harder, hmm?"

She blinked up at me, cheeks flushed, skirts still rucked up about her waist, and nodded enthusiastically.

I winked at her. "I love your spirit, Delilah."

I reached down and unfastened my trousers, freeing my aching cock from confinement, and I saw her eyes widen when I wrapped my fist around it, slowly sliding it up and down.

"That's not going to fit. Anywhere," she declared, the haze of pleasure beginning to fade from her expression.

"I promise you, it will. You just have to trust me. I made you feel good before, right?" I tilted my head at her as I knelt between her parted thighs, the remnants of her pleasure still dripping from her cunt onto the stage.

She pulled her lip between her teeth, nibbling it uncertainly for a moment before she nodded cautiously.

"Then trust that I know how to make this pleasurable for you as well." I waited for her to nod again.

When she did, I grinned and ran my fingers through her slickness, causing her to jump and squirm.

"All of this is going to help. And you're nice and relaxed now that I've made you come, I promise you're going to love this." I smiled reassuringly, absolutely no doubt that she would give in.

"Okay, Felix. Let me see what it's all about," she whispered.

I slid my hand up to the crown of my cock and rubbed it up and down over her, again and again, nudging her still-sensitive bundle of nerves, until she was writhing beneath me, hips subconsciously tilting toward me.

I slid the first couple of inches into her tight channel and the moan she unleashed would have brought the house down if anyone else had been there to witness it. I rocked back and forth, using my fingers to rub and massage until her walls fluttered around me. I pulled back a bit more then surged forward, seating myself down to the base. I paused my movement and met her gaze, checking that she was okay.

Her eyes were unfocused, but when I placed a quick kiss against her lips she zeroed in on mine and gave me a beatific smile.

She raised herself onto her elbows and declared. "Felix, now I see why they're all so mad at you. Nothing is ever going to feel like this again, is it?"

Before I could come up with a clever reply, another voice rang out in the theatre.

"No, it isn't." The voice came out of the darkness where the audience would have been.

I jerked my head in that direction but couldn't see anything in the shadows past the edge of the stage.

Delilah squealed and frantically started shoving at my chest, trying to push her skirts down to cover herself.

I eased out of her and slowly stood, tucking myself back into my pants as I stepped closer to the edge of the stage. I placed the bulk of my body between whoever was out there and Delilah's exposed lower half.

"Who's there?" I called, crossing my arms over my chest.

"Oh, don't worry, Felix. You'll find out soon enough," the voice called out.

I could hear their footsteps receding even over the sounds of Delilah frantically hissing my name.

I turned back to her once I was fairly sure we were alone again, noting she'd tidied her hair and covered herself while my back was turned. I sighed, looking down briefly at the bulge that remained in the front of my pants.

Something told me I'd be taking care of that on my own later.

"Right. So I guess that means you'd like me to take you home then?" I raised a brow at her.

"Are you crazy? If my father saw you within a mile of our property he'd shoot you on sight." She shook her head vehemently, but I saw her glance down at my pants with a brief, wistful expression.

I grinned at her. "It wouldn't be the first time someone's father tried to shoot me. But come on, I'll at least get you close enough that I don't have to worry about someone nabbing you on the way and finishing what I'd only just started."

She rolled her eyes at me, but I could see her glance back down again.

"Unless...you wanted to help me out with this?" I took a step closer.

She shook her head at me, hissing, "Felix! We just got caught fornicating in a public place by who knows who! Do you think it's a good idea to resume our activities?"

I took another step closer, sliding my hand into my pants and palming my cock. "Cat's already out of the bag, love. We might as well get our kicks before I escort you to the edge of your property. What do you say? Is that sweet cunt still pulsing, begging to be filled?"

She let out a little whimper, and I grinned, taking another step toward her.

She looked around uncertainly, but I saw the way her stance shifted from one foot to the other.

"You're aching, aren't you, love? Your muscles still clenching. Let me finish us off. I'd hate for you to go tell your friends that I didn't satisfy every single need you had. I have a reputation to uphold, after all."

"Okay. Fine," she hissed. "But we should probably make it fast. You know, in case whoever that was decides to come back." Her eyes shone with a tinge of excitement, and I knew that some part of her relished the idea of someone watching us.

That made two of us.

"Good girl," I crooned as I slid up against her, nudging her toward the wall that surrounded the stage.

I bent down slowly, maintaining eye contact with her as I grasped the hem of her skirt and began working it back up to her hips. I held onto it with one hand while I freed my cock from my pants with the other, nearly coming just from the feel of my hand grazing against it.

"I'm going to pick you up and I want you to wrap your legs around my waist, okay, love?"

She nodded eagerly, and when I lifted her slight frame, I groaned to feel her wet heat pressed against me as she slid her legs around my waist.

I notched myself against her opening, happy to note she was still soaked from my earlier attentions. "God, this tight, wet little cunt feels so good teasing the head of my cock."

She moaned and wiggled against me, as much as she could in her position.

When I slid home, she threw her head back on a moan, and I buried my head in her throat, licking and biting the tendons there as I started off slow and steady but, before long, ended up rutting against her like a man possessed. With every thrust I could feel her tightening around me more and more.

"Use one of those gorgeous little hands to rub yourself, love. I want to feel you choke the life out of me when you come," I panted into her ear.

When one of her hands tentatively slid between our bodies, I paused my movement and leaned back, letting her rest against the wall while I watched what she was doing.

"Just like that, love. Does that feel good?" I crooned at her.

"Mm-hmm, yes, god, yes, it feels amazing," she moaned, muscles clenching and releasing around me.

"That's a good girl. Think about this when you're lying in your bed touching yourself. Think about how it feels when I drive my cock inside you."

She let out a cry, almost a sob.

"You'll feel so empty, but you can slide those fingers inside and remember. You'll fuck yourself with your own hand until you're screaming into your pillow, careful not to wake Daddy with your lusty moans, won't you?"

I drew back and drove back inside, sheathing myself to the hilt inside her, over and over again while she stroked herself and, when I heard her hold her breath, I took one finger and reached behind her, stroking her tiny, puckered hole, just teasing it with the tip of my finger until she screamed and clenched around me, pulling me over the edge with her.

I exploded inside her, keeping up small movements to draw out our pleasure until she was hung around my neck like a limpet, completely wrung out from pleasure.

"*Good girl*," I whispered against her lips.

Chapter Three

FELICITY

I could tell at a glance that she'd been at it for quite some time. She was swaying back and forth, bouncing from tree to tree as she meandered through the forest, muttering under her breath about how she should have known better.

"Stupid, foolish Serafina believed that drugstore cowboy actually wanted me, but he was so convincing, and he's so fucking pretty, and that cock. Oh my goddess, that cock. Arghh. I could just…kill him. I hate him. I truly hate him."

Her constant rambling drew an amused snort out of me which had her whirling around, looking for the source of the sound.

"Who's there?" she slurred. "I'm…armed!" she called with more force.

"With what? A half-empty jug of moonshine?" I laughed.

At my words she spun in my direction, eyes

attempting to focus on me with great difficulty. "No. It's..." She lifted the jug in her hand. "Well, mostly empty, as it turns out."

Her shoulders slumped, and I took pity on her. "I'm not here to do you harm, girl. You can put down your weapon."

She narrowed her eyes in my direction. "Are you mocking me? Because I don't think that's wise. Even in my current...condition, I'm still a force to be reckoned with," she asserted, which would have been slightly more menacing if she hadn't hiccupped halfway through her declaration.

"Well, well, well...does this drunk little kitten have claws?" I widened my eyes at her before putting my hands on my hips and widening my stance.

"Go ahead then. Give me your worst," I urged.

Her mouth dropped open as she gaped at me. "What? No. Why? I..." She looked around the forest where we stood, like she was trying to remember how she'd ended up there. "I don't want to hurt you. I don't think, anyway."

"What a relief," I quipped, smirking at her. "Do you mind if I ask what exactly a drunken witch is doing wandering around the forest muttering to herself about pretty assholes with convincing cocks?"

She drew herself up to her full height, not exactly an intimidating figure, but I appreciated the effort. "I'm heartbroken. And I'm drowning my sorrows in moon-shine," she declared.

"I see." I slid a hand up and cupped my chin. "Are

you even of age to drink that?" I tipped my head at the jug in her hand.

She narrowed her eyes on me, sweeping them down to my booted feet and then back up again. "I'd guess no younger than yourself."

I tossed my head back, a laugh escaping into the night sky. "Appearances can be deceiving, lamb."

Her confusion was apparent, but she didn't question me further.

"I think it's time for you to make your way back to your bed, little witch."

"Sera," she declared.

"I'm sorry?" I tilted my head at her.

"Well, you keep calling me 'little witch', but my name is Sera. Serafina, actually." She blinked up at me, and I realized that she'd taken a few steps closer during our exchange.

"It's nice to meet you, Serafina. I'm Felicity." I watched her closely as she took another step closer and until she stood mere inches away.

"You're beautiful," she stated, tilting her head left and right as she studied me. "What *are* you?"

"What do you think I am?"

She walked around me once, only the slightest hitch in her step from the moonshine. When she'd come back around to face me, she shrugged. "I don't know. Are you a witch? I don't think you're a witch. I think I'd know if you were a witch, and you don't feel like a witch. I'm a witch, did you know that?" Her rambling dialogue was adorable, and I didn't even attempt to hold back my delighted laughter.

"Yes, little witch, I know what you are." I couldn't help but soak in her beauty. She was nearly angelic in appearance. Long silver hair flew in wild tendrils around her face, small twigs and leaves tangled in it from her romp through the forest, and her adorable button nose was slightly upturned, giving her an impish appeal. Her eyes were a deep midnight blue at the iris, which was surrounded by a ring of silver; they appeared to glow from within as she stared up at me. She was flawless.

A thud resonated inside my chest as I studied her. If I didn't know it was impossible, I would have been tempted to think she'd cast a spell over me, my response to her was so intense.

"But if you're not a witch, then what are you?" she asked.

"I'm many things, none of them important at this very moment. What *is* important, though, is that it's time for you to be out of the forest this night. You need to get back to your bed where you can sleep off the effects of the spirits." I gestured to the jug she still clutched.

She looked down at it in surprise, like she'd forgotten she still held it. "I don't think I want it anymore."

"That's good, little witch. Why don't you hand it over and I'll walk you home? Make sure no harm comes to you between here and there." I held out a hand, indicating the pathway leading out of the forest.

"How would you protect me?" she asked. "You're just a wisp of a girl yourself."

"I am many things, Sera, but a girl I have never been. I'll tell you what. Let's get you to bed, and if you wake in the morning with any recollection of our meeting, come back here tomorrow night, and maybe I'll tell you all about me and then you can tell me what has you in such a state."

She gasped and a frown appeared on her face. "Felix. Ugh. I'm so furious at him. He's a cad. A…a…" Her face scrunched up in consternation.

"An asshole?" I supplied helpfully.

"Yes!" She nodded enthusiastically. "Exactly. He's an asshole. I should *curse* him. That would teach him."

I nodded, having no confidence she would remember anything of our meeting when she woke in the morning. "Then that's what we'll do. But first, sleep, little witch."

Chapter Four

FELIX

There should have been chanting.

Mist.

Maybe even some trees swaying in a breeze that no one else could feel.

Instead…it was eerily quiet.

I awoke to find myself bound by an unseen force, unable to move anything except my eyes, which, for their part, spun wildly to take in my surroundings. I was in the middle of a clearing in the forest; a full moon loomed ominously above my head, providing enough light that I could see the ground at my feet for several feet in every direction. It had been swept clean of forest debris and a pentagram appeared to have been drawn around me using some type of white powder.

Witchcraft. *Dammit.*

My attention was drawn away from the forest floor when I heard a low sound coming from the other side of the clearing; I wasn't alone. It wasn't quite a chant, but an eerie sound I'd never heard before and couldn't identify. As it intensified, I began to feel as if I were being crushed into a size and shape that no longer resembled my old form.

When the pressure had reached a crescendo, the pain becoming so intense I feared that was the end of me, the sound stopped abruptly, taking the pressure with it, leaving the clearing silent, but for my audible gasping.

A face leaned forward into the circle of light cast by a lone candle. It had been placed on a stump in the center of the clearing and the light from it had obscured anything beyond it to my vision. A flash of recognition struck me as she met my eyes briefly before she pursed her lips on an exhale and the candle went dark.

I should have known that in the next moment— everything would change.

The pressure I'd felt before had become a stabbing pain in my back that nearly drove me to my knees, but at least I no longer felt like I was being crushed to death by an invisible fist. I maintained my feet, but barely, and still struggled to breathe. I settled my gaze back on my former lover and her companion, who I could finally see once the flame between us had been extinguished.

I narrowed my eyes. I'd thought Serafina was lovely to look at the night I'd taken her back to my boarding house—and undoubtedly, she still was. The woman before me, however, lacked the air of the ingénue that she'd carried the night we'd been together. When she met my gaze across the clearing, none of the good humor that she'd shown me before remained in her expression. Actually, if I had to guess at the emotion on her face, I'd have said she was well and truly incensed. Good.

That made two of us.

"What the fuck have you done to me?" I growled at the two women who'd apparently been the ones to toss a bag over my head as I was leaving my favorite speakeasy just an hour prior. I cocked my head at Serafina; certain she was at the root of it. I'd had my suspicions she was a witch during our tryst a month past, but current circumstances had erased any doubt.

"Does he have wings?" Serafina gestured toward me in annoyance. "Why does he have wings?" She rounded on her companion with an accusatory look.

The redheaded woman shrugged, unconcerned. "I don't know, love," she drawled. "When Dave did this, he said the gent ended up with a tail. Hey, mate?" She cocked her head at me. "Do you have a tail?"

I growled before turning in circles in an attempt to determine if I had, in fact, gained a tail.

"No tail, then," the redhead confirmed with a wave of her hands in the direction of my backside.

Sera turned to look at her with wide eyes. "This was supposed to curse him! Why does he have wings?"

Still clearly unbothered, the other woman shrugged and rolled her eyes at her. "Not sure, but if I had to give it my best guess, I'd say...balance?"

Sera studied me for a moment, gritting her teeth audibly, before addressing her companion again. "What do you mean 'balance'? Look at him! If anything, the wings have just made him *more* ridiculously attractive. I wanted to *curse* him, not make him irresistible to the opposite sex." She crossed her arms over her chest, and I half expected her to stomp her foot to emphasize her point.

Wings. I had fucking wings. I could feel the weight of them tugging on the muscles in my shoulders and, as I shifted on my feet to keep both of the women in my direct line of sigh, I could feel the tips of them brushing against the legs of my trousers. No matter which way I twisted and turned, however, I couldn't get a true grasp of their size in my peripheral vision. How they'd managed to sprout into existence was a mystery, but I was sure the witch before me had the answers I sought.

I cut my eyes to the other woman, careful not to give either of them my back as they faced off. Who knew what other fresh hell they had planned for me if I didn't keep my guard up.

"Like I said—balance. I won't swear to it, but I'd guess this is the universe's way of making sure witches aren't just going around cursing cads to Hell willy-nilly over a hangnail. A balance must be maintained, Serafina. I'm willing to bet the rest of your terms were honored, but the balance demands he be granted a boon or two in exchange for your vengeance."

"Ugh," Sera groaned before she turned back to survey me. "So, how do we know if the rest worked?"

Felicity stared at her blankly. "Um, kitten? Aren't you the witch amongst us? It seems to me you should be able to decipher that for yourself."

"I'm sorry to interrupt this month's conclave of the local chapter of fucking crazy women, but do either of you, by chance, want to explain to me what the fuck you've done to me? And is it permanent? Because I am notably freaking the fuck out at the moment." The pain in my shoulders had faded to a dull ache, but my body as a whole felt like it'd been through a ringer. I ached from my neck down to the soles of my feet, and as much as I knew I should be equal parts angry and terrified, a pervasive exhaustion was ruling out all other emotions.

Neither of them acknowledged my questions, or that I had spoken at all, truly.

The redhead had assumed a position lounging on a fallen log in the clearing, her posture that of someone totally unconcerned with the potential consequences of their actions. She studied me with her head tilted to the side in curiosity, but offered no hint that Serafina's anger, my confusion, or the wings that had sprouted from my shoulder blades gave her reason to worry.

She continued as if I hadn't spoken at all. "But you're right about one thing. The wings really do nothing to lessen his appeal. Pity."

I narrowed my gaze on her before a thought occurred to me suddenly. "Wait. Does this mean I can fly?"

She tossed her head back in raucous laughter. "Mate. You're what...a hand over six feet tall? Do you know how big those wings would have to be for you to be able to fly?" She shook her head, still chuckling. "No, I don't think flight is in your future. Which means that, like most things males have to offer, *those* are likely just for show." She smirked at having crushed my hope while summarily insulting not only myself, but the entire male gender.

She stood to her full height and turned toward Serafina. "We'd best be going then. I'll have to show him the ropes."

Sera's shoulders slumped but she nodded. "But you'll come back, won't you?" There was something in her voice that told me her request wasn't entirely to do with me.

"I'll be around." Her accomplice winked at her before putting a hand on my shoulder, and with a sideways tilt of the world, snatched me to Hell.

Chapter Five

FELIX

WELCOME TO HELL—A BEGINNER'S GUIDE

"*T*hese will be your chambers for the duration of your...stay." The redhead, Felicity, gestured lazily with a hand through an open door offering me a smirk, while I continued to gape at her.

I'd been attempting not to regurgitate the moonshine I'd consumed earlier in the night since the world had righted itself once again and she'd commanded me to follow her. Her demeanor hadn't changed since she'd taken me out of the clearing in the forest, though. She was the picture of nonchalance.

"Is this something you two do often? Curse men for not wanting to tie themselves to a single woman for the rest of their existence and snatch them to...where even are we?" I looked around incredulously.

"It's actually my first time." She winked at me. "How'd we do?"

My mouth dropped open. "Do you expect me to commend you?"

She shrugged. "I suppose that's a bit much to hope for, but you should probably be grateful. If I'd gone along with her original request you'd be a lot less here and a lot more dead. Best keep that in mind before you verbally flay me for my involvement."

"Dead?" I choked out. "My mother warned me my cock was going to get me in trouble one of these days, but dead seems a bit extreme."

"I agree..." She looked down at the front of my pants with a brow raised. "And I took a peek—call it curiosity—while you were incapacitated. I must say, it would have been a terrible waste. Even flaccid, that appendage of yours is quite impressive."

I was torn between preening and running screaming from her presence as fast as I could.

I was also oddly aroused. *Not now, cock.*

"So, how exactly does this work?" I asked her, surveying my new accommodations. "Do I get a hand-book for the newly cursed?"

She slid me a side-eye before shaking her head. "Honestly, mate, I don't know. It's not like this is a common occurrence for me. I pulled in a favor from someone with a good bit more power than me, but Sera-fina holds the reins on this one. It's her curse."

"Then shouldn't she be here explaining what exactly this entails?" I widened my eyes, feeling annoyance finally overtaking the shock I'd been feeling for the past few hours.

Felicity laughed. Outright cackled at my question. "She can't come here, Felix. She can never come here."

"And why the hell not?" I threw out.

Felicity's expression shuttered and her face went entirely blank. "That's not my secret to tell. But I know enough about this curse to be able to give you the basics. She'll have to fill you in on the rest once you learn how to move topside on your own. But heed this warning, Felix, you have to try and remain as invisible here as you can. Do not draw unnecessary attention to yourself. The Denizens of Hell will not take kindly to your presence here, and if they turn on you, there will be nothing anyone can do to save you. Least of all me."

After that cryptic warning she proceeded to lay out the rules of my curse in an oddly mechanical tone, completely at odds with her laconic attitude up until that point. "You are, for all intents and purposes, immortal. At least, for now." She leveled me with another blank look. "Once you learn how to use those" —she gestured at my wings—"because I can only assume that's what they're for, you'll be able to travel topside. In that dimension you will be invisible. Unable to be seen or heard by humanity. You may walk among them, but they will never witness your passing." She paused. "Unless…"

"Unless?" I leaned toward her, already feeling the

sting of the sentence I'd been given merely for scorning the wrong woman.

"Look, Felix, I'm not condoning Sera's choices here, but you got yourself into this mess. She wants you to learn your lesson, but she did grant you the possibility of redemption."

"What. Possibility?" I gritted my teeth.

"If you touch a human, skin to skin, you'll become visible to that person. They'll be able to see, hear, and touch you—and vice versa."

I knew there was more to this, there had to be more to this. "What is the catch?"

"You only have three attempts to learn your lesson. Up until you touch a third person, your immortality, and any other gifts that have come as a result of it, will remain intact." She took a deep breath.

"And then? What happens when I touch the third person?"

"Your mortality will return. You'll be restored to your previous form and your clock, if you will, will restart toward an inevitable end." She bit her lip.

"What else?"

"If you don't choose wisely. If you touch that third person and one of the three aren't your soulmate, you'll be cursed to live out your natural life completely alone. Your existence on that plane will be worse than a mere case of invisibility. You'll be a living ghost. Until you die." She shrugged and offered me a sympathetic look.

I sat down hard on a chair that suddenly appeared behind me as I stared at Felicity. The ramifications of what she'd just told me just kept hitting harder and harder, like waves crashing against a shore. Each one more powerful than the last. "I have three chances to learn how to...love someone?"

She gave me a look that might have almost been pity. "Yes, Felix. That was the loophole. She believes you incapable of ever loving anyone but yourself, so by setting this curse upon you, she thinks she's guaranteed your misery. Either in Hell, or above."

I rubbed my hands over my face, attempting to conceal my shock and my dread. Because, as angry as I was with Serafina for what she'd done, I feared I agreed with her.

I don't believe myself capable of loving another human either.

I stared blankly at the shirt in my hands. It was shredded in the back and there were streaks of blood here and there, though not nearly as much as I would have assumed, given how much it hurt when I grew wings in the span of a few minutes.

Felicity had left me to my own devices in my "chambers" after our little talk, and I wondered if, or when, she would return, because I didn't have the faintest idea what to do about dressing myself. Or getting something to eat. Now that the exhaustion had gone, my stomach was reminding me that another need now took precedence.

I heard a snort from behind me and whipped around

to find the woman in question leaning against my doorway.

"Guess we'll need to get you something else to wear. I'll check with Dave and see if he's got anything we can...modify."

I just blinked at her. The entirety of the situation too big to grasp. "What am I supposed to do now?"

I thought I caught a glimpse of something that might have been compassion in her gaze before she replied. "No one can answer that for you, Felix. But for now, let's see about getting you some clean clothes. And how about some food?"

I looked back down at the shirt I still clutched in my hands. "Okay. I still have a lot of questions, though."

"Of course you do. And I'll answer what I can. Some...well, some of it, you'll just have to figure out for yourself." She waved at me to follow her, and without any other option, I did.

PART II

THE IN-BETWEEN

"Hell is empty,
and all the devils are here."

-*William Shakespeare* - The Tempest

Chapter Six

FELIX

I flicked my wings sharply, unfurling them before they resumed their position draped down my back. When I closed my eyes, the world tilted on its axis. When the ground righted itself beneath my feet, I blinked, letting my eyes adjust to the low light as I surveyed my surroundings.

I placed a hand against the dirty brick wall to steady myself. No matter how many years had passed since the first time I'd jumped from one dimension to the other, the slight feeling of vertigo never went away. I swallowed hard to choke down the queasy feeling in my stomach.

The alley I'd blinked into was adjacent to one of my favorite places to watch humanity in all its messy glory. It was part Irish pub, part nightclub; on a given day one might encounter everyone from cranky, retired fishmongers during the daylight hours to a more...contemporary crowd at night when the music turned up and the lights went down.

I'd stumbled upon the pub quite by accident nearly forty years prior, and it had since become a regular spot for me. I'd observed how it had changed over the years from my perch in the corner of the catwalk that over-looked the bar. I'd seen the inlaid wood floor become more and more scuffed, while the windows had to be replaced so often due to rowdy patrons that the glass never had an opportunity to become cloudy. I'd watched the dress of those same rowdy patrons as it went from bell-bottoms to flannel to ripped skinny jeans —and back again.

If my longevity had taught me anything, it was that there was no portion of the human experience that escaped its own cyclical nature. Everything came back around.

Everything.

"Fancy seeing you here," the husky voice whispered in my ear, startling me out of my thoughts.

See what I meant?

Everything came back around.

"Sera." I cut my eyes in her direction feigning an annoyed expression as I rubbed a hand against the back of my neck where she'd made the hair stand on end.

While my own extended lifespan had been a given, as a term of the curse she'd placed upon me over a century prior, her own had come as a bit of a surprise. To no one more so than Sera herself. While I still bore some hard feelings about her having cursed me, I had to admit that simply being perceived in the human world gave me such joy after so long in isolation that I'd learned to tolerate her company.

In small doses.

I studied her out of the corner of my eye as she leaned against the wall next to me, noting that a century had been very kind to her indeed. While I remained frozen in the state I'd been that night in the forest, she appeared to have aged perhaps a decade. Enough that her curves had filled out a bit. Her beauty had matured in a way that women tended to lament in their thirties but that I couldn't help but appreciate. She no longer carried her girlish innocence, but that did nothing to diminish her appeal. Sadly, I couldn't find it in myself to take solace in her. That hadn't worked out well for me the first time around and, besides, I had an inkling that her affections were pointed in an altogether different direction of late.

"Are you stalking me?" I quipped, cocking a brow at her.

She ignored my question and continued studying our surroundings, a thoughtful look on her face. "Did you ever think we'd be around to see such change in this world?" Her normally playful tone had a somber note to it.

I narrowed my eyes at her, trying to discern her mood. "Well, certainly not before you took me for a trip to the forest." She rolled her eyes at me but kept quiet as I continued. "Being a spectator in this world for the last century has been both a blessing and the most heinous curse you could have bestowed upon me, Sera. It's given me perspective that I wouldn't have otherwise had, but it's been torture to watch it while never being able to engage."

And that was the crux of it. I'd spent the first twenty-five years of my existence grabbing every visceral experience that my human life could grant me, denying myself no pleasure or indulgence, and I'd spent the last century a ghost in the world I'd been born into. I craved human interaction with a strength that astounded me. But fear held me back. I was paralyzed by the knowledge that the wrong choice would be the beginning of the end for me. The start of living out the remainder of my mortal life in the same solitude that I'd suffered for the last century. Or worse.

My immortality was both the greatest gift and the thing that locked me in stasis—unable to move beyond what I had become. Serafina could never have predicted the gravity of the cage she'd placed me in a century ago; how it would shape me into something completely new at the same time that it trapped me in this reality.

Fear would do that to a man.

"Do you regret it?" She cast a sidelong glance at me.

"What? Debauching you?" I grinned. "Only the parts that came after."

She rolled her eyes. "You'd be long in your grave by now if I hadn't cursed you."

"And blissfully unaware of Nickelback. It's a trade-off." I shrugged.

"Felix...be serious. Would you go back and change the events that brought you here?" She turned and met my gaze with hers, imploring me to give her honesty.

"I'm a better man today for what you did to me,

Sera. I'll never thank you for it, but I'd likely have died a selfish cunt if you hadn't forced me to change my ways." I shrugged my shoulders, offering her a forced smile that I knew didn't reach my eyes. "So, in that respect, I don't regret it. But I don't know how to escape this cage you've cursed me with, and that may be the biggest tragedy of it. Your curse was extreme, but I may have deserved it. The only problem is that the ultimate goal may not be something I'm capable of." I turned my head toward the mouth of the alley, hearing the sounds of revelry cranking up in the bar next door.

"Then you're not done yet, Felix." She pushed away from the wall and turned away from me, sauntering toward the street in front of us. "Never underestimate the power of love, you just have to be open to it. Have a little faith."

I stood staring at the spot where she'd stood for a long time after she'd gone. I still had doubts that I was capable of the kind of love that would be required to break the curse, but perhaps she had a point.

Had I been open to it?

Chapter Seven

SILAS

The mail slot on my door let out a metal screech when it opened; the nut brown hand of Oscar the mailman appeared briefly as he shoved the stack of mail through before it landed in a heap on top of the existing pile already collected there.

Afternoon, Silas!" he called, observing our routine.

"Otis," I returned.

"Have a good day, Silas!" he called again, altogether too cheerful, but given he was regularly my only point of contact with real live humans, I was inclined to give him a pass on the unnecessary good cheer.

"Thanks, Otis. Same to you."

I waited until I heard his feet retreat across the wooden planks of my front porch before I stepped away from the door, completely ignoring the growing stack of unopened mail there.

My cell phone had been chirping incessantly since

early that morning, and I knew it was my agent, but my particular neuroses meant I had to be in exactly the right headspace to actually answer the call. I hadn't gotten there yet.

I studied the cup of coffee gripped in my hand and decided it needed to be four degrees warmer overall before I drank it.

Maybe, after that, I'd be ready to talk to him.

As it turned out, I didn't feel ready to talk to him until I'd washed two loads of laundry and refolded all the towels in the linen closet, but once I'd done that I was somewhat soothed. I finally picked up my phone when Henry's face showed up on it for the fifteenth time that day.

"Silas, for fuck's sake, I know you heard me, would you say something?" I could picture Henry's face in my mind, red-cheeked and apoplectic.

I was gaping at my phone, simultaneously exceptionally gratified and terror-stricken.

"I heard you," I coughed out.

I backed away from my phone where it was perched on the corner of my antique writing desk in my study. Bands of late afternoon sunlight had created a striped pattern on the floor, and I found myself mesmerized by the fact that only the very tips of my toes were bathed in sunlight while the rest of my feet were hidden in shadow.

"Silas? Silas," he huffed, clearly excited but under-whelmed with my response to his news. "Silas, it's the New York Times. This is a moment most writers wait their entire career for and never actually achieve. This is a really big deal."

I was nodding, forgetting momentarily that he couldn't see me. "I...yes. I understand. That's great. My coffee's getting cold, can I call you back? Maybe next week." I was already reaching for the giant red button at the bottom of the screen when Henry screeched at me.

"No! Don't hang up, Silas. We've got to talk about this. You'll need to do interviews. Appearances. Signings! We need to talk logistics." Henry knew about my *special* considerations, so the fact that he thought landing on the New York Times Best Seller list was going to change anything about, it was proof-positive that he thought it was all an affectation on my part, not a legitimate diagnosis.

"You know I can't do that. I won't do it." I shook my head resolutely. "I can't. That was the deal when I signed with you."

"And that was all fine and good when you were a nobody, Silas. The reclusive author who never shows his face was a great gimmick, but it's time for you to come out into the real world!" He was frustrated, I could hear it in his voice, but he still didn't understand.

"It's not a gimmick," I whispered. "I would if I could."

He was still squawking on the other end of the line when I disconnected the call and slumped down to the floor next to my desk. Swiping my hand in and out of the bands of sunlight and enjoying the way the light illuminated the lines in my palm in turns as I moved it in and out of the shadow.

"It's not a gimmick," I whispered again to the empty house.

"*I would if I could.*"

Chapter Eight

SILAS

FOUR YEARS AGO

The headline threw me for a loop. What even was I seeing?

Federal law enforcement to question author of crime thriller series in connection with string of serial murders.

I grabbed my phone from where it rested on the charging stand next to my laptop, frantically hitting the number for my agent.

"Silas? Shit, I've been trying to get a hold of you all morning. Look, this is bad, but it's not your fault, okay? Silas?" James's voice sounded like it was coming at me from underwater. How odd. Wait, maybe that was me, not him. Was I under water?

"Come on, buddy, talk to me. We're going to get in front of this. Just because someone decided to use your book as an instruction manual for serial killers doesn't mean you're libel. The authorities have been in touch with me and they just want to talk to you, see if you have any information that might help them track this psycho down. I've already got our lawyers on standby and one of them will accompany you to the meeting."

My body went cold at his words. "Lawyers? Why would I need a lawyer, James? I didn't do anything wrong!"

"I know. I know you didn't. They'll just be there as a precaution, just to make sure the feds treat you right while you're with them. They aren't charging you with anything."

"Charging me?! *Could* they charge me?" My voice had ratcheted up into a register I couldn't normally achieve.

I pushed away from my desk, frantically pulling on the ends of my hair and feeling like I might be having a heart attack. I could hear my heartbeat in my ears, drumming like the four horsemen of the apocalypse were coming right for me.

"Just try to stay calm. I'll call you back when I have more information. Have a drink. Stay away from the news. I'll be in touch." James ended the call, and I stared at the darkened screen of my phone for endless minutes while trying to wrap my brain around the predicament I found myself in.

Just yesterday, I'd been a best-selling crime fiction author quickly on my way to becoming one of the up- and-coming literary darlings of the decade.

Today, I was being villainized in the headlines as the

man who'd written a primer for the most prolific serial killer to exist in the US in the last fifteen years.

Fuck my life.

Chapter Nine

FELIX

FOUR YEARS AGO

I'd found all manner of things to occupy my time over the course of the last century, but most activities lost their luster after a while when they were all solitary in nature. I'd read more books than I could count, and despite having no presence in the moral plane, I could affect objects around me, I just couldn't be seen or heard in the process. So if I say... pulled a book from a shelf and sat down in a comfy chair in the corner to read, what would be perceivable to anyone around me would only be the indentation in the chair cushion and what appeared to be a floating book with turning pages.

Had I, on occasion, taken great joy in giving people a jolt with that particular trick?

Perhaps.

I never said I was a mature being.

Most of the time, however, I simply "borrowed" a book for a while before returning it to its place on the shelf when I finished it.

I'd recently discovered crime thrillers, and there was one author that I particularly enjoyed reading. There was just something about the way he crafted the story that made you feel as if you'd been transported into the mind of the killer he wrote about. His books were fast-paced and so well written that I found myself flying through the first four books in his series in a matter of days, but when I went searching for the next one there was nothing to find. As a matter of fact, it seemed as if the author had simply ceased to exist after the publication of his last novel in the series.

It piqued my curiosity enough that I began digging. I had all the time in the world to satisfy my curiosity, and something told me this would be a story worth getting to the bottom of.

I sat in the public library at one of the computers Felicity had shown me how to use—typing in queries and only occasionally noticed the people around me who were throwing questioning glances to where I sat. I was sure they all thought the cubby was haunted, given that the words on the screen jumped around as I typed in search after search trying to get to the bottom of the mystery. I enjoyed the wide berth they gave my spot and the wide-eyed stares they directed at the keyboard as I worked.

What I eventually discovered about the author began

a side quest that gave me more purpose than I'd felt in a very long time.

Federal law enforcement to question author of crime thriller series in connection with string of serial murders.

Well. *Color me intrigued.*

"Felicity, I need a phone," I declared as I strode through her doorway, belatedly realizing she was not alone.

"Perhaps you should first learn how to knock before entering a lady's room?" She met my stare over the head of the man—demon?—currently positioned between her legs. When he attempted to raise his head, she gently placed her hand on the back of it and admonished him.

"No, no. It's just Felix. Keep going, you're almost there. But use your fingers…ahh, just like that." She threw her head back with a gasp before returning her gaze to mine.

"So, a phone, you say? And why is that? Who are you going to call, Felix?" She quirked a brow at me.

"I can't keep going to the library to do research. They're going to decide it's haunted, and as much as that thought amuses me, I need to be able to work without worry that someone is going to plop into my lap at any given moment."

"Hmm. What are you researching now?" She moaned before addressing the other man. "Yes, that's much better. Do you happen know the alphabet?"

At that, he did raise his head. "I'm a demon, Felicity,

not an imbecile. I know the fucking alphabet. I know five of them, actually."

"Fantastic. Well done, you. Start with the first one and don't stop until I'm screaming then, hmm?" She pushed his head back down and studied him momentarily with her head cocked to the side. "Good boy."

She offered him a pat on the head while I watched. Despite my need to get to the bottom of my own mystery, I felt my pants tighten as I observed the picture they made. Felicity was spread out across her black satin sheets; all the other blankets having been pushed onto the floor surrounding her bed. She wore a black corset, but her breasts were spilling over the top, and her skirt had been rucked up to her hips, exposing what was arguably a very lovely cunt to her partner.

For his part, he wore black leather pants and not much else, leaving his heavily tattooed torso exposed to my view. Long dark hair was wrapped in what I believe they now referred to as a "man-bun," which gave her a lovely handle with which to steer his ministrations. There were no outward indications that I could see that would label him "demon," though he *was* larger than any human man I'd ever encountered. It was hard to tell from his prone position, but I'd have wagered he was well over seven feet tall. The muscles in his back shifted under his tan skin as he changed position and I heard Felicity gasp again at whatever he'd done.

I studied where one of his huge hands gripped her thigh, forcing her legs open wider to accommodate the breadth of his shoulders, while his other hand stroked her between her legs, teasing one hole and then the other, his shoulders shaking with a chuckle every time she jumped and shuddered.

He may have been playing the submissive for her at that moment, but something told me it was only an act.

"See something you like?" Her question pulled me from my study of their compromising position. "You know you're always invited, my friend." She winked at me, and I slid my hand down to the button of my pants.

"Is that so? It looks like you're being well serviced. What could I possibly offer?" I took a step closer to the bed.

In an impressively acrobatic feat, she clamped her thighs tight around his shoulders and flipped them both, so he landed on his back with her riding his face. He groaned and his hands reached back and parted her to show me her glistening core, sliding his fingers in and out of her slowly, urging her to grind down onto his face.

Felicity looked back at me over her shoulder. "Like I said, there's always room for one more."

I grinned before reaching up and pulling my shirt over my head and unfastening my pants. "Far be it from me to pass up such a…" I leaned forward and swiped my finger through her juices before sliding it into my mouth to savor. "Delicious opportunity."

I climbed onto the bed, straddling the other man's torso as I did, before I addressed him. "Any issues having another man's cock so near your mouth?"

He lifted her up off his face long enough to shoot me a grin. "None at all." His tongue extended from his mouth to offer her clit a languorous lick before he pulled her back down to his face, keeping his hands in place so she was completely bared to me.

I pushed her forward until she knelt on all fours on top of him, and pulled my aching cock from my pants, swiping it up and down the length of her cunt, coating myself in her juices. I jerked when his tongue darted over the head of my cock. "Mmm. I can see that."

I pushed my hips forward until the head slipped inside her, feeling her walls grip it greedily, trying to pull me in the rest of the way, but I remained just barely inside, teasing her as I reached over to the bedside table and grabbed a clear glass bottle.

"Is this what I think it is?" I inquired with an arched brow.

She looked back at me over her shoulder again. "Even half-demons need lubricant for ass-play, Felix."

I laughed as I pulled the cork out of the bottle, sliding out of her before drizzling the liquid over my cock and using my hand to coat it fully before I slid my slick fingers over her tiny, puckered hole, dipping one inside to get her nice and slick. "This may be my favorite invention of the modern age."

"Lube dates back to the ancient Romans, Felix, just because you've just discovered it doesn't mean it's new," she snarked at me before she gasped when I pushed the head of my cock against her ass and snapped my hips, breaching her tight ring of muscle. "Oh fuck. That cock. I forget when you don't come visit me for a while." Another gasp. "Felix..." she whined. "Give it to me."

I smoothed a hand over one of her cheeks, fully

intending to land a smack there, when a giant hand reached up and wrapped around my wrist, squeezing uncomfortably. I looked down as if I'd be able to meet his gaze, and he waggled a finger at me.

Okay then. No spanking the half-demon. Hmm. *Interesting.*

"Never let it be said I'm not generous," I quipped before pulling back slightly, watching her stretch around me beautifully. I thrust again and gained another couple of inches, groaning at how tight she was wrapped around me. I pulled back a bit, and when I pushed forward again I kept going until my hips met hers and she keened beneath me.

"Oh, fuck. Yes. I'm going to come all over his face if you keep that up." Her head was thrown back, bright red hair spilling down her back in an irresistible fall that I couldn't help but wrap around my fist.

One of the demon's hands brushed against my balls as he slid three fingers into her pussy and he moved so I could coordinate my thrusts to counter his. I slid in and out of her ass as he slid his fingers in and out of her pussy, and all the while I could feel her shuddering as he tended to her clit.

Some days, I thought it might be nice to be a woman, with so many ways that a man—or men—could pleasure her simultaneously, but then I remembered how inept the vast majority of the population was in this area and changed my mind. Finding one man who knew his way around a woman's body had to be hard enough; finding more than one to do it at the same time seemed like a herculean task.

Felicity's moans had grown louder, but I could tell she was having trouble getting there. I reached behind me and unfastened his pants as I spoke. "I think she needs more, so please don't kill me for what I'm about to do."

I gripped his cock in my hand, pumping him a couple of times, unnecessarily, because he was already hard enough to hammer nails from what I could feel. I carefully withdrew from her before reaching my arm around her and lifting, dragging both of us down his body until his face was revealed to me, glistening from her juices.

I raised my brow at him and he grinned.

I positioned her so she could sink down onto his cock that I still held in my fist. I watched, fascinated, as her pussy stretched to accommodate his girth before I ran my thumb around her tight back hole again.

"Are you ready for more?" I asked her.

"Yes!" She was grinding on his dick, and I had to hold her hips to keep her still so I could ease back into her ass. The fit was quite a bit tighter now that she was riding his cock as well.

"Mmm," I groaned. "Do you like being so full of us? Because this feels fucking amazing for me. I can feel all your muscles clamping down. So fucking tight."

"Less talking, Felix. As much as I adore your filthy mouth, right now I just need you to destroy me." Felicity's whole body shuddered and trembled as she chased her orgasm.

I met his gaze over her shoulder and watched him slide two of his fingers in his mouth before he fitted his hand between their bodies. I knew the moment he made contact with her clit, and whatever it was he did sent her into keening orgasm that nearly dragged me right over the edge with her. She was clamped around the two of us so tightly that neither of us would be able to move until she'd released us, so I just rocked my hips, helping her ride out her high as she shuddered and slumped between us. When she'd settled enough that I could feel her muscles relax again, I stroked my hand down her spine, loving the way the sweat coated her skin.

"Can you take more, love?" I asked. I could feel his cock twitching against the thin wall that separated us, and knew it wouldn't take much for me to fuck her so well that we both came.

"Make it fast," she replied, her voice muffled with her face pressed into his shoulder. "I'm about to pass out from the best orgasm I've had in a decade."

I chuckled but then put on my serious face. "Good girl. You don't have to do anything but lie there and take it while we fuck you raw. Just rest while we fill you up until you're overflowing." Her muscles clamped down and it drew an irreverent laugh out of me. "No, no. You're tired. No clamping down. You just lie there while we use your body. This isn't for you, it's for us." She peeled one eye open long enough to offer me a glare that had me laughing again, but I shook my head in admonition. "Just lie there and take these cocks. You're ours to use now."

When she stretched languidly and pushed her ass into me, I knew she was on board and there was something about the idea of her handing over that control that turned me on to no end.

I pulled my hips away from hers, sliding until I'd almost pulled out entirely. I drizzled more of the lube from the bottle onto my cock and the place where she and I were connected. His hand came up and swiped the excess, dragging it down to where they were connected as well. When I set the bottle back down I met his gaze over her shoulder, and he tilted his head at me in a silent "It's your show."

I slid my hand around my cock, stroking her softly where she was stretched around me, watching her skin pebble as I did. "Brace yourself."

I slid home as I curled myself over her back, grazing my teeth against the tendon in her neck and feeling her arch into me as I did. Then I began fucking them in earnest. Using my entire body to rock her against his cock, creating a rhythm that, based on the way his face began to tighten and his eyes rolled back in his head, was pleasing to everyone involved.

"Oh, fuck," he groaned, thrusting his hips upward. "I'm coming."

I upped my pace, feeling his cock jerking inside her pussy as he unloaded inside her. "You feel him painting your insides, Felicity? Are you ready to have us spilling out of both of your holes?"

She nodded enthusiastically without saying anything, but I could feel her tightening around me and I knew she was about to come again.

I reached around her and found his fingers still avidly

stroking her clit and I slid my hand on top of his, adding more pressure, squeezing her clit gently between our fingers as I pulled back one last time and surged forward. She clamped down on me as my balls drew up and hot seed exploded from the head of my cock, the waves of pleasure almost too much to take as I rocked against them both.

I rested my forehead against her back, trying to catch my breath, when I heard him speak again. "We should invite him to join more often."

Felicity started laughing, still pressed between us, with two cocks still resting inside her well used body, and before long all three of us were laughing.

When I pulled out of her, I gently lifted her off him and stared, fascinated, as I watched our cum spill out of her, landing on his abdomen. She crawled off him and flopped onto her back next to him, throwing an arm over her eyes. I stayed where I was, mesmerized by the way our combined cum looked pooling against the ridges of tattooed muscle just above where his cock was already starting to harden again.

I glanced up to meet his eyes, only to find him staring at me heatedly. "Is that a perk of your nature? No refractory period?"

His lips parted to show me all his teeth, half grin, half leer. "No, I think that's just because you're still sitting on me and staring at my cock like you want to know what it feels like in your mouth. Have you ever had a cock in your mouth?" he asked.

I shook my head. "I haven't. Never really had the opportunity." I shrugged returning my perusal to his now fully erect cock. "I'm not against it." I licked my lips.

"Go ahead then. I guarantee it tastes fucking amazing right now because it just came out of Felicity's delicious pussy. Why don't you lick it clean for me?"

I returned back to my previous thought that his submission to Felicity had been out of character. This one was not submissive in the least.

I reached down and swirled my fingers through our seed where it was spilled onto his stomach, spreading it over his skin before again wrapping my hand around him. He groaned in response.

"I've never said no to trying new things."

I slid down his body, feeling my own cock harden as the head of it dragged against his leather pants on my way down. I darted my tongue out when I reached the base of him, pressing the tip of it into the sensitive dip there and feeling his hips jerk in response. I looked up the expanse of his body to see he'd pulled his arms behind his head, propping himself up so he could watch me.

I flattened my tongue and let my saliva coat him as I slid my mouth up to his crown, savoring the combined taste of all three of us on my tongue. I swirled it around his head, noting it was probably large enough that a woman would have a hard time wrapping her mouth around it. Me, on the other hand? I didn't have any problems in that department, and I opened my mouth around the head, sliding down over him slowly, sucking my cheeks in, enjoying the feel of him in my mouth. Enjoying the fullness.

I groaned, and he matched the sound with his own.

"Fuck. Felix. That mouth. Can you take more?"

I shot him a look before I hollowed my cheeks and slid my mouth down his cock until he'd sunk into the back of my throat with my lips pressed against his pelvis.

"Definitely," he gasped. "Need to invite him to play." He jerked. "More." He shuddered. "Often."

I chuckled around his length, making him jump and curse, before I slid one hand into his pants where they were still gathered at his hips, sliding my fingers over the patch of skin between his balls and his ass, putting just a little pressure there before I kept going, my hands still slick from the lube I'd used on Felicity, I slid a finger between his cheeks and felt him shudder again.

"Oh, fuck. Do it," he grunted.

I slid my middle finger into his ass and rubbed the tip of it against the sensitive nerve endings there as I continued fucking him with my mouth, letting him slide deep into my throat and swallowing hard to massage him as he did. When his balls began to draw up, I pulled my finger out and added another, giving him a little stretch before pumping them both in and out of his ass as he groaned and cursed, his cock kicking in my mouth as he came down my throat.

I gave him another couple of strokes of my fingers in his ass before I slowly withdrew them, languidly pulling my mouth away from his cock at the same time until I was hovered over him with a very satisfied smirk on my face.

"How'd I do?"

FOUR YEARS AGO

"Good afternoon, Silas. Thank you for coming in today. Can I get you something to drink? Coffee? Water?" The officer in the ill-fitting suit held a hand out for me to shake before gesturing at the conference table.

"Whiskey?" I deadpanned.

"Ha-ha, unfortunately I can't offer that, though I can understand why you'd prefer it." He shrugged uncomfortably, and I relented. Rubbing my hands down the legs of my pants to wipe away the sweat.

"Coffee, thanks," I said before surveying the room and selecting a chair where my back was to the wall. I'd always hated having my back to the door and that feeling was magnified under the current circumstances.

He nodded enthusiastically and made his way over

to the sideboard in the room, pouring coffee into a little paper cup and setting it on the table in front of me.

"Cream? Sugar?" He raised a brow.

"Black is fine. Thanks." I wrapped my hands around the cup, enjoying the heat that radiated through them at the contact. I'd been cold since I saw the first headline and nothing had been able to warm me up since.

"Okay, first of all, I want to be clear that you are not being charged with anything. We've brought you in today to ask for your help in tracking down our target and substantiating our case against him so he can go away for a very long time.

"With that being said, I'd like your permission to record this interview. It will go on record, however your identity will be protected when this goes to court; if you're called to testify, we'll close the court for that portion of the hearing. I can't guarantee your anonymity during the course of the investigation, but I promise you we'll do everything we can to protect you." He folded his hands in front of him but his eyes kept dragging to the recording device on the table between us.

"I think the world already knows that it was my words that 'inspired' your guy to go on this spree, so I think the cat is already out of the bag…but I do appreciate anything you can do on that front." I nodded toward the recorder. "Go ahead."

"Okay, thank you for your cooperation." He reached over and pressed a button on the device before he addressed me again. "For the record, can you please state your full name?"

I cleared my throat, suddenly nervous, despite the

fact I'd told him it was okay to record. "Silas Allen Wells."

"Thank you, Mr. Wells. And can you please state your age and occupation for the record?"

"I'm thirty-three years old and I'm a writer. An author, I guess. I write books." For someone whose professional description included being "good with words," I'd suddenly found myself stumbling over all mine.

"Thank you. Now, I'm going to give you a little bit of background and then ask you some questions. Are you squeamish, Mr. Wells?"

It didn't miss me that he'd begun our conversation calling me Silas and now I was Mr. Wells but I shook my head cautiously. "One can't really write the kind of books I write and also be squeamish."

"Good. Okay, so we'll just jump right in then. Let the record show that I'm providing evidence photos: numbers one through five for Mr. Wells to observe." He slid a folder across the table and tapped on the cover with a finger. "Take your time."

I took a deep breath and lifted the cover, sliding the five glossy photos out and spreading them across the table in front of me. The first showed a young woman, her body half in, half out of a culvert in what looked like a park or wooded area. She had clearly been grossly mistreated prior to her death, and all the signs pointed to her having been dragged for a distance either before or after she'd been killed. I slid my gaze to the next photo, noting it was the same woman, but she'd been rolled over and the photo was zoomed in on her right shoulder blade where it appeared she'd been branded. I closed my eyes. Any hope that this case had nothing to do with me flew out the window.

I took a deep breath and surveyed the other three photos that were close-ups of other details at the crime scene, but I'd seen everything I needed to. Whoever had done this to her had done so using my words as an instruction manual.

I felt sick. Dizzy. The sound of my heartbeat in my ears again reminded me of what I imagined the hooves of the four horsemen of the apocalypse would sound like as they came straight for you.

This poor girl was dead. Because of something I'd come up with out of my imagination. This was my fault.

It was all my fault.

James sat down across from me at my kitchen table. His expression gave nothing away, but I didn't need to be psychic to guess what was about to happen.

"Silas, I like you—you know that, right?" He started with the platitude of all platitudes, and I snorted, looking just past his shoulder, refusing to make eye contact while he abandoned ship. I knew what this was.

"Yeah, James. I know." I reached for the glass of whiskey I was finally allowed to have now that I'd returned to the safety of my own home. I took a healthy sip before he cleared his throat to continue.

"The publisher...they just don't think it's a good idea to continue your working relationship. You obviously are going to have to lay low for a little while until the dust settles on this case, and, even then, I'm sure you aren't going to want to finish this series. You know. Under the circumstances." He grimaced.

"So they're dropping me." I leveled him with a tired stare. "And what about the advance? Am I supposed to be able to pay that back?"

"Well..." He hedged. "Part of that was for this last book, which you delivered!" He smiled like that was an accomplishment I could ever be proud of again. "So they'll just want half of it back. You know. For the next book, which you aren't going to write. Right?"

I rolled my eyes at him. "No, James, I will not be writing the next book. Or maybe any book ever again after this," I muttered, tilting the glass to my lips again.

"There's one more thing..." His eyes shifted away from mine before his shoulders dropped and he said the next bit like he was ashamed. "I have to drop you, too. The agency, they just feel like it's best if they distance themselves from the...um...situation."

"From me, you mean." I raised a brow at him before I waved my hand in his direction and dismissed him. "It's fine, James. I just need you to get the fuck out of my house now so I can get blackout drunk and pretend I live in a different timeline."

He stood, and I could feel him staring at me awkwardly as he shuffled in place for a moment, but I eventually heard the click of the front door latching closed behind him, and I breathed a sigh of relief.

I scooped the whiskey bottle off the table and tucked it under my arm. I left the glass where it sat as I headed to my bedroom to hide for the rest of the night at least. Maybe even for the rest of the week.

PART III

NOW

"All great ideas are dangerous."

-Oscar Wilde

Chapter Eleven

FELIX

I'd been sitting on the catwalk overlooking the bar for hours with my legs draped between the spindles of the railing, my forehead pressed to the warm wood—watching the mass of bodies moving below with an envy so visceral I could nearly feel the brush of their bodies against my own.

One man that seemed to always be at the center of the crowd caught my attention. His smile wide and his expression open; a wink tossed out occasionally when someone danced close to him. There was something magnetic about him. The way he moved, the carefree way in which he carried himself, the way he skimmed a hand along a shoulder as he passed by his fellow dancers on the way to the bar.

I'd discovered a side effect of my long life, not to mention my exile from humanity, was that I'd gained an appreciation for humans, regardless of their form; I'd begun to see the soul flickering inside their form and it was that force which drew me to a person. Sexual attraction hadn't been a factor on that plane of existence in so long that I couldn't even recall what it was like to select a companion purely on the basis of whether I wanted to stick my cock in them. In hindsight, I truly had been a woefully shallow man.

As I sat on the ledge, watching him as he moved, I got flickers of a vision, ephemeral in nature, but my brow drew up even at the brief glimpses I saw. Something was coming for him. Something terrible.

I tore my gaze from him and studied the rest of the crowded bar, looking from face to face, trying to determine if there was one amongst them who bore him ill will, but my search didn't provide any additional premonition. The flighty nature of that particular gift never failed to drive me to the edge of madness. Why bother showing me anything if I couldn't draw enough information from the visions to stop something bad happening?

I growled in frustration and returned my gaze to the place where he'd been standing moments before, only to find the spot empty. I panned through the crowd, searching for his dark head of hair, but couldn't find him.

I climbed to my feet quickly, feeling my wings twitch on my back as if they, too, were offering a warning. I cleared the railing and landed with my booted feet in the middle of the bar, sprinting the length of it with no one the wiser before I jumped off the end and bolted out the front door. The bell jangled, announcing my departure, but no one paid any attention.

I paused on the walk outside in the midst of the people gathered out there smoking, talking, and laughing amongst themselves. I tilted my head to listen; when I heard a grunt coming from the alleyway that I had dropped into hours prior, my feet immediately turned in that direction.

I dodged through the gathered people, occasionally brushing a shoulder with my own, careful to keep from making skin-to-skin contact with any of them. I noted their startled glances as they looked around, trying to understand what they'd felt but hadn't seen.

By the time I broke free of the crowd, I took off at a dead run toward the corner and ducked into the mouth of the alleyway; the sight before me triggering a rage that I'd seldom experienced in my long life.

The beautiful man I'd been watching in the club was being held up by two burly men, his arms banded cruelly behind his back, while a third man was landing vicious blows to his face and stomach. By the time I reached them deep in the recesses of the alley, they'd dropped him to the dirty ground where he curled in on himself. His hands were cradled around his head in an attempt to avoid the booted feet that were pummeling his body relentlessly.

The three men stood around him, hurling vicious words as they kicked and spat at him, and I heard the sound of bone snapping just as I knelt down and wrapped my gloved hand around a rusty steel pipe that someone had been kind enough to discard there.

I was risking drawing attention to myself, but how could I simply stand by and watch the assault continue?

It wasn't in me. I weighed my options in the moment it took for another grunt to sound out from the man and decided consequences could be damned.

I swung my impromptu weapon at the first man's head with all my strength. The sound it made on contact was wildly satisfying, and it drew a grim smile to my face as I spun to the next man while his friend crumpled to the ground—unconscious with one strike.

The second and third men went down in a similar fashion to the first, unable to defend against an assailant they couldn't see coming as I spun from one to the next, wielding the steel bar with deadly precision. In mere moments, I stood over all three of them with my chest heaving with adrenaline.

A choking sound from their victim had me spinning around and dropping to my knees in front of him, hands hovering over his body, but not touching. Never touching.

He gasped and the wet sound of it told me his injuries were substantial. *Goddammit.* I'd been too slow.

A cough erupted from his throat and bright red blood sprayed on the dirty concrete in front of him with the sound.

"I know you're there." His voice was thready.

He fought to gather another breath and I could see in his face what it cost him to do so.

"I know you're there," he repeated. "I don't know who, or what, you are, but thank you for trying to save me."

Something in my chest spasmed at the finality of his words. *Thank you for trying to save me.*

I'd tried. But failed.

"Please." There was a catch in his voice. "I don't want to die alone in a dirty alley. Please."

I hung my head, every sense of self-preservation I'd maintained over the past one-hundred years fighting with the need to comfort him in his final moments. I slid my black glove off my left hand and reached out slowly, my hand trembling, not certain until the last moment if I could make myself do it, but wanting to with every fiber of my being.

The feel of his skin under my hand was jarring, foreign—*nirvana*.

I closed my eyes, allowing myself to soak in the sensation. When I reopened them, it was to meet his own pain-clouded gaze. His eyes widened as he took in my appearance. I knew what he was seeing, but I couldn't imagine it would make much sense to him.

He coughed again and the arm he'd wrapped around his middle curled up further, tightening around his rib cage as if he hoped to be able to return his insides into their proper position by sheer will alone. "Are you..." he barely grated out the words. "Are you an angel?"

One side of my mouth tipped up in a rueful expression. "Hardly."

"Well, whatever you are. Thank you. For trying." Every word he uttered cost him and the pool of blood that had collected on the ground in front of him was steadily growing, telling me his time was running out. "Will you stay with me?"

I nodded, settling down in front of him more firmly,

feeling the pool of blood seep through my pants legs. I kept my hand wrapped around the side of his head, making sure, even when his eyes were shut in agony, he could feel that he wasn't alone.

"What's your name?" I asked.

"Kyle," he whispered. "What's yours?"

I offered him a tip of my imaginary hat. "Felix."

He stared at me for a moment, but I couldn't be sure he was actually seeing me. "Felix? Can I tell you something?"

I cocked my head, torn between comforting him and trying to draw the attention of a passerby so they could get him help, even though I could tell that no help would be able to get there soon enough to change his path. My vision had shown me that, and, once again, I cursed that particular gift.

"You can tell me anything," I replied, feeling that ache in my chest again. I didn't want to watch this man die.

"I'm gay," he rasped. "That's why they…"

I nodded, feeling the anger stir in my gut again. "I'd deduced as much from the barbs they were flinging."

"My family, they disowned me. All but Anka. My twin sister." His eyes went distant, and he stopped breathing for long enough I thought maybe he'd passed on.

He regained focus after a moment and took another thin, wheezing breath. "This will kill her."

"Tell me about her," I whispered. Willing to offer him anything to give comfort in that moment.

"Her name is Anka Kelly. She's…beautiful. Her soul.

It's..." A rivulet of blood was now streaming from one of his nostrils as well as from the corner of his mouth. "She's the best person I know." For the next while, in between choking breaths and pained expressions, he told me about his twin. How he loved her. How he admired her strength of character. How, of all the people in the world that were supposed to love him, she was the only one who had ever done it well.

"Will you..." His words cut off and his face clenched as a spasm ran through his body.

I slid my hand from where it cupped his jaw down to grip the hand that cradled his ribs, wrapping mine around his fully.

I offered a comforting squeeze. "I'll check on her."

He was silent for a long time. A tear leaked from his eye, rolling over the patrician bones of his nose and dropped into the puddle of blood beneath him. "Thank you."

I watched the beautiful man as he struggled for his last breath, wishing there was something more I could do to offer him comfort, but knowing there truly was nothing. I watched his light grow dimmer and dimmer until, with one last gasp, it ceased to exist entirely.

And still, I remained. If, over the next brief while, my tears joined his own, there was no one to witness their fall.

Chapter Twelve

FELIX

"*To everything, there is a season and a time to every purpose under Heaven: a time to be born and a time to die; a time to plant and a time to pluck up that which is planted; a time to kill and a time to heal…*"

The preacher's voice was quiet in the stillness, as if he'd toned it down to account for the fact that only one mourner stood for his sermon that morning.

From my vantage point, I watched her face as she listened to him drone on as she stood over her brother's grave. She was clad in a black sheath with her hair pulled back into a severe bun secured at the nape of her graceful neck. I could see the resemblance to her brother clearly. He'd told me they were twins, but I'd have known even if he hadn't now that I was standing mere feet away from her. They shared the same patrician features, the same dark hair, the same bright green eyes; hers were red-rimmed when she lifted her sunglasses to wipe away her tears and they appeared to glow in the sunlight.

She didn't make a scene during the sermon; didn't throw herself against her brother's casket with a wail, or even shift her stance. She simply stood quietly, listening to the priest, though she did wince when he got to the part about a time to kill.

Aside from that, her face remained impassive but for the tears that ran down her porcelain cheeks.

There was the slightest tremble in her hands when she took the white rose she'd clutched throughout the service and placed it lovingly on top of his casket. When she placed her hand on the top of it I saw her lips move, though no sound came out. *I'll be seeing you, little brother.*

The priest paused as he passed her, placing his hand on her shoulder as he offered a word of consolation before he began the long walk to where his car was parked.

Anka remained frozen there, and my feet twitched against the manicured grass, yearning to go offer comfort; knowing I couldn't. I watched for long minutes, hoping someone would come and take her hand, offer her an arm to lean on, but no one came.

Finally, she shook her head violently, swiped at her tears one last time, and turned to head in the same direction the priest had gone. Her head was held high, her spine stiff, but that tremble in her hands remained as she crossed the too-green grass, opened her car door, and slid into the driver's seat. She pulled the door closed behind her with a quiet snick and wrapped her hands around the steering wheel, but didn't reach to crank the engine.

I cocked my head, stepping closer so I could study her face as she sat staring straight ahead at the rows and rows of gravestones across the way. I wondered what she was seeing.

My own grief nearly took me to my knees when she opened her mouth and threw her head back against the headrest letting out an anguished scream.

That scream echoed in my mind for hours after she'd gathered herself and driven away from the cemetery. Hours that I watched the light go from the mellow butter of morning light to the harsh brightness of the noonday sun, and eventually, a creeping purple twilight as it descended upon the landscape. I knew I should go, but something held me there.

"I told you it would kill her."

I jerked my head around, eyes widening comically at the nearly see-through version of Kyle camped out on the lawn next to me.

"The fuck?" I whispered, to no one in particular.

He offered me a sad smile. "You look like you've seen a ghost. You really should get out more, Felix."

I stared at him wide-eyed for a beat before I turned my head slowly back to the view I'd been staring at for the better part of the day. Neat rows of headstones laid out one after another up and down the gentle hills of the cemetery, the landscape broken up occasionally by giant oak trees that offered shade to the handful of final resting places nearby.

"How are you here?" I asked him.

I saw him shrug out of the corner of my eye.

"Not sure. I always heard most ghosts have unresolved business. Maybe that's it."

I turned to look at him again. "Do you have unresolved business?"

"Well, I guess there's the matter of the assholes that put me here, but other than that I'm not really sure."

I clenched my jaw before I shook my head resolutely. "That business is...no longer unresolved."

His mouth dropped open in shock. "Felix, you naughty boy! Did you avenge me after only having just met me? How romantic. Pardon me while I swoon." He put his hands underneath his chin and batted his lashes at me.

I rolled my eyes and ran my fingers through the grass near my hip, pulling a blade out and placing it between my teeth, enjoying the crisp green taste of it bursting on my tongue. "They had it coming. And they probably already had brain damage from taking a pipe to the head, so I was really just saving any loved ones they might've had from a lifetime of spoon feeding them baby food out of a jar."

"Ah." He nodded, amusement sparkling in his eyes. "Your version of community service then. Just doing your part to help humanity, hmm?"

I grinned. "Exactly."

"So, if that isn't my unresolved business. What do you think it might be?"

I studied him for a minute, noting that, as we'd spoken, he'd become more substantial—taking on a solidity he'd lacked when he first appeared. "Anka?" I asked.

He turned his gaze to where her car had sat hours before. "Anka," he confirmed.

I studied Felicity over the rim of my glass, taking a long sip and relishing the burn as the whiskey flowed down my throat.

"Why arn you staring at me like that?"

She snorted and tilted her head to the left and then back to the right as she studied me from different angles.

"I'm staring at you because, in the span of a century, I've never seen you so smashed that you can't form intelligible language. I think…" She placed her hand on her chin. "I think I'm worried about you. Which is obviously cause for great concern. I don't…worry."

I tossed my head back on a laugh, but thought better of it when the room spun wildly with the movement.

"Does no worry 'bout mes. I's so fines," I assured her sagely.

"Clearly," she offered drolly. "So what's with the monkey suit?"

I blinked at her slowly before I realized she was referring to the black pants and waistcoat I'd worn to the funeral. "Respects. I paid 'em."

Her eyebrows ratcheted up to her hairline. "I have questions. First of all, who the hell do you actually respect? And second of all, you remember no one can see you—right?"

I slapped my fist against my chest. "I see me."

"Okay, deep thinker, so who did you pay your respects to?" She turned in her chair and refilled her glass from the second—third?—bottle of whiskey of the night before she returned her unwavering stare back to me.

"Kyle." I leaned forward, resting my head in my hands as I stared at the floor between my boots.

"Felix." I watched her booted feet shift impatiently in my peripheral vision. "Who the fuck is Kyle?"

"Was. *Was* Kyle." I sniffled.

I heard her huff in frustration. "I comprehend you've had enough whiskey to drown an upper demon, but try and focus, will you?" She waved her hand below my face.

"I touched him. He died," I whispered before raising my gaze to meet hers once again. "Was so sad, Licity."

"Wait a fucking minute. Felix, are you telling me you touched someone and they died? Holy fuck, I need to go talk to Dave." She started to rise from her chair but I stopped her.

"No, no, no. He dying *then* I touched." My eyes welled with tears again before I implored her. "How do I stop?"

Felicity leaned forward, placing her face close to mine before she answered. "Felix, is this the first time you've ever mourned someone?"

I thought about it for a moment before I nodded slowly.

"What about your family? Your mother?" she asked, incredulous.

I shook my head. "She lived a long, long time. She was happy." I stared into the distance over her head before I continued. "He was so young. And so pretty. Full of life. Then *meanness* took him." I spat the last part.

"What did you do, Felix?" She raised a brow at me and looked over her shoulder like she was expecting a knock on the door any moment.

I shrugged. "I killed the meanness." I placed my finger over my lips and dropped my voice to a whisper. "But no one saw. Shhh."

Chapter Fourteen

FELIX

I watched as she made her way through the bustling historic district, hips swaying in time to the music coming from the taqueria on the corner. She was oblivious to the looks that followed her as she passed the outdoor tables packed with happy hour patrons, as she never took her eyes away from the book in her hands. I growled at anyone that stared too long as I followed along behind her. They couldn't *hear* me, but it assuaged my irritation somewhat.

She was enchanting that day, as usual. Her dark locks danced in the crisp fall breeze, a strand wrapping itself around her neck before she absentmindedly pulled it away and tucked it behind her ear, only for it to break free immediately in a show of rebellion. The urge to put my hand out and see if it would wrap so lovingly around my own fingers was a compulsion I could barely resist.

Was it as soft as it looked? I was dying to know, and

even my awareness of the consequences of such an act barely dampened the urge. I forced my hand into a fist at my side as I kept pace behind her.

She couldn't see me. But if I touched her? Oh, she'd feel that.

I almost grabbed her when she stumbled as she stepped off the curb to cross the street, barely checking the flow of traffic before she moved forward. I'd appointed myself her personal guardian, completely without her knowledge naturally, so the thought of allowing her to wander into danger was abhorrent.

She jerked her head up, and I imagined her jade green eyes widening to take in her surroundings as she regained her footing. Thankfully, she took more care with her steps until she'd reached the sidewalk on the next block, but then her head immediately tilted back down, once again focused on the words on the page before her.

I knew she was headed home to an empty house since her oxygen-thief ex had moved along, and while I knew I couldn't do anything to fill that gap for her personally, I wondered if there was something else I could do about it. What was the use of having a mostly omniscient invisible demon guardian if they didn't, on occasion, wave their magic wand and move things around on your behalf?

I tilted my head and grinned at the thought of all I could do with my *magic wand* if my circumstances were different, but that was as far as I allowed that train of thought to progress. It would do no good.

The grin on my face turned feral as an idea began to form.

A cunning, if devious, idea.

I just had to figure out a way to put it into play. It would take time, of course. But that made no difference to me. After all...I had nothing *but* time.

Chapter Fifteen

FELIX

"You're plotting."

I whipped my head around, only to find another of the creatures that had decided to haunt me for all eternity leaned up against the side of the building that housed the taqueria. I greeted her with narrowed eyes.

"Must you always sneak up on me?"

"Must you always be so jumpy?" she fired back.

I considered her question momentarily. "Oddly enough, you're not the first...ah, person to point that out of late."

"So, what brings you topside on this glorious fall evening, Felix?"

I'd begun walking, knowing she'd keep pace with me until her curiosity had been satisfied. She was like a terrier that way, refusing to relax her grip until she'd gotten what she was after.

I stopped walking and turned toward her, causing

her to draw up quickly. When we were facing off, I cocked my head at her. "What is it that you're after, Serafina?"

She shrugged, looking off to the side briefly before she met my gaze again. "What makes you think I'm after something?

"Because you're always after something." I rolled my eyes.

"Maybe I just want to check on your progress. See how your humanity is coming along."

I might have believed her if she hadn't cut her eyes off to the side again, mid-sentence.

"Mm-hmm. I see. Well, of course you'd have an... academic interest in my development. On account of you being the one who put me in this position." I cocked a brow at her. Not believing for a minute that was the reason for her appearance.

"Exactly. I feel...responsible. For your personal growth. I'm like your emotional parole officer. Just here for my check-in." She was nodding so enthusiastically that she resembled one of those hula girl bobble heads I'd seen people stick to their car dash.

"Of course, of course. That's reasonable. But just in case there's more to your visit, are you sure there isn't anything else you'd like to know? Perhaps something you'd like to ask me?" I bit my lip, eager for her to confirm my long-standing suspicion.

She adopted a nonchalant pose, staring off down the road, that didn't fool me for a moment. "Well, I..."

Something happened in her face then. A brief crack in her normally sarcastic mien. The smallest glimpse of the girl she'd been before I—and who knew how many others in her life—had hardened her heart.

I softened toward her in that moment and the twinge of guilt still remained after a century.

She turned to face me again and let me see it for a moment. "How is she?"

Ah. As I'd thought. But…was poor Serafina getting her heart broken again? I found the notion quite a bit more disheartening than I would have thought myself capable of on her behalf.

I pictured Felicity as I'd last seen her, when Davanos had come to collect her from my rooms the night of Kyle's funeral. They'd both stared down at me pityingly before he'd urged her to leave me to pass out in peace. He'd used the toe of his boot to slide a trashcan closer to the side of my chair and he'd scooped her over his shoulder.

Somehow I didn't think relaying that particular vision would do anything for Sera's peace of mind.

"I believe she's well. Have you two not been in touch lately?" I asked carefully. I didn't particularly want to involve myself in that love triangle, if there was one, but a part of me did feel I owed Sera an ear if she needed someone to talk to.

She shook her head. "It's been a bit. I'm sure she's really busy. Demon stuff. Probably takes up a lot of time, I'm guessing." She looked up at me with wide eyes.

"Oh, sure. Demon stuff. Very time consuming. Mayhem, mischief, and the like. Always someone to torment. Her schedule is grueling, I'm sure."

Sera just stared at me, unblinking, before she

responded. "Yeah. That's what I figured." She looked down at her bare wrist. "Well, would you look at the time. I didn't realize. I have to run, but I'll see you around, Felix."

I leaned back against the building, offering her a sympathetic smile. "Okay, Sera. I'll be seeing you."

I'd twitched my wings and beamed myself back to Hell with a side quest that I hadn't intended on. But, if for no other reason than my own curiosity, I wanted to know: did any part of Felicity return Serafina's affection?

Chapter Sixteen

FELIX

The idea that had begun to form the last time I'd followed Anka had taken root in my brain and become more and more real as time passed. I'd finally thought of a way to make my stupid, flighty power of omniscience do some good for once.

I'd need Felicity's help for part of it, but I knew she wouldn't mind. We'd grown close in the last century. In a weird way, I thought she and I might be friends, aside from that part where she helped Serafina curse me. I'd never actually had a friend before, and something told me most people didn't partner up with a demon to double-team their friends. But maybe more people should. So, yeah, I thought we were friend-like, at least.

I shook my head at my own inner dialogue and reached to open her door before I thought better of it and knocked.

I heard whispering coming from the other side of the

door, followed by a grunt that definitely didn't come from Felicity.

"Who is it?" she called in a falsetto.

I choked back a laugh and swiped my hand over my face. "Felix."

I heard another grunt, followed by Felicity whisper-shouting. "Stop being such a big baby. It's not that big."

"I'll be the judge of that," the other, much deeper, voice responded drolly.

"Oh, for fuck's sake, I've had bigger in my pinky finger," she snarked back.

I cocked my head to the side. I'd made some assumptions about what was happening on the other side of the door, but her last statement had me more than a little confused.

More shuffling happened on the other side of the door, followed by a muffled curse and Felicity screaming, "I got it!"

"Uhh. Should I come back later?" I called.

"Come in, Felix," Felicity responded.

When I opened the door I was greeted by a scene that simply didn't add up. Dave was laying across her bed while she straddled his naked thighs. His wrists were tied to opposite corners of her bed, but Felicity was still fully clothed. I tried to piece it all together but Felicity interrupted my perusal before I could make sense out of the scene.

"Dave here had a splinter in his ass and he was being a big baby about it. Weren't you, big guy?" She smacked him on his ass cheek and he growled at her.

"For the love of fuck, Felicity, stop calling me Dave.

You know that's not my name." He tugged on the restraints that held his wrists and both snapped with what appeared to be very little effort on his part.

She rolled her eyes at me dramatically. "I know that's not your name, but Davanos sounds like you're some big, bad demon and we all know you're just a big ol' teddy bear." She climbed off the bed and straightened her clothing, while he stood and grabbed a pair of pants that were draped over the footboard of the bed.

I averted my eyes as he did, but couldn't help but flash back to the last time the three of us had shared this space. It'd been a while, but those memories still remained crystal clear in my mind.

Davanos's chuckle drew my eyes back up to meet his. "You're blushing, Felix." His deep voice rumbled out of his chest.

"Yeah, well, live-action porn just replayed in my brain for a minute there." I shrugged.

"Mmm. That was a good night. You should come back around more often, friend." He shot me a wicked grin.

"I'll keep that in mind."

I saw Felicity gesturing at him out of the corner of my eye but when I turned toward her she struck a nonchalant pose, draped over a velvet chaise in front of her fireplace.

"So, to what do we owe this visit, Felix?" She studied her cuticles like she hadn't just been waving frantically at Davanos.

"Well, it's actually good that I caught you both. I need a favor and it's a bit outside of my...wheelhouse."

Davanos went to join Felicity on the chaise, scooping her up as if she weighed nothing and taking her spot before setting her in his lap. Something had changed about them, but I couldn't put my finger on it. I'd have to come back to that mystery later, however. I had more important things to deal with at that moment.

"I need to give someone a vision," I stated.

"A vision," Felicity repeated.

"Well…a dream," I corrected.

"A dream," Davanos repeated.

"Sort of." I hedged, looking off to the side as I tried to find the right words. "I need to convey a lot of information to someone without them knowing I'm the one who did it. Or, more to the point, I need them to think *they* are the ones who came up with it."

They both stared at me blankly for a moment before Felicity turned and looked back at Davanos over her shoulder. "Do we want to know?"

He shook his head solemnly. "Absolutely not."

She nodded at him before she returned her gaze to meet mine. "And…if we somehow knew someone that could help you perform such a feat…what would we get out of it?"

I grinned at her. "The personal gratification of knowing you'd done something to help better the lives of two humans?"

"Nope. Does nothing for me. Try again," she declined.

"Hm. What could I do for you that would entice you?" I raised a brow.

Davanos cleared his throat. "I can think of a couple

things." He grunted when Felicity's elbow made contact with the washboard surface of his abs. I'd never seen him wear a shirt. Poor little demon. Maybe he didn't own one.

"Not that." He swatted the side of her ass.

He looked at me, and I swore I saw his pupils swirl for a split second before he spoke again. "You can owe me…a favor."

Felicity frowned. "What about me?"

He raised his brow at her, "I'm the one who's helping him."

She huffed and rolled her eyes. "Semantics."

Something told me I was going to end up regretting my next words, but I couldn't shake the idea that I had a chance to help not only Anka, but also my other little pet project, so without an ounce of self-preservation, I met Davanos's gaze. "Done."

"Felix…" Felicity cautioned. "You don't know what you're getting yourself into."

Davanos chuckled, and it sent chills down my spine. That had probably been a terrible idea.

I was sure it would be fine, though. Surely he wouldn't ask for anything too terrible.

Right?

The lawn looked like it hadn't been cut in a few weeks, but other than that the house in front of us was well maintained. Cute, even. If that was a thing. A mid-century craftsman bungalow with a long low porch stretching across the front of it, big eaves with windows across the breadth of the structure. Since it was 2 a.m., only one light shone from inside, and my guess was it was just there to deter anyone with bad intentions. Lucky for me, I didn't have bad intentions, and if I did a thirty-watt bulb wouldn't have done much to dissuade me.

I turned my head to study the mammoth next to me and gave him a jaunty salute. "This is the spot. Are you ready?"

Davanos shot me a look. "We're not here to pull some mission impossible shit. Just point me to the man and let me get back to my girl before she finds someone else to entertain her for the evening."

My eyebrows shot up to my hairline. "Your girl? It's that serious, huh?"

He grumbled. "She may not know it yet. But she'll come around eventually."

I tossed my head back on a silent laugh. "Oh boy. You've got your work cut out for you. That one has been a wild card from day one, if I had to guess. You trying to put a ring on it?"

He turned his head slowly and looked down at me; no small feat considering I was well over six feet myself. "I'm a demon, Felix. We do not 'put a ring on it.'"

"Oh. Well…then, what do you do? I mean…is there a ritual or something?" My mind raced with the possibilities.

He snorted. "No, I simply ask, and if she consents, the next time I fuck her I shape her insides to fit only my cock. From that day on, no one else will ever be able to satisfy her like I can."

My jaw dropped at his words. "Are you fucking serious right now? That's a whole new level of commitment. What happens if you decide you don't want to be with her at some point?"

His stare was unwavering. "I won't."

"But what if you do?" I repeated.

"I won't."

"But…what if you do?"

His hand shot out and wrapped around my neck, placing enough pressure on it that I knew he could have me writhing on the ground in seconds if he wanted to. "I. Won't."

"Okay, buddy. I hear you. Fidelity big amongst the demon crowd. Got it," I wheezed out.

When he released my neck I took a few gasping breaths, rubbing the skin there to try and re-establish the circulation.

He nodded, clearly having made his point to his satisfaction.

When I'd regained full use of my windpipe I started toward the front door, and I could hear him following closely. On the porch I started lifting flowerpots and looking under the doormat.

"What are you doing, Felix?" he asked, head cocked to the side.

"Looking for a key. Humans are notorious for locking themselves out of their homes. They stupidly tend to leave extra keys laying around in spots they consider 'hidden.'"

Davanos rolled his eyes and wrapped one of the giant mitts he called a hand around my bicep. In a blink, we stood on the other side of the door.

"Handy trick. You should take up a career of breaking and entering. You'd be aces at it," I quipped.

He looked around before he replied, "I didn't break. Only entered."

I rolled my eyes. "Demons. So literal." I took a step toward the stairs the led to the second floor where I assumed the bedrooms were, and he stopped me again.

"This man. Who is he to you?"

I paused with my foot on the first tread, turning to look at him over my shoulder. "Just one step toward my redemption, Dave."

He studied me for another minute. "If you say so. Lead the way, Felix."

I continued up the steps and was surprised to find that his footfalls behind me were far quieter than I would have imagined.

I grinned when I heard him mutter, "And stop calling me Dave."

If I had to guess, I'd have said that Silas was a very restless sleeper. Perhaps even violent. As we stood at the foot of his bed studying him, the covers were wrapped around him more than once, like he'd rolled in his sleep. One arm was stretched out to his side, as if he were reaching for something even in slumber, and the other rested over his heart.

It had never occurred to me that one could tell a lot about the mental state of a human being just based on the position they slept in, but nothing about the way he currently laid in his bed screamed "peaceful."

Davanos stepped to the side of the bed and looked at me expectantly.

We'd discussed the logistics of this particular gift of his on the way there, so I knew he needed to be touching both me and Silas in order to be the conduit through which the information I wanted him to have would be transferred.

I had a sudden thought, however. "What if he wakes up when you touch him?" I whispered.

"He won't," Davanos stated calmly.

"But what if he does?" I repeated. I was suddenly having déjà vu.

The big demon rolled his eyes at me. "When I touch him he will go into a deeper sleep. He'll wake feeling better rested than it appears he has in quite some time." He gestured vaguely at the way Silas was twisted amongst the sheets.

"Okay," I whispered. But still, I remained where I stood.

"Have you changed your mind, Felix? Because you will still owe me a favor even if you back out at this point," he reminded me.

There was a low hum in the back of my mind, warning that whatever favor Davanos would ask of me wasn't going to be something I would be thrilled to do for him, but that wasn't the problem. I honestly wasn't sure how to put everything I wanted Silas to know in his brain in a form that he'd actually be able to do anything with it.

"What if he wakes up and has no recollection of anything we"—I gestured at his head—"put in there?"

"He won't."

"But what if he does?" I repeated.

The growl that Davanos let out should have woken then dead, but Silas remained still in his bed.

"You are getting on my last nerve, Felix. Do it, or don't do it. But if you question me one more time, I'm going to fill your mouth so full that you cannot talk. Again." He shot me a combination of an annoyed glare and a leer.

The color rushed to my face as the rest of the blood in my body took a trip farther south. Intriguing. But not the time. "Fine. Fine. Let's do this," I grumbled.

Stepping closer to the side of the bed, I watched as Davanos placed his hand on Silas's head, instantly causing the man's face to relax into a deep slumber. When he nodded at me, I placed my hand on top of his and began the slow work of "feeding" Silas the story of Anka. But with just a *few* tweaks.

I wondered if Davanos was getting all the information I was sending to Silas as the go-between, and my curiosity was answered when I got to the part about the unicorn horn. His snort was a low rumble.

Good to know he had a sense of humor. Something told me that was going to come in handy for me in the future.

Chapter Seventeen

ANKA

I was running late. I'd closed up shop at the normal time but then gotten distracted on my way home by the new window display at the local bookstore. I'd passed by on my way to work that morning and hadn't noticed anything special, but on my return trip the display had been completely reworked and there was a book on a stand in the window that I simply couldn't pass up. I'd never heard of the author before, but the cover had drawn me in. It was stunning, with a design on the front that seemed to shift and change as I moved closer, revealing something new with each step I took. When I'd spotted the silver painted edges they had sealed the deal. I'd had to go inside and buy it on the spot.

I didn't make the rules.

Now, I was rushing to get my front door open before poor Mags exploded in the entryway. I could hear her whining at me as I jingled the keys, far less coordinated in my effort to hurry.

"I'm sorry, babygirl, hold on, I'm coming!"

I got the door open and my tricolored mountain of fur burst past me in a blur, her powerful haunches pushing as fast as she could to get to the edge of the grass. I could almost hear her sigh as she squatted, and I immediately jumped to apologize again.

"I'm sorry, I'm sorry. There was a new book in the window. You know I'm weak, Mags."

She gave me a judgy expression, as only dogs can do, but I knew she'd get over it as soon as her bladder was empty. In the next moment, her attention was diverted from my transgression by two squirrels that dropped down to chase one another around the base of the giant oak in our front yard. Mags bounded that way in a bid to make friends, but the squirrels ran for their lives, darting back up the tree trunk and out of her reach, chittering angrily all the way.

"Come on, sweet girl, those squirrels don't want to play with you." When she returned to my side I scratched behind her ears before tugging her back toward our little bungalow. "Come inside and I'll get your dinner. We can go for a walk after you eat."

Once I had her settled with dinner, I walked down the short hallway to my bedroom, already pulling the top I'd worn to work over my head with visions of leggings and a hoodie dancing in my head. We were in the early days of fall, and it was my favorite season, if for no other reason than the temperature justified wearing a hoodie as soon as the sun began drifting toward the horizon.

A few minutes later I was pulling my favorite one over my head as I walked back to the kitchen and was greeted by the sound of Mags pawing at the kitchen window, chuffing and fussing at something on the other side of the glass.

"Come on, girl, no amount of barking at the window is going to make them want to be your friends," I assured her wryly, assuming the object of her fascination was her tiny squirrel nemeses. "Let's go for a walk, it'll get your mind off it."

It was our normal routine. She'd eat her dinner while I snacked on something that required little to no effort cooking-wise, then we'd go for a walk. When we got back home, I'd curl up on the couch with a book while she laid on my feet, happily gnawing on her bone.

Quiet.

Zero drama.

That was my life, and it was exactly the way I liked it since I'd kicked my ex, Ted, to the curb. It had been an easy decision to make when I'd found him getting pegged by his assistant in his office during their lunch hour. I'd stared, gaping, as the containers I'd brought with me dropped from my hands to splatter my shoes and his designer rug with what was arguably the best chowder one could get in the tristate area.

Dammit.

I'd been stunned by the scene before me, and a little hurt, but not really all that surprised. He'd always been a flight risk. To be honest, I'd been more offended that he hadn't let *me* peg him than I was that it was happening at all. I'd always wanted to try that. Add to that the chowder that was, at that moment, congealing on the tips of my designer boots and I was having a

very

bad

day.

Sigh.

I'd really been craving that chowder.

I shrugged off the memory and grabbed Mags's leash from the hook before I snapped it to her collar. My new book was waiting for me to spread those pages after our walk and I couldn't wait. I'd been in a bit of a slump since I'd finished my last read and I needed some ammunition for my...imagination.

Self-care was a lot more fun when I had a book boyfriend to keep me company.

She wiped her brow with the back of her arm, leaving a trail of flour in its wake as she huffed and stared at her creation. She couldn't put her finger on what it was about it that she didn't love, but she was reluctant to give up for the night and go home. Even knowing that a good night's sleep would probably do wonders for her creativity, she found that lately she'd been less and less inclined to rush home after work. That probably had a lot to do with her boyfriend, Bill.

She wasn't sure how he'd ended up living with her in her quaint little bungalow on the edge of town. It seemed like one day he'd shown up to have dinner and brought an overnight bag with him and he just…never left? She hadn't been bothered enough by his presumption to kick him out, but more and more lately it had become apparent that they weren't going to work out.

Which was why, when the end of her workday approached, she tended to work longer and longer hours to avoid him. She surveyed the three-tier confection in front of her again before she sighed and admitted defeat, carefully pulling a cover over the cake and sliding the tray it sat on into one of the giant cake coolers at the back of the kitchen. Like it or not, she was going to have to try again tomorrow. And she was probably going to have to kick Bill out.

I jerked awake from the dream and looked around, confused. Mags was snoring softly sprawled across my feet at the other end of the sofa and my book was laying open on my chest. I blinked sleepily and rubbed my face, trying to get my wits about me enough that I could remember what I'd been dreaming about.

I wiggled my toes, causing Maggie to raise her head and look at me questioningly. "Come on, girl, let's go to bed."

She stretched her large frame languidly before she climbed down off the sofa, and I swung my legs to the floor to follow her ambling form to my room.

Once I'd brushed my teeth and rinsed my face, I climbed into bed and patted the mattress next to me, waiting for her to hop up next to me and circle three times before she settled down with a contented doggy grunt.

I shut off the bedside lamp and laid there staring at

the ceiling as images from my dream flashed before my eyes. I'd only gotten halfway through the first chapter of the book but I'd been delighted to discover that the main female character was a baker—like me. I couldn't remember exactly what I'd read just before I fell asleep, but snippets from my dream were teasing the edges of my subconscious, just out of reach, and I felt like I'd dreamed about something from the book. Unfortunately, the harder I tried to chase the thread of thought, the more insubstantial it became until I finally drifted back off to sleep, no closer to recalling what it had been about.

Chapter Eighteen

ANKA

"Ms. Osbourne?" I called out, craning my neck to see over the heads of the customers gathered in the small cafe at the front of the bakery. The smell of cinnamon and rich coffee combined to create a signature scent I didn't think I'd ever tire of. As the lead pastry chef at Dough Me, Baby, I was in charge of all the specialty cake and pastry orders that came in, either by walk-ins or through our website, and my most recent creation was ready to leave with one of my favorite customers. Her orders, without fail, challenged my creativity and made me giggle, and today's request was no different.

The tiny woman of indeterminate age stepped up to the counter, her bright blue hair piled on top of her head in a chaotic explosion of color while a multicolored poncho draped over her thin frame; both ensured she stood out among every crowd she wandered into. Add to that the bejeweled, oversized cat-eye glasses she wore and the naughty grin she had plastered over her kindly, wrinkled face, and I couldn't help but match her expression as I slid her box across the counter to her. I put my hand on the lid before she could open it.

"You have to tell me what the occasion is, Ms. Osbourne." I refused to move my hand, despite her efforts to peek at my creation without answering my question.

Finally, she gave up and pretended to huff before she relented. "I've joined a book club," she declared. "They said everyone has to bring a treat to the meetings and I wanted my treat to be appropriate!" She shrugged, but the glint in her eye said she was hoping to shock the book club members with her contribution.

I let out a loud laugh before I slapped my hand over my mouth and leaned in. "Ms. Osbourne, I have to ask...what sort of books does your book club read?"

She leaned forward conspiratorially and cupped her hand around her mouth, cutting her eyes to the rest of the customers before she spoke only for my ears. "It's... *adult* fiction." She leaned back and gave me a big-eyed expression, tilting her head like she wondered if I'd understood the implication.

I let out a teasing gasp and clutched my imaginary pearls. "*Ms. Osbourne!* Are you telling me you've joined a *dirty* book club?" It took everything in me to contain my absolute glee at the thought.

Her dentures glinted in the fluorescent lighting when she smiled at me. "Yes, dear! Isn't that fantastic? I can't wait. Our first book was all about knots? I didn't even know what that was until I started reading, but now I'm obsessed!"

I had zero chance of containing my cackle at that. "Good for you, ma'am! In that case, I think your treats will go over fabulously at book club. But, perhaps, it's better that you wait until you get home to look these over, okay?" I glanced around at the other people standing in line with a look full of meaning.

She slid the box off the counter and cradled it in her arms protectively. "Okay, dear, I certainly wouldn't want to shock the rest of your customers, would I? I'm sure they're perfect and I'll definitely see you next week!"

With a wink and a whiff of Chanel, she made her way out of the jingling front door and onto the side-walk, soon disappearing into the lunch crowd who were hurrying back and forth in front of the shop. I shook my head and grabbed the next order from the printer before making my way back to the kitchen. I hoped the penis-shaped eclairs I'd made for her met all her expectations.

In hindsight, maybe I should have doubled the filling.

I was wiping up the counters in the back, the low hum of the custom dishwasher the only noise aside from the squeak of my shoes against the checkerboard linoleum as I moved around the kitchen. I hummed "Season of the Witch" (a la Lana Del Rey) under my breath as I returned the kitchen to the pristine condition it had been in when I started my day.

I had the next day off and didn't want to leave Nelson, our other baker, with a mess to start his shift. I loved him madly, but his sass game was strong, and I knew I'd never hear the end of it if I didn't leave the kitchen spotless.

I dropped the last rag into the cleaning solution by the door and surveyed my work before I shut off the lights and headed to the front door, keys jingling in my hand. It'd been a long day and I knew Mags would be ready to take a walk the minute I got home.

The crab bisque at We've Got Crabs was straight-up food porn and her mouth watered from the smell; she hummed under her breath, swinging the plastic bag as she made her way toward Bill's office. She was still iffy on whether or not she really wanted to be in a long-term relationship with him, but she figured she could at least give it a real effort and see if it went anywhere.

Which was why she'd decided to take her lunch break away from the bakery that day and surprise him with one of their favorite treats. His office door was closed as she approached, but she knew he often did that if he was on the phone with a client, so she didn't knock before entering, for fear of disturbing a call.

She should have knocked.

God, she should have knocked.

Several things happened at once when she stepped into

his office. Bill looked up from his position bent over the end of his desk, his face reddening immediately. His assistant, still mostly dressed in her skirt and blouse, though the former was hiked up over her hips to accommodate the harness, pulled back from her position behind him. An accompanying squelch sounded in the dead silence as she pulled her hips away from his, removing what turned out to be a very festive looking unicorn horn from his ass and drawing an unintentional groan from him as she did. That thing was...huge.

Anna paused to stare at it, almost in admiration, before she raised her gaze to that of his assistant, who was biting her lip and looking at Anna apologetically.

"Anna, wait..." Bill exclaimed as he leaned down and began maniacally grabbing for his pants where they were gathered around his ankles.

The bag of chowder slipped from Anna's fingers and hit the floor, the containers popping open and splattering the viscous concoction across his Berber rug and the toes of her Louboutin's. She peeled her eyes from the uncomfortable scene in front of her and lowered them to study the Rorschach pattern the soup made at her feet. Dammit. That was going to ruin her favorite heels.

"I can explain..." he began again, and she held up a hand to stop him.

"There's nothing to explain, Bill. I'll be going home now to set your things on the drive. If you get there quick enough you may be able to grab them before I set them on fire." She held out her hand. "Key, please."

Bill hung his head and dug around in his pocket until he pulled out his key ring, pulling the key to her house off the ring with shaking fingers before placing it in the palm of her hand.

"For the record," Anna tossed over her shoulder as she turned to leave, "I would have been down for that if you'd asked."

I raised my eyes from the pages before me and stared at Mags, who, for her part, seemed wildly unconcerned about the fact that the book I was reading bore a striking similarity to my own life. *Striking.*

"Mags, I don't know what's going on right now, but this is starting to freak me out." I put my bookmark back in between the pages to mark my spot and carefully placed the book on the table in front of me, using my foot to slide it as far away as possible.

I didn't know if I wanted to read more of it. I wasn't sure I'd be able to stop myself either.

Seriously, what the fuck was going on?

Chapter Nineteen

FELIX

*S*he'd become my new favorite hobby. My obsession, if you will. My favorite pastime was watching her as she moved through her world. She normally seemed like a pretty happy person, but I occasionally caught brief glimpses of something else brewing beneath the surface. A tinge of sadness. In those moments I knew she was thinking of Kyle and my heart echoed her sadness.

"What are you up to, Felix?" Kyle's voice echoed in my ear, and I whipped around, looking for him.

A deep laugh resonated from my other side. "Honestly, sneaking up on you is the most fun I've had since I died. I think living in Hell has made you jumpy, friend."

I rolled my eyes. "Show yourself, you fiend."

Another chuckle rang through the air and his form slowly began to appear standing on my right. "So, stalking my sister again, eh?"

My spine stiffened and my wings ruffled in response. "You're the one who asked me to keep an eye on her."

He studied me for a moment. "I did. But I think you've taken the request to a whole new level of dedication. How many times has she worn that top this month?"

"Only three..." I winced. "Okay. So maybe I've become a bit obsessed.

He laughed again. "A bit? Something tells me your interest has taken a turn away from being her guardian to something more...carnal in nature?"

I bit my lip. "It's not like I can do anything about it. You don't need to play the protective brother to protect her from me."

He rested his chin on his hand, continuing to study me closely. "How exactly does that work, anyway? I assumed you have to touch someone in order to be visible to them, based on our interaction, but why don't you just go around touching everyone so that you're not so lonely all the time?"

I wasn't sure if there were any rules about telling people about the curse, but I supposed it was probably safe to tell Kyle. On account of him being dead and all.

"I was cursed a long time ago. Over a century, actually. I...um, well, I'll just call it like it was. I was a self-absorbed cunt. The witch who cursed me made it such that I have a certain amount of opportunities to change my ways. Every person I touch, skin-to-skin, uses one of those opportunities. Eventually, if I haven't found a way to truly love, romantically, one of the people I've touched, I'll be forced to live out the rest of my mortal life like a ghost…" I winced, shooting him an apologetic look.

"Nothing to be sorry for, Felix. It's not your fault I'm dead." He waved a hand at the world in general. "It was evil that put me here, not you."

I nodded. "I know. But I still wish I'd been faster."

He smiled at me sadly. "So do I, Felix. But let's get back to your curse. How many chances do you get to redeem yourself, if you will?"

I didn't truly want to answer that question. Because I didn't want to make him feel any guilt about what I'd done.

He just maintained his stare until I gave him a sheepish grin. "Three?"

His eyes widened. "Three. Three? As in…me and two other people? Ever?"

I nodded.

"Who was the first?" His ghosty eyebrows had disappeared into his hairline.

I just stared at him until realization dawned on his face. "Me? Felix. What the fuck? Why would you waste one of *three* chances of redemption on a man who was dying? Are you insane?"

I shrugged, brushing off his incredulity. "It was the right thing to do. And look at us now. If I hadn't revealed myself to you, who knows if you'd be wandering the afterlife with no one to sneak up on."

I could feel the weight of his stare against the side of my face.

"It's more than that, Felix. Why did you do it?" he repeated.

I sighed. "I felt compelled to. I couldn't just leave you to die in that alley, bleeding out and thinking you were alone."

He turned his head and looked into the distance before he responded. "Well. Maybe that was a step in the right direction then. For you, not for me." He chuckled.

I nodded. "You were the first person I ever mourned, and I only knew you for moments before you passed. I'd say that's some personal growth, at least. But it doesn't get me any closer to finding the kind of love that will break this curse."

He jerked his head in the direction of Anka's house, where she was chasing Mags around the sofa, trying to get a shoe out of her mouth. "Do you think she gets you closer to that?"

I shook my head with a resolute air that I didn't feel down in my soul. "No, I'm just here to uphold the promise I made to you. I'm just making sure she's okay after everything."

He rolled his lips inward, trying to contain a grin. "I see. So, following her to and from work every day and sitting on her lawn watching her play with Maggie is all just in the spirit of making sure she's not mourning me too much?"

"Absolutely. Purely out of concern for her emotional well-being. Nothing else to it."

Kyle patted me on the back, turning to walk away

from me. As his body began to fade back to translucent, his voice drifted back to me. *"If you say so, buddy."*

I stayed where I was until darkness had settled in around me like a cloak. Anka was curled up on the sofa in her living room, Maggie curled up at her feet, with the book in her hands, and I watched her face closely to see if my plan was showing any evidence of working. Her brow had been furrowed for the past hour as she turned page after page, sometimes flipping backward a few pages before returning to her spot.

Occasionally, she would look around the room, squinting her eyes as if she was trying to peer through the glass into the darkness. I wondered if she could somehow feel my eyes on her, despite my current condition.

I watched her until she'd closed the book and placed it on the table in front of her, using her toe to push it to the opposite edge of the surface. She turned to Maggie and said something, but I couldn't decipher the words from where I sat. When she stood and grabbed her laptop, pulling it into her lap, I grinned. If I had learned anything at all about Anka Kelly in the time I'd been watching her, this mystery would be too much for her to ignore.

I hoped Silas was ready for his quiet little world to be turned upside down, because something told me Anka wouldn't quit until she figured out how the hell he'd managed to write the story of her life before it had even happened.

I let my wings unfurl and the world tilted as I returned to Hell, satisfied for the moment that everything was moving right along.

I just loved it when a plan came together.

"Girl, you've wiped that counter eight times. If it ain't clean by now I don't think anything can help it."

Nelson leaned a hip against the prep table and arched a perfectly manicured eyebrow at me. In typical Nelson fashion, he had on his chef's coat, but this one had unicorns printed all over it. I'd snickered when he walked in with it that morning. He'd just grinned at me and pointed finger guns at me. "Ka-pow!" I fucking couldn't with him.

"What's on your mind, cupcake?" he asked, since I hadn't replied.

I knew there was no way for me to explain what was on my mind without sounding like a certifiable lunatic, but if I didn't talk about it with someone, I was going to drive myself crazy wondering if I was crazy. The ouroboros of insanity was strong in this scenario.

"You remember me telling you that I grabbed a new

book last week? Like…that when I walked past the store I felt compelled to buy it?" I reached into my work locker and pulled out my messenger bag as I spoke.

"What's new about you obsessively needing new smut to feed your addiction?" He leered at me, and I laughed.

"Well, it's strange…" I pulled out the gorgeous book and started flipping pages before I handed it to him with my finger marking the spot I wanted to show him. "Just humor me. Read this?"

He gave me a long look but took the book from my hand and started at the spot I'd marked. Before long, his diamond encrusted eyebrow piercing had climbed so far up his forehead that it looked like he was wearing a barrette. When he raised his eyes back to mine they were comically large. "Bitchhhh. What in the fuck is this?"

I shrugged. "It's weird, right? At first I just thought it was a really fun coincidence. I picked up a book at random and it happened to have a main character who was a pastry chef. Cool, right? But when I got to that part you just read I started to get paranoid. Now I'm scared to read any further. Do I have a stalker, Nel?"

He craned his neck around the corner, like he was checking to see if someone had snuck in the kitchen with us in the last five minutes. "I think you gotta keep reading, girl. Maybe it's just really coincidental?"

I tilted my head and I could feel how dubious my expression was. "Nelson. She caught her boyfriend getting pegged by his assistant. With a unicorn horn.

The soup? Everything about that scene happened to me, except I can't fucking afford Louboutin's!"

He'd already flipped to the next page before I'd finished my rant, and I could see his eyes skimming the page before he let out a relieved breath. "Babygirl, you're fine. I just read forward and I know this part hasn't happened to you. I know that unicorn thing is a wild coincidence, but I think you're good. Look!"

He passed the book back to me and I read the page he'd just skimmed. But where it had reassured him, it only made the color drain from my face the further I read.

"You. Nasty. Ho. Tell me you didn't!" He thumped me on my forehead. "And you didn't tell me! That's it. We're breaking up."

I hung my head in shame. "He's a shitbag, but he has a really great cock, Nel!"

Anna climbed onto the barstool and heaved a sigh of relief. It had been a long day and she'd been on her feet for most of it. When she'd passed the taqueria on her way home from work, it was like her feet made the decision all on their own, and before she knew it, she'd waved her favorite bartender over and ordered a jumbo frozen margarita and a family-sized bowl of queso. Sometimes a girl just needed tequila and inadvisable quantities of melted cheese to make everything feel all better.

She'd just taken the first happy sip of her drink when a hand landed on the barstool next to her, swiveling it around to make room for the last person she wanted to run into on that particular day. Or any day, really.

"*Mind if I join you?*" *Bill asked tentatively.*

"*I'd rather you didn't. But it's a free country, Bill, I can't stop you.*" *She returned her focus to the tequila in front of her before scooping up a healthy bit of queso with a perfectly crisp tortilla chip, humming as it hit her tongue and her taste buds did a happy dance.*

"*I just want to try and explain. So maybe we could at least still be friends? Or get some closure?*" *He leaned his elbows on the bar top in front of him and offered her a side-long glance.*

She hmphed *at him.*

"*Okay, then at least maybe make it where you don't hate my guts?*" *he implored.*

Anna looked back down at her queso sadly, giving up on the thought of this being a relaxing stop on her way home from work. She looked back at him. "*You have five minutes. But that's it, Bill. Then you walk away and leave me and my tequila and cheese in peace. I've already had a long day, and I'm not really in the mood for whatever excuse you want to spout at me.*"

He nodded enthusiastically, far too happy with her acquiescence for her own sanity.

"*Look, Anna, I know I wasn't exactly winning any boyfriend of the year awards when we were together, and I want to apologize for that. When we first got together I thought maybe you were the one. You know...the one. But the longer we were together the more it became apparent that you didn't actually need me, and, well, I'm sure you can understand what that started to do to my self-esteem.*"

He was staring at the side of her face, likely waiting for her to assuage something for him but she just signaled to the bartender. "Hey, Miguel! Could I get two shots of tequila, please? Make it top-shelf or I may throw myself into traffic."

Miguel snorted and cut his eyes over to where Bill still stared at her hopefully. "Heard. Coming right up."

She ignored Bill's stare until Miguel placed the shots in front of her but when Bill reached for one of them she smacked the back of his hand. Hard. "Nope. Those are both for me. You want tequila? You get your own."

His face fell, but he lifted a finger to signal Miguel who found himself suddenly so busy at the other end of the bar that Anna guessed it would be at least twenty-four to thirty-six hours before Bill got that drink. She fucking loved Miguel.

"Okay. Now that I'm properly medicated. Let me clear something up for you. Me not needing you didn't hurt your 'self-esteem,' Bill, it hurt your ego. Those two things are not one and the same, but I can understand why you'd have a hard time differentiating between the two. And you're right. I didn't need you. As a matter of fact, I still can't remember ever actually asking you to move into my house. You just showed up one day and never left, and the sex was good and I'm a really fucking nice person, so I never kicked you out. But when you insert yourself into someone's life in a perma-nent way without an actual invitation, you don't get to be butthurt they aren't falling to their knees to thank you for being there."

She felt the giggle start up in her throat and she tried to keep it in. She really did. But when the word "butthurt" came out of her mouth, she'd immediately flashed back to the moment when his assistant had pulled the giant unicorn horn out of his ass, and maybe the tequila had begun to kick in a little, because she couldn't hold it back.

Bill frowned at her as the giggle escalated into a full-blown bout of hysterics. She laughed so hard and long that tears began pouring down her face.

"It's not funny," he groused.

"Oh, Bill, trust me when I say that is the only funny thing about that situation." She continued reveling in her hilarity for another few moments. Periodically muttering "butthurt" under her breath and starting up a whole new round of giggles.

"Are you done?" he asked, annoyed.

Anna swiped her fingers under her eyes to clear away her tears before she straightened her expression and turned to address him. She wanted to make sure there were no miscommunications in what she was about to say. "Bill, please hear me when I say this, because I want to be perfectly clear. Every single moment we've been apart I've wanted to come running back, just so I could tell you this."

His face lit up with false hope. "Yes, Anna?"

She gazed deep into his eyes. "I literally do not know what I ever saw in you. Like...it's truly astonishing. So trust me, no one in the history of the world has ever been more done with anyone than I am with you at this very moment."

He winced, as if she'd screamed the words at him, and Miguel must have heard a little of her speech and taken pity on Bill, because a shot of tequila appeared in front of him magically.

He tossed it back immediately before he looked back at her one last time. "So I guess there's nothing left to say."

She saluted him before picking up her melted margarita and draining the glass. "Nothing left to say."

The porcelain sink was stained with rust rings and she kept her eyes locked on them so she wouldn't mistakenly look into the mirror just inches from her face and be confronted with the consequences of too much tequila. Her stomach rolled and she thought maybe she was going to puke up her precious queso, but thankfully, the feeling passed.

The constant motion wasn't helping her equilibrium, but then a hand snaked into the front of her panties and slid over her clit expertly, circling the bundle of nerves in a way that complemented what he was doing behind her with his dick quite nicely and her attention was diverted.

"Fuck, Anna, I've missed this pussy," he groaned.

"No talking. If you say one more word, I will stand up and walk out of here and finish myself off when I get home," she grunted at him.

"Okay, okay. No talking." He doubled his efforts, slamming into her from behind and she could feel the beginnings of an orgasm creeping through her veins. Bill was a terrible boyfriend, but he had a magnificent cock.

"I can feel you tightening up on my cock," he whispered.

"I said," she panted, "shut the fuck up." She slid her hand into her panties and knocked his out of the way so she could finish herself off before he had a chance to chase her O away with the sound of his voice.

The orgasm rolled through her body, and she rode it out as long as she could, pushing back against him and grinding as the sensations peaked and then began to fade, leaving room for the clarity she'd briefly lost sight of.

Bill was still thrusting against her, probably getting close to his own finish, but suddenly she couldn't stand the thought of him being inside her for one more moment. She put a hand behind her, placing it on his abdomen, forcing him to stop his movement.

"What's wrong?" he asked, confused.

"I'm really done now." She slid forward off his cock and grabbed a paper towel from the dispenser, swiping it between her legs before stepping into one of the stalls and dropping it in the trash can in there.

"Are you fucking kidding me?" he gritted through his teeth, still standing there with his dick at attention.

She met his gaze in the mirror as she quickly washed her hands. "Nope. Not even a little bit. I hope you have the life you deserve, Bill. And next time? Leave me and my tequila alone, 'kay? Thanks."

She walked out of the bathroom with her head held high and a smirk gracing her face. Maybe there was something to be said for closure after all.

She felt amazing!

I stood from my desk, scuffing across the wooden floor toward the kitchen. Just as I reached for the coffee pot, a knock on the door stopped me in my tracks. I cocked my head to the side. Otis never knocked. He…knew not to knock. Knew I wouldn't answer. Maybe it was just a door-to-door salesman.

Another knock. "Hello? Is anyone in there?" a woman's voice called through the door.

I crept closer, keeping my steps light and avoiding the creaky board halfway across the foyer. I could see the woman standing on the other side of the door, her figure fuzzy through the frosted glass.

"Look, I…this is going to sound crazy. But I've been looking everywhere for you. I…need to know who you are…" I heard her mumble to herself, *"Fucking hell, Anka, you sound like a psychopath."*

"Let me try again. My name is Anka Kelly. And I

think you wrote a book about my life. Except that...it hasn't all happened yet. And I really need to talk to you."

I stepped closer to the door, risking that she'd be able to discern my shadow through the glass but too intrigued not to get a closer look. I peered at her through the thin strip of glass between the frost and the frame, and heard my heart start to beat like a drum; *felt* it beat. Once. Twice.

How the hell was my main character standing on my front step?

Chapter Twenty-Two

ANKA

"*M*other. *Fucker.*" I stomped back down the stairs, across a cute, if mildly neglected, front lawn, to where my car was parked on the street. I knew someone was in there, but they wouldn't open the door, and I still didn't know for absolutely certain that I'd found the right place.

My online stalking skills weren't terrible, but it wasn't like I'd ever actually *tried* to find someone on the internet who didn't want to be found. This house—purchased under the LLC the book was copyrighted to—had been my only lead, and I'd only managed to find that because it was a matter of public record. If whoever had been standing on the opposite side of that door refused to open it, I didn't know what else to do. At least, nothing else that wouldn't get me arrested for trespassing or harassment.

I slipped into the driver's seat and cranked the engine before I leaned forward and rested my head against the steering wheel, trying to figure out what to do next. This situation had consumed me. I knew that book was written about my life. What I didn't know was *how*.

My phone interrupted my meltdown with a ding announcing a text message.

Nelson: Well?

Anka: Strike out.

Nelson: What do you mean, strike out?

Anka: Whoever lives here wouldn't even open the door. I don't know what to do, Nel. I feel like I'm losing my mind.

Nelson: Bitchhhhh. You're not losing your mind. This shit is cray-ze. We'll figure something out, babygirl. I'll come over tonight and me, you, and Mags can have a girls' night and make a new plan.

I smiled in spite of myself. I fucking loved that man.

Anka: Okay. I'll see you soon.

"The thing is, I don't even know if the person in that house is the one who wrote the book. Like…what if it was a completely wrong lead? How am I supposed to know if I'm even on the right track?"

I squeezed a thin line of icing along the edge of my latest confection for Ms. Osborne while I waited for Nelson to respond.

"I think you should go back, just keep trying until he, or she, opens the door and tells you you're crazy and to get off their lawn." He stepped closer as he transferred the layer of cake he'd just pulled from the oven to a resting tray near me. I heard him snort out loud before he spoke again. "Girl. What in the fuck are you making right now?" He gestured to the table in front of me.

"It's a Saint Andrew's cross. How does it look?" I turned to gauge his reaction over my shoulder.

Nelson wrapped his hand over his mouth with his elbow resting in his other hand while his body began shaking. "Please tell me that's for that little old lady you're always snickering with at the counter. What the fuck does she even know about kink?"

I laughed. "It is! And, as it turns out, she's getting quite the education. She joined an adult book club and she's been learning all sorts of new things. Last week she had me make glazed sweet bread knots for her to take to their meeting."

I waited till the count of five before Nelson threw his head back in a cackle. "Knots. Jesusfuckingchrist. That's the best thing I've heard all week."

"So, this week, she asked me to do a Saint Andrew's cross. I've just got to add the restraints once I'm done with this part. What do you think I should make them out of?" I studied my creation thoughtfully.

"I try never to think about edible restraint systems while I'm at work," he quipped, stepping to the door of the kitchen. "I'm going to check the stock out front." He left me with the sound of his laughter drifting through the door.

"Fondant. I could make the restraints out of fondant. They'll taste like shit, but at least they'll technically be edible." With that decided, I moved toward the cabinet where the day's fondant was stored in an airtight container, pulling out just enough that I thought I'd be able to form four tiny cuffs out of it. I added a few drops of black coloring to it and folded it in until I had the right color and got to work.

"Anka, dear! This is fantastic! I can almost hear the heavy breathing!" Ms. Osborne's eyes sparkled behind her rhinestone-encrusted glasses.

Thankfully, it was after the lunch rush, so the cafe was empty for this week's reveal to my favorite client. I didn't need a Yelp review about NSFW pastries being waved in front of someone while they were trying to eat their tuna on rye.

"I'm so glad you like it!" I grinned.

"And the brass accessories are so pretty! You've outdone yourself, darling!" She closed the lid and pulled her wallet out of her giant purse.

"Thank you! I was afraid I got a little carried away, but this was fun!" I heard Nelson snort from the kitchen and used the heel of my boot to push the swinging door closed as I rang her up. "I can't wait to see what you come up with for me to do next week."

Ms. Osborne winked at me, a devilish look in her eye. "I'll let you know as soon as they pick a new book. I'm sure you'll be up to the task, though, dear. You haven't let me down yet."

"Have a good day, Ms. Osborne. As always, it's been a pleasure doing business with you."

The bell jangled as she waved and disappeared out the door, and I pushed my way through the swinging door into the kitchen just in time to see Nelson sliding my book back into my locker.

"What are you up to, mister?" I put my hands on my hips.

"Just checking to see if you've had any more ill-advised run-ins with your ex, girlfriend. I'm not about to get caught off-guard by your libido again." He gave me a shit-eating grin.

"Fuck you," I grumbled, laughing under my breath. "It was just the one time. We'll call it temporary insanity."

He shot me a smug expression. "Mm-hmm. That's what they all say."

Chapter Twenty-Four

ANKA

"*I*'m sorry, miss. But we cannot give out that information. As I'm sure you can under-stand, our authors' private information is exactly that. Private. Have you considered sending him a message on social media?" The perky voice on the other end of the line was gatekeeping the hell out of his information, and while I appreciated the dedication she gave to her job, it wasn't doing anything to help me at that moment.

"I understand what you're saying, but this particular author doesn't appear to *have* any social media and I really need to get in touch with him. Isn't there anything you can do?"

There was silence on the other end of the line for a moment before she sighed. "I can send a message to his agent and see if they'd be willing to talk to you. But that's the best I can do. I make no promises that they will even respond."

"Yes. Please. Thank you. I really appreciate it." I

waited patiently as she took my name and email address and phone number down before she curtly thanked me for calling and disconnected the call.

I stared at the darkened screen on my phone for longer than I'd admit to anyone, trying to figure out if that bitch had hung up on me. I finally decided it wasn't worth my energy to figure out and slid it back into my pocket before looking around the house, wondering what I could do in the meantime to occupy myself. I didn't hold out a ton of hope that I was going to get a call from his agent, but it was the only lead I had going.

I'd shoved the book into my messenger bag and I could almost feel it calling to me, despite the fact that it was tucked away out of sight.

I stared at the bag where it lay on my kitchen counter, chewing my lip. Did I want to read more? Was there any chance I had this all wrong?

Maggie let out a plaintive whine and jumped up, placing her paws on the counter and nudging my bag with her nose.

"You think I should just stop being a scaredy-cat and read some more, girl?" I asked her.

She turned to look at me over her shoulder and wagged her tail before returning her attention to my bag.

I sighed. "Okay. But if there's some more freaky shit in this book, you're going to be the one keeping me company while I'm awake all night staring at the door like a paranoid freak."

Woof.

"Okay, okay. I heard you the first time." I dragged

the bag by its handle and carried it over to the sofa. I curled up in my usual reading spot and flipped it open, grabbing the book and placing it in my lap. I stared at the holographic design on the front, still wondering what about it compelled me to buy it. It was like some sort of witchcraft was involved.

I snorted at the turn my thoughts had taken. *What the fuck, Anka? Witchcraft?* Ridiculous.

Anna woke the next morning feeling rejuvenated. She'd never given much credence to the idea of closure, but something about the run in with Bill the night before had obviously done something good for her mental state. She felt better than she had in months and she rolled over in bed, stretching leisurely before she climbed out of bed and headed to the bathroom to wash her face and brush her teeth. She didn't have to be at work until later in the day and she had every intention of spending her morning leisurely enjoying a good book and no less than two full cups of uninterrupted coffee.

When she walked back into her bedroom, face scrubbed and teeth minty fresh, she drew up short when she noticed a piece of paper on her bed that hadn't been there when she'd woken up. At least, she didn't think it had been there.

She looked all around her bedroom for a sign of anything out of place, but everything else looked just as she'd left it. What the hell?

Gingerly, she stepped closer to the bed and lifted the piece of paper with two fingers, flipping it over to reveal the words scrawled on the opposite side.

Glad you got a good night's sleep, beautiful.

I'll see you later.

Anna felt her brows lift all the way to her hairline as chills spread across her body and the hair on the back of her neck stood on end. She dropped the note back to her bed and backed away toward the door slowly before the creepy feeling of being watched forced her to turn away from her bed and scan her room. The door to her closet stood open, and she could see straight into it, so she was fairly certain no one was lurking in there waiting to pounce on her. She ducked down and lifted the comforter so she could see under the bed, but the only things hiding under there were a couple of boxes and some dust bunnies.

She dropped the blanket and turned toward the door again, wrapping her hand around the doorknob and turning it slowly, a tremor passing through her body before she made herself fling it open, but no one waited for her on the other side.

She cut her gaze back toward the bed where the note still lay where she'd dropped it. What was going on? Did she have a stalker? She was a pastry chef, not someone famous, why the hell would anyone even want to stalk her?

I closed the book, feeling my skin begin to crawl with the feeling of being watched, but I wasn't sure if the feeling was because I actually was being watched or just a feeling the resonated from what I'd just read.

I was somewhat reassured—I hadn't woken up the

day after my run-in with Ted to a mysterious note on my bed. So, maybe this really was all a huge coincidence. But I found myself suddenly worried that I was going to wake up one morning soon to find a note on my bed and that paranoia canceled out any reassurance I felt.

I needed to find the author of that book before I lost my mind.

Chapter Twenty-Five

SILAS

It'd been so long since I'd written anything that I forgot how good it made me feel. The act of creating stories in my head had never stopped, but the trauma associated with the last time I'd written anything for the world to see had overshadowed any creative urges I'd had in the past four years. That was, until recently.

Six months ago, I'd woken up from the most vivid dream I recalled ever having. A story had poured out of me after that; nearly faster than I could get the words on the screen.

It was like I was possessed. I *had* to write that book. It was a compulsion. And, thankfully, it was unlike anything I'd written before, so somehow it managed not to trigger any of my phobias.

It was the complete opposite of the edgy crime-thrillers I'd written before; it was funny, and smart, and gripping—and it felt real to me in a way that nothing I'd ever written had before. Like I was always meant to write that book.

Six days after the first morning I woke up with my mind filled with the story of Anna Kellen, I typed "The End" on the first draft of an eighty-thousand-word manuscript. I sat with it for a few days, waiting for my inner monologue to start up, telling me this was a horrible idea, but I eventually sent it to my old editor to see if she'd be willing to take a look at it.

What happened over the next couple of months still astounded me when I thought back on it. My editor, the only person I had worked with professionally in my past life, loved the book. She loved it so much, in fact, that she sent it to an agent friend of hers, imploring him to take a look, and before I knew it I had a new agent, a new publishing house, and they were fast-tracking the book for a quick release.

I created a new pen name, for obvious reasons, and for the first time in four years I had the tiniest hope that my writing career didn't have to be over with after all.

I didn't know how it had happened, but the feeling was something I'd equate with coming above ground after having lived in the dark for years on end. I could see the sun shining again and I wanted to sob with how bright and beautiful it was.

THE NEW NAME TO KNOW IN THE PUBLISHING WORLD IS ABBOT FRANKLIN. HIS DEBUT NOVEL FINDING ANNA HAS ALREADY CHARTED ON THE NEW YORK TIMES AND

USA TODAY BEST SELLER LISTS IN ONLY THE THIRD WEEK OF PUBLICATION, AND THIS UNAPOLOGETIC ODE TO A WOMAN'S ABILITY TO OVERCOME AND THRIVE ALL LIFE'S SO-CALLED "NORMAL" UPS AND DOWNS IS SURE TO REMAIN THERE FOR MANY WEEKS TO COME. FRANKLIN POINTS OUT THE RIDICULOUSNESS OF THE FEMALE EXPERI-ENCE WITHOUT GETTING PEDANTIC OR CROSSING THE LINE INTO CONDESCENSION. THIS IS A CLEAR-WINDOW LOOK INTO THE LIFE OF A WOMAN WHO REFUSES TO BE PLACED IN A BOX. IT'S A LOVE LETTER TO THE FEMALE GENDER FROM A MAN WHO, CONTRARY TO MOST, ACTU-ALLY SEEMS TO "GET IT." AND WE LOVE HIM FOR IT.

ASHLYNN RHYS – USA TODAY

I always tried to avoid the reviews. But I'd opened my email that morning to a screenshotted message from Henry. I grinned when I read what he'd sent. Being one of the few men on the planet known for "getting" the female experience was a far cry from how I'd been known when I'd left the bookish world years before.

Now, if I could just convince him that I didn't need to go on a book tour, everything would be perfect. I could stay right there in my cozy little house and write my stories and keep my life simple and happy. There was absolutely no need to shake things up. Everything was exactly as I wanted it. It was a bit lonely from time to time, but Otis would be by in a bit to drop the mail. That always broke up the day.

Chapter Twenty-Six

SILAS

NOW

We'd been over this a hundred times in the past couple of months and my frustration had only grown in that time.

"Nothing has changed, Henry. I know that's not what you were hoping to hear, but I can't go on a book tour. I just can't. And I wish I could explain to you why I can't, but I can't do that either. You're just going to have to trust that I have my reasons."

"But, Silas, this could be your big break! If you don't go out there and promote this book, you could lose the momentum. It's my job to advise you on the best way to help your career, and I'm advising you to get over whatever hermit tendencies you're harboring and get your ass out there and shake some hands, schmooze some

readers, create a goddamn social media presence. Something! Help me, help you!"

I snorted. "Nice *Jerry Maguire* throwback, Henry, but
you really don't know what you're asking. I'm sorry, but
this was a term of my contract when I signed with you.
If you can't work within those constraints, I'll have to
find a new agent."

I could almost hear his teeth grinding before he
finally responded. "No. You're right. I'm sorry I've been
pushing so hard. I just know that with some strategic
appearances we could really capitalize on the success
your book is having already and turn it into an
international sensation!"

I grimaced. "I understand you think that would be
an enticement to me, but that sounds awful. I don't
want to be an international sensation. I want to make
enough money off these books to keep me in whiskey
and keep the lights on, so that I can keep writing more
books. If I'm an international sensation I can't imagine
that maintaining my anonymity would be possible, and
that's non-negotiable, Henry. I'm serious."

"Fine, fine. I hear you, Silas. I hear you. What if I
asked the publisher to create some social media
accounts for you and they just have one of the interns
run it? It's a compromise! We can protect your identity,
but still give the fans something that feels like they're
getting access to you?"

I thought about it for a minute, trying to imagine if
there was some way his suggestion could backfire for
me, but it seemed like a fair ask, and I knew I needed to

give him something since I was vetoing any possibility of me appearing in person to promote the book.

"I'll tell you what—I'll do it. I'm not going to post any pictures of myself, but I'll create something, okay?"

I could almost hear his relief over the phone line. "Yes! Thank you, Silas. This is going to be great! You'll see!"

I had my doubts about how great it would be, but for the sake of Henry I faked some enthusiasm. "Yep! I'm sure it's going to be the best. What could possibly go wrong?"

"That's the spirit! I have a meeting so I have to run, but we'll talk soon, okay, buddy?"

His entire demeanor had changed since I'd agreed to create a presence on social media. He'd gone from cajoling and irritated to us suddenly being buddies again and I tried to contain my eye-roll.

"I can hardly wait," I deadpanned before disconnecting the call.

@shebakes commented on your post
@shebakes liked your post
@shebakes followed you
You have a new message request.

Whoever @shebakes was had, in the span of the last hour, liked every single thing I'd posted in the past few days, even the blurry picture I'd posted of my coffee cup sitting next to my laptop that morning.

Her comments were intriguing, if vague, and I clicked on her profile to satisfy my own curiosity about my new follower since she seemed to be such an avid fan.

When her page opened up on my screen, I heard a ringing sound start up in my ears.

It was *her*.

The woman who'd shown up on my front porch the other day, and if I'd thought my view of her through the sliver of unfrosted glass on my front door had been mistaken, the pictures now staring back at me from my screen removed any doubt.

The woman who called herself @shebakes was the exact image I'd carried in my head for my main character the entire time I'd been writing the book. The exact image that still lived in my mind.

The ringing sound got louder and louder and my heart did that weird thud thing again. Even with all of my neurosis tied to the horrendous events of four years prior, I'd never once questioned my own sanity. But now? The irrefutable evidence was staring back at me, smiling a huge smile with a ridiculous sombrero gracing her dark chocolate locks, her eyes sparkling as she tipped a shot glass to her lips.

The post was dated a few months prior.

The caption sealed my fate.

Happy birthday, little brother. I'm having my shot and yours since you're not here to celebrate with me. I miss you every single day. RIP.

My hand shook as I slid the mouse over to the little arrow that led to my inbox. I let it hover over that indicator for so long that the sun shifted its position in the sky outside my window, but I finally opened the message. Reading it only convinced me further. I was losing my mind. It was the only explanation.

> Hi. I really hope you're the one reading this and not some intern at your publishing house but look…I don't know how to say this without sounding like I'm certifiable, but I really need to talk to you. I…think your book is about my life and…well, some of it hasn't happened yet, and I don't understand what's going on.
>
> I swear I'm not some crazy stalker lady and since I'm not aware of having a stalker of my own, I just really want to get to the bottom of how the hell you wrote a book about my life?
>
> Please. I'm begging you. Please respond. Or send me an email. Or call me. Just…don't leave me on read. Okay?

She'd closed out the message by providing her email address and her phone number which, even according to my own very basic understanding of online behavior, seemed wildly irresponsible on her part.

Didn't she have any sense of self-preservation?

Chapter Twenty-Seven

FELIX

The world tilted nauseatingly and I plopped onto my ass in the middle of Silas's lawn, swallowing convulsively until I was sure I wasn't going to throw up all over his uncut grass.

I wondered briefly if anyone would be able to see it if I did. What an odd fucking thing to not know about my own situation, but there it was.

Once I'd regained my balance and the certainty that the contents of my stomach would remain in their rightful place, I stood and made my way up the front stairs, pausing in the dim circle cast by his porch light.

I'd dropped in on him from time to time over the past few years, but my visits had increased in their frequency and duration since Davanos and I had paid him our visit.

Silas was a paradox for me, and I'd spent a lot of time just trying to figure out what made him tick. On the one hand, he was chock full of neurosis (under-standable) and he held onto them like they were the only thing protecting him from the cold, cruel world outside his front door. But, on the other hand, I'd observed him often enough to see flashes of the capable and confident man he likely was before a psychopath had used his life's work as a macabre instruction manual for murder.

That man intrigued me to no end.

Since Davanos wasn't with me to zap me to the other side of Silas's door this time, I had to resort to breaking and entering, though less breaking and more just entering.

As I'd predicted, Silas kept a key hidden in a fake little rock tucked in the corner of his porch. I'd seen his agent use it one day, and filed the information away for future use.

I walked the perimeter of the house until I found Silas hunched over his laptop in his study, his hands threaded through his dark hair, glasses askew on his face and his expression unidentifiable. I jogged back to the front door and availed myself of the spare key, slip-ping in quietly and easing the door back to as silently as possible.

I made my way down the hall that ran the length of the first floor, until I stood in the doorway to his study, somewhat concerned that he hadn't moved a muscle in the minutes I'd been gone. I crept closer, cautiously, until I was leaning down behind his laptop, and it was only from that angle that I could determine his eyes were moving, so I was slightly reassured he hadn't had a stroke and died in that position.

I straightened to my full height and stepped around to the other side of his desk, stopping just behind him so I could see what he was looking at on his screen. When I realized what it was, it all began to make sense.

This was the one part of my plan that had been a bit of a wild card. My flighty gift of premonition hadn't shown me how this part would play out. Felicity had guessed it was because there were simply too many variables at play.

My veins buzzed with excitement, though, because Silas was staring at a picture of Anka from one of her social media profiles.

I remembered the night she'd taken that picture. I hadn't realized it was her birthday until I'd followed her home from work and she stopped at her favorite taqueria.

I'd chosen a spot close by to observe her from, and Kyle had appeared, his expression sad as he watched his twin settle onto a stool at the bar.

I'd turned to look at him, noting his expression. "What troubles you, friend?" I'd asked.

He usually had something snarky to say to me about stalking his sister, but that day he'd been quiet. I didn't think ghosts could cry, but, if they could, I'd have guessed by his expression that Kyle would have been.

"It's our birthday," he whispered.

My wings twitched when he spoke, and a brief flash of

premonition struck me, but it was gone before I could examine it too closely.

"Well. I guess, just her birthday now," he added.

"I'm sorry, friend. Are you sure you want to be here right now? Doesn't this just rub salt in your proverbial wound?" I raised a brow at him questioningly.

He nodded. "Even if she doesn't know I'm here. I don't want her to be alone today."

I gave him an understanding smile. "You're a good brother."

"It was the only thing I was ever really good at," he responded sadly.

A few moments later, Anka had been joined by her friend Nelson, and the mood for us all took a turn for the better. Nelson immediately signaled the bartender, Miguel, and pointed at Anka, making a hat out of his hands above her head and Miguel nodded, snickering.

"Nelson, you dick. I purposely didn't tell him it was my birthday." Anka smacked him on the arm.

"You get the hat, bitch, then you get the tequila, and I'm here to make sure you laugh at least once tonight. Then I'll take you home and tuck you into bed. Because that's what best friends are for. Well, that, and telling you that those pants make your ass look atrocious." He gave her a blank stare, and she burst out laughing.

He clapped his hands together. "My work here is done, then! Garçon! Tequila!"

Miguel, clearly accustomed to Nelson's antics, had just rolled his eyes at him and dropped the oversized sombrero on top of Anka's head before he poured three shots of tequila, sliding one in front of Nelson and the other two in front of Anka with a nod.

"His is on the house, Amiga." He tapped a finger on the second shot in front of her and we'd both watched as her eyes misted up briefly.

"Thanks, Miguel." She coughed, swiping at her eyes before turning toward Nelson and lifting one of the shots up to her lips.

"Take a picture for me?" she asked.

"Yes, ma'am." Nelson's response was unusually reserved. He lifted his phone and snapped a picture of her grinning at the camera right before she downed the shot and carefully removed the hat from her head, placing it on the bar in front of her.

"I miss him," she said, staring at the bottles lined up on the shelf behind the bar. "Every fucking day."

"I know, baby. I know." Nelson put an arm over her shoulder and leaned his head toward hers, just holding her while she struggled to get her emotions under control.

I turned to look at my friend and he'd almost faded entirely from sight. He opened his mouth but nothing came out.

"It's okay. You can go." I gave him an understanding nod.

He just nodded back and tipped an imaginary hat in my direction before he gave her one last sad look and disappeared from my sight entirely.

"I'm losing my mind," Silas spoke to the empty room, and I wondered if, on some level, he knew he wasn't truly alone.

I felt a stab of guilt. When I'd devised my plan, I had only intended to help Anka and Silas, not make either of them doubt their own mental acuity.

Silas shook his head and shut the lid to his laptop, reaching for a glass near his elbow and taking a healthy sip. "That's the only explanation. A psychotic break. My god, did I actually stalk this woman? Have I been possessed? Oh my god, I'm going to have to respond to her. What the hell do I even say? *'Oh, sorry miss, I think I may have accidentally stalked you for months on end while in a fugue state that I have no recollection of. Either that or I'm a victim of some sort of demon possession.'* Jesus Christ," he muttered, letting his head fall back into his hands. "I'm going to have to check myself into a psych ward."

It was that last statement that had me reevaluating my plan. *Perhaps* there were aspects of this I hadn't considered fully.

I watched Silas drain the remaining amber liquid in his glass before he reached for the bottle to refill it and something came over me. Temporary insanity, perhaps.

I pinched the fingertip of my glove in between my teeth, tugging my hand free. I reached out and placed my hand on the bottle as he was reaching for it so his hand landed on mine instead of the liquid escape he'd been reaching for.

I hadn't thought through my spur of the moment decision long enough to have guessed what Silas's reaction would be to a full-grown half-demon with wings appearing out of thin air in the middle of his study, but I worried I'd broken him when he just slid back into his chair and stared at me blearily.

I watched him for any indication that he was on the verge of screaming, or running, or possibly launching that bottle of whiskey at my head, but he just stared, silent. He remained silent for so long that I was compelled to fill the space.

"If it helps, you're definitely *not* losing your mind." I grinned at him and shrugged.

Chapter Twenty-Eight

ANKA

The kitchen at work looked like a bomb had gone off. I stepped in and stared around the room in horror, feeling the soles of my boots sticking to the floor as I shifted to take it all in.

"Nelson? Are you in here?" I called in a borderline panic.

"Here!" he called, but I still couldn't see him.

"Marco!"

A giggle drifted to me from the opposite side of the room. "Polo!"

I turned toward the sound and found Nelson sitting on the floor with his back propped against the wall, legs outstretched in front of him, covered head to toe in what appeared to be flour and little chunks of drying dough.

My eyes bulged as I took in his appearance. "Um, babe?" I swirled my finger over my head to encompass the room as a whole before pointing at him. "What the hell happened here?"

He lifted a cup of coffee to his lips, taking a long sip before he grinned at me. "Well, first there was a mishap with that fucking industrial mixer and that caused the first explosion of dough, most of which landed on me." He gestured vaguely at the drying bits that clung to his coat and hair. "Then, the conveyor belt on the dough sheeter decided to take a shit, and when I tried to fix it I think I just made it worse, and a little puff of smoke came out and I called in reinforcements. But in the meantime, I am having a coffee. Because fuck this day, girl."

I put my hand over my mouth to hide my snicker but he still narrowed his eyes at me. I made my way through the mess, trying not to step in any of the larger clumps, and when I reached his side of the room I bent down and held my hand out to him, getting a good whiff of his coffee when I did.

"Now your laissez faire attitude about this makes much more sense. How much Baileys is in that cup?"

He tucked the mug closer into his chest protectively. "Back away from the emotional support Baileys. It's medicinal."

I shook my head at him, chuckling in spite of myself. "You can keep your emotional support Baileys, but I need you to get your ass up and help me get this kitchen cleaned up. Ms. Osborne will be here in a couple of hours and I have to finish up her order."

"Ohh, what's the crazy little bird asked for this time?" He climbed to his feet, brushing the flour off his ass in a ridiculous attempt to fix himself.

"Well, it's essentially just donuts." I bit my lip and choked back my snicker.

"Donuts," he deadpanned with a skeptical look on his face.

"Yep. Donuts," I responded cheerfully as I made my way over to the industrial refrigerator on the opposite side of the room. I opened one of the huge doors and slid the tray I'd prepped the day before out for his inspection.

They really did look like little donuts...or they would until I'd finished decorating them.

His dubious expression didn't waver as we teamed up to put the kitchen back together. It took both of us working diligently for the next hour, but when we were done it was so clean that you could have eaten off the floor if you'd wanted to. Just in time for me to start icing Ms. Osborne's "donuts."

Nelson pulled up a stool and parked his ass on it with another cup of coffee in hand—and what I could only assume was another healthy dose of emotional support Baileys.

When I turned to look at him with a raised brow he just gave me an innocent look. "What? I can't make croissants without a dough sheeter. So, I'm just going to sit here and enjoy my coffee while I watch you make what I goddamn well know are not *donuts* for that spicy little cupcake."

I just grinned and shook my head, returning my attention to the details in front of me. It was always the details that made these projects the most fun, and I couldn't wait to see her expression when she picked up this order.

I iced all the little circles with different colors and when I started adding designs to them I cut my eyes over at Nelson but he was just watching me with a confused look on his face.

I grinned and continued adding swirls and pinstripes and Celtic knots to some of them. On one of the larger ones, I used a thin pipette to draw a rooster on it. Another had little smiley faces all the way around the outside edge.

I heard a snort from the peanut gallery and grinned as I put the finishing touches on the last one before stepping back to survey my work.

"You've outdone yourself with these, girl." Nelson was shaking his head and laughing. "That little old lady is gonna love her little cock rings."

"This one was challenging, I really wasn't sure what I was going to decorate them with, but a quick Google search gave me some ideas." I winked.

"Here you go, Ms. Osborne. And also, could I ask the title of this week's book? You know...for science?" I grinned as she flipped open the lid on her order, cackling when she saw the different designs on them.

"Oh, of course, dear! This week it was *Save Me, I'm Lost* by L.J. Daniel! And it was absolutely magnificent, highly recommend!" She closed the lid on her box and handed me her card to pay for them.

"Great! Thanks, Ms. Osborne, I'll add it to my TBR! Have fun at your meeting tonight!"

"I always do, dear!" She winked and headed out the door, leaving me with the next few hours of my work day to prep for the following day, now that the repair guy had fixed whatever Nelson had broken that morning in the kitchen.

I pushed through the swinging door only to find Nelson perched on top of one of the prep tables with the book open in front of him.

"Well, that's not sanitary," I quipped at him.

"Eh, fuck it. I'll wipe it down when I get done here. I needed to see what else you've been up to lately that you haven't told me about."

"So far, I haven't read anything else that's happened to me, but I can't lie. That part about the note on her bed has me freaking all the way out. Nel, if I come out of my bathroom one morning to a note on my bed, I'm going to freak the fuck out."

"Girl, that mountain of fur you call a dog would never just let someone meander into your bedroom without raising hell. I think you're safe."

"Nelson, Mags loves me, but she's far from a guard dog. She'd be more likely to point them toward the valuables instead of chasing them off."

When I got home that night I took Mags for a walk, trying like hell to ignore the feeling of being watched the whole time. I usually felt pretty safe with my ninety-pound Bernese mountain dog by my side, but I couldn't seem to shake the feeling that there were eyes on me everywhere I went. I finally gave up and turned us back toward home, just wanting to hole up in my bed and read until I, hopefully, passed out.

Back at the house, I refreshed Mags's water and tucked her into her bed in the living room. She gave me big sad eyes, but I didn't relent.

"Mommy needs some alone time, Mags. You can't unsee that, trust me." I scratched her behind her ears and went to my room, pulling the door closed behind me.

I unzipped my hoodie and let it slide off my shoulders until it landed on the floor. I slipped my bra out from under my tank top, breathing a sigh of relief as I tossed it to the floor to land near my hoodie. I toed off my tennis shoes and shimmied my jeans down my legs, letting them all land wherever they fell to be a tomorrow problem.

I grabbed my e-reader and fluffed the pillows up before I climbed into bed, clad only in my panties and tank top.

There was no way in hell I was reading any more of the book I'd just bought, not if I wanted to actually relax. No, what I needed was a good old-fashioned book boyfriend. Or two.

I unlocked the screen and did a quick scan through my already read library. No surprises needed, just a reliable O and a good night's sleep. I pulled up one of my favorites, a reverse harem retelling of *Alice in Wonder-*

land, and went straight to a scene I'd bookmarked that I knew would do the trick.

I'd read that book so many times I nearly had it memorized, so the scene was set before I even started reading.

I turned off my lamp and slid down in the bed, enjoying the slide of the sheets against my bare legs as I got comfortable. Within the first few sentences, I could already feel myself getting wet between my legs and I slid a hand into my panties, groaning as I parted my lips and slid two fingers over my clit, pushing them down to my entrance. My hips jerked involuntarily when I grazed myself there, and I dragged the moisture back up toward my clit, leisurely stroking as I read about a very lucky woman getting double teamed by a set of gorgeous twins. My hand began moving faster as she straddled one of them, sinking down and gasping as he filled her, rocking against him, until his brother paused her movements, pouring lube over her ass and rubbing the tip of his cock against her there. He teased her with it, asking if she wanted to take them both, and I moaned out loud, knowing I was getting to the good part.

I could feel my nipples pebble against the material of my tank top, so incredibly sensitive that every movement of my body shot a thrill down to my clit as the material moved against them.

I briefly considered pulling my vibrator out of my bedside drawer, but my orgasm was already so close I didn't want to take a chance of losing it. So I just kept reading, my hand gliding over my entire pussy, the heel of it stimulating my clit as my fingers dipped inside to slide against my inner walls, making me want to cry with how empty I felt, even as the first wave of my orgasm radiated outward.

Just as one of the twins finally sank his cock into her ass, I screamed and came so hard I saw black dots in my vision.

I laid there, panting, just barely stroking myself to draw out the sensations until exhaustion began to take over.

I rolled over and pulled a clean towel from the basket by the bed, cleaning myself as best I could before I laid back, enjoying the glow until my eyelids fell shut and a deep, dreamless sleep took over.

Chapter Twenty-Nine

SILAS

I stared down at my hand where it rested on top of his. I looked at them blankly for a beat before snatching mine back like I'd been burned. When I shoved my chair away from the desk, the force sent me wheeling across the floor at speed. Perhaps not the best idea in my current state.

Before I even came to a stop, my inner dialogue started a running commentary in my head:

This isn't real.

I'm having a delusion. A full-on psychotic break.

There's definitely not a giant man-bird standing in my study. Bird-man?

Are those fucking wings?

My hands are tingling. Maybe I'm having a stroke.

Do I smell toast? I read somewhere that you smell toast when you are having a stroke.

Oh wait…I actually made toast earlier, so if I smell toast, does that mean my house smells like toast or I'm having a stroke? *The literature on strokes didn't properly account for that culinary possibility; a gross oversight on their part, in my personal opinion.*

The figment of my imagination stands there staring at me with an amused expression on his face, like he can hear all my inner thoughts as they circle through my brain. Either he's psychic, or I've been speaking aloud this entire time. The jury is still out.

For my part, I'm pretty sure my face has frozen in a permanent expression of shock and bewilderment. There is a possibility my mouth is hanging open like a fish out of water.

Wait…did he just speak?

My mental break can talk?

What the fuck?

Too much whiskey. You've definitely had too much whiskey, Silas.

"What?" I finally formed an intelligible word.

He grinned at me, repeating himself slowly. "I *said.*" He drew the word out. "You're definitely not losing your mind."

I blinked at him dumbly. While I appreciated the reassurance, I wasn't sure I could take his word for it. On account of me being 88 percent certain he was a hallucination.

"Hi Silas, it's nice to finally meet you." He offered me a little wave, and I smacked the heel of my hand against my temple. Maybe this was a glitch. I could probably jolt my brain and get everything back online.

Maybe shock therapy would help.

"Silas," he called. "Eyes over here, buddy."

I reluctantly returned my gaze to his.

"I'm Felix. And you aren't having a mental break. I'm not a figment of your psychoses, and shock therapy isn't going to do anything to make me go away, but you're welcome to try it. Sounds kinky."

I slammed my eyes shut and shook my head. "This isn't real. This isn't happening. I just need to go to bed and wake up tomorrow with a psychiatrist on speed-dial. Everything is going to be fine."

My delusion snorted at me. "I repeat. You aren't having a mental breakdown. I'm as real as you are." He reached over and knocked a book off my desk.

"The fuck did you do that for?" I gasped. How dare my delusion abuse one of my books?

"I'm trying to prove to you that I'm real. Could a hallucination have knocked that book off your desk?" He crossed his arms, again causing his wings to swish around at his back.

"Well, it could if my hallucination was really just a manifestation of my own mental illness, in which case it would have actually been me that knocked the book off, so that doesn't prove your point."

He rolled his eyes at me dramatically. "Fine. What can I do to prove to you that I'm real?"

I thought about it for a moment; setting aside the fact that simply entertaining this conversation only confirmed my worst mental health fears.

"It'd have to be something complicated. Something that requires multiple steps." I nodded, secure in the knowledge that I'd put an end to that conversation.

I pushed out of my chair and started pacing, returning to my previous train of thought. There'd been a counselor I'd spoken with after the thing with the serial killer a few years back, maybe they could recommend a doctor for me.

Would I need to check myself into a facility? I mean, if I was having full-blown visual hallucinations, it seemed like that might be the best course of action. I'd need someone to water my plants. I wondered how long I'd have to be away.

I didn't want to leave my house. In fact, I hadn't left my house in almost four years, but maybe they could sedate me. That's what they did when they came and got people destined for the institution, right?

I started curling my arms around myself, trying to figure out how bad the straight-jacket was going to hurt when they strapped me in it. I'd injured my left shoulder playing baseball in college and it still ached whenever it rained.

I started mumbling to myself at some point. "Maybe they can skip the straight-jacket, on account of my shoulder injury."

I spun back toward my desk to grab my phone and the strange bird-man intercepted my trajectory. I sidestepped him, determined to get to my phone and call someone to come get me before I completely lost it.

"Silas. Buddy, I really think you need to get out more, because you're starting to lose it. Look at me. I'm real. Flesh and blood and bone." He pounded on his own chest, and I had to admit that the solid *thunk* of his fist hitting his chest was somewhat convincing.

He insinuated himself between me and my desk, grabbing my shoulders and giving me a little shake while I slammed my eyes closed.

I heard him sigh a moment before he spoke. "Sorry, buddy, but it's time to snap out of it." And then he grabbed my face in both of his hands and laid a smacking kiss on my mouth.

My eyes popped open and bulged. I took a step backward, staring at him incredulously, dangerously close to sounding like a broken record. "The fuck did you do that for?"

"Well, it seemed like you were really starting to crack up there, so I just wanted to snap you out of it. Did it work?" He crossed his arms over his chest and his wings flared a bit behind him again, rustling against the floor.

"Uh. Maybe?" I blinked at him dumbly. "You're real?"

"That's what I've been trying to tell you for the last ten minutes while your cheese has slowly been sliding off your cracker. Are you back with me now?"

I looked around the room, confirming I was still standing in my study and, impossibly, having a conversation with a giant bird-man.

I nodded slowly. "Yes. I'm…with you. But I either need coffee or a whole lot more whiskey."

"I think we better go with coffee, bud. It's gonna be a long night."

I watched him make his way down the hallway toward my kitchen like he'd been there a hundred times before. I followed behind him and, when he opened the cabinet where I kept the coffee, I narrowed my eyes on him.

"Yeah. I think you've got a lot of explaining to do."

He peered at me over his shoulder with a wink. "Indeed I do, buddy. And look! A hallucination could never work this ridiculous contraption you call a coffee maker."

Chapter Thirty

FELIX

There was a common myth about coffee's miraculous ability to sober a person up. It hadn't taken me a century to figure out that was most certainly not the case.

Silas was staring at me over the rim of his coffee cup, and I was having a bit of a moment myself, on account of having burned two of my three chances at redemption at that point, with no indication that true love had found me. Or that I had found *it*. Was I one of those self-sabotagers?

"Any moment now, I'm thinking you're going to come out with some revelatory words that will explain the presence of a bird-man in my house." He raised a brow at me.

"Made-demon."

"Excuse me?"

"I'm not a 'bird-man,' as you keep calling me. I'm cursed. A made-demon," I announced cheerfully.

"Oh, well, that clears things right up. Thank you for that," he muttered drolly.

I sighed. "It's a long story."

He planted his mug on the table and leveled me with a stare. "One would have to assume so. Might as well get on with it, because my nighty-night clock started ticking the moment you took the whiskey away."

"Let me get this straight. You...debauched a *witch*. And she *cursed* you with wings and immortality?" Incredulous didn't appropriately capture Silas's tone.

"It hasn't been all fun and games!" I responded, offended.

"Yeah. It sounds really terrible. But also, are you stupid?" He got up and went to the coffee pot, refilling his cup.

"It's not as if I knew she was a witch when the debauching started. Well, not entirely, at least. I may have had suspicions. And apparently, she didn't think I was capable of loving another human more than I loved myself. So she designed the 'perfect' curse for me."

"And?" He turned to look at me over his shoulder.

"And what?" I knew what he was asking, but the answer wasn't a simple one to give.

"Are you capable of loving another human more than you love yourself?"

I went to speak, but he cut me off. "And I do *not* mean with your dick."

I snapped my mouth shut.

When he resumed his seat across the table from me, I shrugged. "I've definitely grown in the past century. I'm a better non-human human." I widened my eyes at him. "I think?"

His expression was dubious.

"What? I even tried to save a man's life a few months back," I cajoled.

"Tried?" He tilted his head.

"Well, technically, he still died. But I definitely tried. And I was really sad when he died."

"It's true. You were." The voice intoned from my right.

I jumped, rounding on Kyle with an accusatory glare.

"Man, it's not my fault you're so jumpy. It's not like you don't know I lurk." He shrugged his shoulders as he became progressively more solid before my eyes.

Silas's gaze was traversing back and forth between me and the space to my immediate right. "What's happening right now? Because I don't think I'm mentally equipped for my hallucination to have a hallucination tonight."

I rolled my eyes in his direction. "We already cleared that up. And I'm not having a hallucination, I have a ghost." I gestured to Kyle on my right.

Kyle saluted Silas, though the gesture went unseen by its intended audience.

"A ghost," Silas intoned.

"Look, no one was more surprised than I was." I shrugged.

"Boy, if that isn't the truth." Kyle was cackling off to my side. "Your face was priceless."

I waved a hand at him in dismissal. "He can't hear you. Your wit is lost on him."

"It wasn't for him." Kyle grinned at me.

"No, seriously, what is happening? Are you having an argument with your imaginary friend, Felix?" Silas was staring at me through his hands that were clasped over his face.

"Do you mind?" I asked Kyle.

He threw his hands in Silas's direction. "By all means, please continue."

"So, I tried to save him. But I was too late. And as a result, I've ended up with a new ward. And a ghost."

Silas stared at me blankly before he shook his head like he was trying to clear it. "We'll come back to the ghost thing. Ward?"

"Well, as Kyle was dying, he asked me to watch over his twin sister, Anka. And, in a sense, that's how you came into the story. No pun intended."

"Felix, I feel like you think you just explained something, but rest assured, the combination of whiskey and a bird-man who just appeared out of thin air in my study has stunted my powers of deduction...I need you to spell this out for me."

"*Made-demon.*" I glared at him.

Kyle was cackling, and if I didn't know better, I'd think that Silas could see and hear him, because even he was chuckling a bit as he cut his eyes back and forth between me and the empty space next to me.

"So I had this genius idea," I explained.

Kyle snorted.

"What?" I snapped at him. "It was a great idea."

"It's full of plot holes, my friend," Kyle pointed out.

"Okay, so it was a great idea. But I may not have considered every eventuality in the making of it," I admitted.

Silas had remained silent throughout my explanation, and I'd begun to worry that I'd overwhelmed him with too much information in such a brief period. He looked nearly catatonic. I just had one more thing I wanted to explain before I sent him off to his bed.

"So, essentially, I fed you the book." I stared at him, waiting for him to acknowledge the genius in my plan.

"You did *what*, now?" His eyebrows slammed up toward his hairline.

"Well, me and Davanos. I needed his help because I don't have that particular skillset. But the story? That part was all me. Well, and you. Because I just gave you the ideas and a few key scenarios and details, but then you really took it and ran with it, didn't you, buddy? I mean…well done, you!" I smiled at him.

"Felix!" He gaped at me. "What in the actual fuck? You…I…the book…you wrote it?" he stammered, looking green.

"No, no! Not at all! Silas, you wrote the book! I just… planted the idea in your head. While you were vulnerable and sleeping. With the help of a higher demon. But he's a really cool guy, you'll love him." I tried to offer him a comforting smile but could tell we were off to the races again with another spiral.

Kyle was shaking next to me, his laughter having turned to convulsions as he listened to me try and explain the situation to Silas.

Silas scooted his chair away from the table with a screech against the floor.

"Okay. That's it. That's the absolute last revelation I can absorb tonight. I'm going to bed. I...don't know if I want you to still be here when I wake up tomorrow or not. So, I'll leave that up to you...both. Good night."

And with that, he turned and headed down the hall toward the stairs, climbing slowly and methodically to the second floor, muttering all the way.

I turned to look at Kyle. "I think that went well."

Chapter Thirty-One

ANKA

"That asshole left me on read." I'd been checking my inbox religiously since I'd reached out to the author of "my book," hoping he would respond to my message, but I was going to have to come to terms with the fact that he wasn't going to answer.

I looked up at Nelson, where he was working on the croissants for the next morning.

"Can you believe that?" I asked him incredulously.

"Sugar, at this point, I don't think anything about this situation would surprise me. But if you've got the right guy and he wouldn't even open his door to hear you out, then leaving you on read doesn't seem so out of character, hmm?"

"But what do I do now?" I wailed, only slightly exacerbating my frustration for the sake of dramatics.

Nelson wiped his hands on his apron and turned to face me. "Well, you could send him a glitter bomb."

"How would that make him talk to me?" I furrowed my brow.

"It wouldn't. But it would be funny, and probably make you feel better." He grinned. "It would definitely make *me* feel better."

I rolled my eyes at him and hopped off the stool I'd been perched on for the last twenty minutes.

"I don't think that's how I want to get his attention. But I really appreciate your thoughtful suggestion."

"I'm here to help, babygirl." He winked before returning to his battle-royale with his nemesis, the dough sheeter.

My phone dinged in my hand and I nearly dropped it in my scramble to unlock the screen.

I threw a hand out and grabbed Nelson's arm. "Oh my god. He responded."

"Guess you should cancel that glitter bomb then," he deadpanned.

"Shut up. I'm reading." I hushed him with a hand over his mouth.

"*Mmrudebish.*" He spoke with my hand pressed to his mouth before he stuck his tongue out and licked me.

"Ew, Nel. That's fucking unsanitary." I wiped my hand on the leg of my jeans.

"Maybe you'll think twice before doing that again then." He *harrumphed* at me.

"Seriously, shhh. I'm reading." I was dragging my finger down the screen to get to the rest of the message.

"Wanna share with the rest of the class? I'm on season four of your personal drama, you know. I'm invested."

"He says there have been some new developments since I showed up on his doorstep. And while he probably would have chalked my message, and my existence, up as insanity and ignored me, whatever has happened since has him reconsidering." I looked up at Nelson with wide eyes. "He wants to meet."

"Yes!" Nelson fist-punched the air. "But make it somewhere public. In case he's a psycho."

I was already shaking my head. "He said, for reasons he's unable to disclose, he can't meet me anywhere. That I'll have to go to his house. Nel, what if he's hideously disfigured and I offend him by staring? What if he has some highly contagious disease? What do I do here?"

"I suppose the option of dropping it and carrying on with your life is off the table?" he asked without even meeting my gaze.

"Obviously," I snorted, shaking my head.

"Do you want me to go with you? I can be your bodyguard." He flexed his, admittedly, impressive biceps before he patted me on my cheek. "Look, unless he really is a psycho, I don't think he'd be inviting you to come back to his house if he had a contagious disease. As for hideously disfigured, are you legit inserting yourself into a modern-day *Beauty and the Beast* moment right now?"

"Okay. You're probably right. But who doesn't want to be in a modern-day version of Beauty and the Beast? Did you see that library?" I was already re-reading the message, only half paying attention to what I was saying.

"Girl, you're preaching to the choir. But only if I get to be Beauty. Otherwise it's just depressing."

I looked up from my phone. "What's depressing?"

He shook his head at me. "You're not even listening, I don't know why I bother."

"Sorry, Nel. I'm overstimulated. I just resigned myself to the fact he wasn't ever going to respond."

"No sweat, babe. So, when is this meeting supposed to occur?"

I shrugged before I realized he couldn't see it with his back turned. "I don't know. He just said 'sooner rather than later.'"

Nel finished feeding the croissant dough through the sheeter and transferred it to a sheet pan to put it back in the cooler. "What do you think happened to change his mind?" he asked over his shoulder as he held the cooler door open with his ass and slid the trays onto one of the shelves.

"I don't even think I can guess at that. I mean…this all seems really fucking crazy. So, I guess that whatever made him a believer must be pretty out there?" I pondered out loud.

He snorted. "Only you, girlfriend. This shit would only happen to you."

I could see a shadow moving back and forth behind the curtains and sweat collected on my palms as the feeling of being observed intensified.

I pulled out my phone and texted Nelson, who I

convinced to stay behind, only by promising to keep him updated every hour on the hour. I'd also shared my location with him, so he could "find my body easier." His words, not mine.

> Anka: I'm here. [grimacing emoji]

Nelson: Great. Any sign of chainsaws? Red balloons?

> Anka: Har. Har. And no.

Nelson: Then why are you still sitting in your car staring at the front of his house?

> Anka: How do you know that's what I'm doing?

Nelson: ... [blinking emoji]

> Anka: Fair. I'm a little nervous. Can you blame me?

Nelson: The only option at this point is to get your skinny ass in there and find out what's going on. Stop stalling. And don't get dead.

> Anka: Okay, okay. Fine. I'm going.

Nelson: Good girl. I'll be texting you in an hour. You better answer.

Anka: [saluting emoji]

I wiped the palm of my hand against the leg of my jeans and reached for the door handle. Outside the car I briefly glanced down at my outfit and then shook my head at myself. Who cared if he liked my outfit? I wasn't here for a date.

I approached his front door as I had a week ago and caught one of the curtains twitching in my peripheral vision just as I raised my hand to knock.

I laid three solid knocks against the wood frame surrounding the frosted glass of his door and took a step back to wait. I could hear footsteps on the other side, and a hushed conversation I couldn't decipher.

When the door opened, I realized nothing could have prepared me for what waited on the other side.

Chapter Thirty-Two

FELIX

I resisted the urge to rub my hands together and cackle like a mad scientist as I observed Anka and Silas meeting face-to-face for the first time. Plot holes, my ass. This plan was coming together beautifully.

Silas cleared his throat nervously and stepped back from the door, holding out a hand to Anka, indicating she should come inside.

"You might want to actually speak to her, Silas. You're being creepy," I reminded him.

He twitched, but didn't look at me to acknowledge my statement.

"You must be shebakes?" He tried to offer her a reassuring smile, but it really just looked like he was constipated from my perspective.

She laughed nervously. "Um, yep. That's me. But you can probably just call me Anka." She held a hand out for him to shake and he stared at it long enough that I reached out and nudged him.

He jumped and wrapped his hand around hers. "Silas. Wells."

"Well, what?" She cocked her head adorably, notably still gripping his hand.

He chuckled nervously, extricating his hand from hers. "Wells. My, um…last name. I don't know why you'd need that. But I thought it might make you feel more comfortable."

"Oh! Oh yeah, for sure. Knowing your full government name. Hang on, let me text my friend, so he knows who to send the authorities after if I go missing," she quipped, pulling out her phone.

Silas's face blanched at her words, but she was speed typing on her phone and didn't see it. When she'd returned her phone to her pocket she smiled up at him and gestured to the open door at her back.

"Should we—shut that?" she asked.

His throat bobbed with a hard swallow as he nodded. "Yeah. We probably should. Would you like a coffee?" he asked. "Or maybe something stronger, all things considered?"

She laughed, a little nervously. "Let's start with coffee. I'll let you know if we need to graduate to hard liquor at some point."

"Deal," he agreed, pushing the door shut behind her and turning to lead the way to the kitchen.

Chapter Thirty-Three

ANKA

What was even happening? Men that looked like him weren't real. I was following Silas to what I assumed was his kitchen as I let my eyes scan his physique from the top of his thick, dark hair that brushed the back of his neck in barely-there curls, down to broad shoulders wrapped in a dark blue Henley, to a trim waist and an ass that in no way indicated this man made his living by sitting on it.

He wore faded blue jeans that lovingly cupped that asset like they'd been specially made for it. My eyes followed his long legs all the way down to...his bare feet? And from what I could see, *sexy* bare feet? What the fuck. Had this man taken a profile from my list of book boyfriends and decided to rob me of all intelligence on our first meeting?

When he'd opened his front door I'd almost swallowed my tongue. Dark eyes had assessed me from behind thick-rimmed glasses and his full lips had split into a nervous smile. The strong line of his jaw would have made him eligible for work on the CW any day of the week, and when you added the perfect five o'clock shadow, my lady-parts came alive in a way they hadn't in quite some time.

Holy hell. Why was this man so gorgeous?

And why had I opted for jeans and a bulky sweater for this visit? I suddenly wished I'd taken more care with my appearance, because I wanted this man to notice me.

That train of thought had me mentally smacking myself. *No, Anka. That's not what we're here for.*

"Do you take cream?" he asked over his shoulder.

"Hmm?" I replied, forcing my eyes up from his assets.

"Cream. Do you take it?" he repeated.

I just stared at him blankly.

"In your coffee?" He turned a little and widened his eyes at me like he wondered if I was slow.

"Oh! Um, yes. In my coffee. Yes."

Chapter Thirty-Four

FELIX

"*D*o you think you could make me some popcorn?" I asked him.

He shot me a nasty look before returning his attention to the coffee maker.

"What?" I replied. "This is the best entertainment I've had in a century. Look at her. She's already half in love with you, and you haven't even started talking yet. This is going really well." I grinned at him, crossing my arms over my chest.

Another glare from him had me cackling.

When he had two cups of coffee poured, he turned and set them on the table before adding a little pitcher of cream and a matching bowl of sugar. How cute. It looked like he'd inherited some china from a long-dead relative that dated back to my own era.

Silas was such an odd mix of modern and old-fashioned, and I knew, down deep in my soul, that he and Anka were a perfect match. Now, I just needed to convince *them* of that fact and my work here would be done.

I ignored the niggling thought in the back of my mind that told me it wouldn't be as simple as all that. I was manifesting, and I was certain my plan was going to work out exactly the way I'd imagined.

Mostly.

Chapter Thirty-Five

SILAS

We both reached for the sugar at the same time, and when our fingers collided, I felt that same zing I had when we shook hands. I stifled any outward reaction to it, however, on account of not wanting to give Felix any more fuel for his gloating. One didn't just get to "play cupid" like some winged guardian demon and have things turn out exactly according to plan. Life seldom worked out that way and, most importantly, I didn't want to give him the satisfaction of having been right. He was cocky enough as it was.

"I'll be honest, I'm not a hundred percent sure where to start with this story, but I'll give it a shot, and then you can, um, ask any questions you want. Or run screaming out the door if you decide I'm insane." I shrugged and grimaced. "Full disclosure, I'm not entirely convinced I'm not insane myself, so either reaction would be fair."

Her eyes widened at my admission, but she rested her elbows on the table in front of her, cupping her coffee between her palms, and urged me to go on. "Okay, I'm ready."

I took a deep breath; I could feel Felix's gaze on the side of my face but forced myself not to glance at him before I started. Anka couldn't see him and the last thing I needed was to add 'staring at imaginary friends' to the reasons that she might try and have me committed.

She hadn't moved in a while. Her face bore a blank expression and she seemed to be staring *through* me without actually perceiving me.

"Anka?" I asked gently, concerned she was having the same internal "am I having a stroke" spiral that I'd had when Felix had appeared to me the first time. "Are you okay? Did you hear what I said?"

My question coincided with a ding from her phone and one or the other managed to snap her out of her stupor. She blinked at me a couple of times before she reached into her back pocket and pulled her phone out, staring at it like she'd never seen one in her life.

She swiped across the screen and read the message before she returned her gaze to mine. "My friend. He's checking in to make sure you haven't hacked me into tiny pieces."

"Oh. Okay." I winced, belatedly considering how frightening it must have been for her to show up here alone. "I'm sorry if my message made you nervous. I assure you, you're perfectly safe here. I won't lay a finger on you."

Felix groaned from his spot at the table. "*Boring.*"

I shot him a quick scowl, miming zipping my mouth, while she was typing out a reply on her phone. By the time she'd hit send and returned her attention to me I was, once again, looking at her.

"So, I think I understood everything that you said, but you'll have to forgive me if absolutely none of it seems plausible. Not that I thought the explanation for you having written a book about a woman you'd never met before would require a *simple* explanation. But... curses? Demons? Witches? Ghosts?" She shook her head and stared down at the tabletop in front of her.

When she lifted her eyes again, I saw tears gathered in corners. "*Kyle?*"

I nodded. Understanding that, of all the things I'd revealed to her over the past hour, that would be the thing that would resonate the most for her. Her twin brother had been taken from her cruelly and without warning. To know that his spirit still lingered? I couldn't imagine how that made her feel.

She sniffed once and then straightened her spine, sitting straighter in her chair. "Is he...is he here right now?"

"Who?" I asked.

"Either of them, I guess. Felix? Kyle?" Her eyes had a slightly wild look about them as she looked around the room, but she was handling this much better than I had. Probably due to the lack of whiskey.

"Yes to the first, and I don't know about Kyle. I can't actually see him," I informed her gently.

"But the...bird-man? He's here right now." She looked around again, like she'd be able to see him if she just looked hard enough.

"Made-demon," Felix grumbled.

I cleared my throat. "Apparently that's a thing for him. He prefers to be referred to as a 'made-demon.'"

Anka snorted. "Okayyy. Noted. The bird-man is sensitive. Got it."

I snickered and shot a look at Felix, noting he'd narrowed his eyes on her. "Don't you dare," I warned him.

He gave me an innocent look, but I could see the mischief brewing beneath the surface of his expression.

I returned my attention to Anka. "You can't see him, not if he doesn't touch you, but he can still affect his environment, if you will. So...if you need proof, because of course you need proof, just ask him to do something. If he's not being an asshole, he'll do it."

"I'm wounded, Silas. I thought we'd made so much progress." Felix put a hand over his heart and gave me sad eyes.

I didn't dignify that with anything but an eye-roll before I gestured at Anka to go ahead.

"I think now might be a good time to graduate to hard liquor," she declared.

I wasn't sure she intended that to be her request of Felix, but he took the idea and ran with it. I watched Anka's eyes widen comically as the bottle of whiskey I'd abandoned the other night levitated to the center of the kitchen table before a cabinet opened and two shot glasses floated over and joined the bottle.

Felix was waving them around like he was a ghost, and I growled at him. "Could you not?"

He cackled. "I'm just having a bit of fun with her for that sensitive comment."

"He's fucking with you," I assured Anka. "He could have simply placed them on the table in front of you, but he's got his panties in a twist about the 'sensitive' comment."

"But Silas." Felix giggled, batting his lashes at me. "I'm not wearing any panties."

I smacked my palm to my forehead. "*Felix.*"

"Fine, fine. I'll behave." He patted me on the back before picking up the bottle and pouring two shots without any more theatrics, all while Anka stared with her jaw hanging open.

"*Holy shit,*" she whispered.

"Yep. That about sums it up," I agreed.

We'd moved to my study and Anka had immediately curled up in one of the armchairs by the fireplace. She'd been oddly quiet since we'd left the kitchen, but I was attempting to be patient, given how much she had to process.

From time to time I'd see her lips move and then she'd shake her head and take another sip of whiskey before returning her attention to the unlit logs stacked in the fireplace.

"I can light it, if you'd like," I offered.

Her head jerked up and she looked around like she'd forgotten where she was for a moment. "I'm sorry?"

"The fire. You keep staring at the fireplace. I can light it, if you want." I stood slowly, careful not to make any sudden moves.

"Oh. Sure, that'd be nice. I—I'm abnormally cold."

I nodded my head understandingly. "Of course. Give me just a moment and I'll have it going. There's also a blanket in the basket right there." I gestured to the wicker basket full of throw-blankets in the corner.

"Thanks," she said, unfolding her legs from beneath her before she stepped over to the basket and grabbed a fuzzy blanket off the top of the stack. She wrapped it around herself before she resumed her seat, tucking her legs back beneath her and watching me get the fire started.

"How are you so calm about all of this?" she asked suddenly.

I shot her an incredulous look over my shoulder before I chuckled. "Calm? No. Nothing about my initial reaction was calm. I've sort of come to terms with it, if that's the way to put it, but that's because I've had a week to process, and that one"—I gestured toward my desk—"he could tell you how absolutely not well I handled his revelation if you could hear him. Rest assured, you're taking it much more gracefully than I did."

She cocked her head. "Wow. And I was here thinking I was over-reacting."

I heard Felix chuckle from where he'd settled himself in my desk chair. "I told you she was great. Didn't I, Silas? I told you she'd handle it like a trooper."

I rolled my eyes at him. "Yes, you mentioned that. Very astute of you, Felix."

"I feel like that's sarcasm, but I'll still take it, buddy. Thank you." He grinned and leaned back in the chair, causing the springs to creak with his weight.

I looked back at Anka and she was staring at the

chair as it rocked backward, slowly shaking her head like she still couldn't believe what she was seeing.

"So, I guess I get how I got dragged into this. But... the one thing you didn't explain is what made Felix bring you into it? Was it just because you're a writer? That seems awfully random." She was staring into the fire I'd gotten stoked up to a roaring blaze in the fireplace.

"Ah. Well..." I cringed a little as I settled into the chair opposite hers. "That's kind of another long story. Do you think you can handle more tonight or would you rather I save that bit for another time? It's not—relevant to current events. Truly."

She turned her head and met my gaze, one brow raised. "Are you telling me it's more outlandish than what you've already shared?" Her tone said she found that possibility completely unfeasible.

I winced and shrugged. "There aren't any demons, at least not of the winged kind, if that's what you're asking. But I can't promise it won't be just as shocking."

Chapter Thirty-Seven

I turned my attention from the crackling logs in front of me to Silas as he squirmed uncomfortably in his chair, avoiding my gaze.

"You know how I said that you'd have to come here if you wanted to talk?" He began, his eyes jumping all over the place as he spoke.

I nodded. "I thought maybe you were horribly disfigured."

At that his face broke into a panty-melting smile. "Ah, a *Beauty and the Beast* fan, eh?" he teased.

"Well, as wild as my theory was at the time, it's nothing compared to the actuality, is it?" I challenged.

He laughed. "True. Well, the real reason for that is I haven't left my house in nearly four years."

I gaped at him. "What? Why, Silas?"

His expression sobered again. "Several years ago, I started writing a crime-thriller series. And much to my surprise, it turned into a nearly overnight success. My career was rocketing to heights that I'd only ever dreamed of."

I furrowed my brow, not understanding. "Okay, but then why…"

He rose from his chair and walked over to his desk, sliding an old newspaper from a drawer there before returning to me and holding it out for me to take.

I studied him quizzically before I reached out and took it, turning it over to read the headline on the front page. Understanding dawned with a mixture of horror and heartbreak. For everyone involved.

"This was you?" I looked up at him.

He nodded sadly. "Yeah. It was the worst time of my life and, before you think it, I'm aware the effect it had on my life was nothing compared to his victims and their families. They endured unimaginable horrors, and I'll never be able to fully relate to everything they went through, are still going through, but this was the end of my life as I knew it. Once the feds questioned me, my identity got leaked to the press. I started getting hate mail and people driving by my house throwing things at the front door. I couldn't go out in public without someone getting in my face screaming about what a monster I was."

He turned away from me and went to stand in front of the fire with his hands tucked into the pockets of his jeans, shoulders hunched defensively. "So—I stopped. I sold my house and moved here. I purchased this house under an LLC, so it wasn't tied to my name, and I effectively disappeared from the public eye. The longer I hid, the harder it became to even consider taking a step out that door and now? Now it's become a compulsion. I can't overcome it."

"You're agoraphobic," I said quietly. "That wasn't one of the scenarios I considered."

He nodded sadly. "When you showed up on the front step a week ago, I panicked. No one ever comes here except for my mailman. I didn't know what to do, and then when I saw you through the glass and you looked exactly as I'd imagined the main character of my book? Yeah. I could have handled that better. I'm sorry, Anka."

I understood. I truly did. But one thing was bothering me about the whole thing.

"But you then used that LLC when you published this book, didn't you?" I asked.

He sighed. "I thought enough time had passed that no one would be looking for me anymore. Plus, this is a completely different genre and I used a different pen name, so I thought I was safe. It was stupid and lazy but I never planned for any of this. I never planned for *you*."

"How could you have?" I quirked a brow at him before looking back at his desk chair that was slowly rocking back and forth.

Chapter Thirty-Eight

FELIX

I felt a pang in my chest as I watched Silas tuck another blanket around Anka's sleeping form, careful not to wake her. When he stepped away and turned to look at me, I offered him my cocky smile, shoving whatever that feeling had been far to the back of my mind.

"I hate to admit this, Felix," he said softly. "But that actually did go a lot better than I thought it would."

"It'd be a real dick move for me to say I told you so, wouldn't it?" I nudged him with my shoulder.

"Yep. It would," he stated as he stepped past me into the hallway, headed toward the kitchen.

I followed along behind him, despite the part of me that wanted to remain where I was, watching Anka as she slept. It didn't seem that my fascination with her had diminished now that she knew I existed. In fact, I suspected it had only grown.

"So, now what?" Silas asked as I joined him in the kitchen.

"What do you mean?" I asked innocently. "The two of you develop an abiding affection for one another—dare we hope, even love—and you ride off into the sunset together. You're an author, surely you know what a happily ever after looks like." I raised my brows at him.

"Felix." He let his head fall toward his chest, like he was exhausted by holding it up. "You know it's not that simple. You're toting around the ghost of her brutally murdered twin, I'm an agoraphobic shut-in, she's clearly had pretty terrible luck with relationships in the past, if the details you 'fed' me are based on any truth. There's a shit-load of baggage here to sort through. Besides, what if she's not even interested? Did that occur to you?"

A grin began to spread across my face. "I notice you didn't say anything about you not being interested."

He lifted his head and his cheeks began to flush. There was a spark in his eye that I suddenly realized had been missing for all the years I'd observed him.

He shrugged and looked off to the side, avoiding eye contact. "She's funny."

"Mm-hmm." I crossed my arms over my chest.

"And she's obviously smart. The fact that she tracked me down..." He shifted from one foot to the other.

"Yep." I agreed.

He finally met my gaze. "She's beautiful," he said in an awed voice.

I smirked. "Told you."

I woke to a cold hearth in front of me and a crick in my neck. I sat up slowly, rotating my head on my shoulders, trying to get some movement back before I stood and looked around the empty room. I pulled my phone out of my pocket to find six unanswered text messages from Nelson.

Nelson: hey babe, how's it going?

Nelson: okay, not gonna lie, I'm a little worried

Nelson: I just tracked your location, you haven't moved in three hours. Are you dead?

Nelson: girl, you better have decided to dick the beast and ride that rolling ladder all the way to an O

> Nelson: no really. Should I call the cops?

> Nelson: ANKA. ERIN. KELLY. You better not be dead.

I winced, immediately typing out a reply.

> Anka: I'm so sorry, Nel. I'm fine, I promise. We talked for a long time and then there was some whiskey and I guess I fell asleep. I'm about to leave. I think.

The three dots popped up immediately, indicating he was typing.

> Nelson: You're out of my will for scaring the shit out of me.

> Anka: I'll make it up to you. [kiss emoji]

I returned my phone to my pocket and tiptoed to the kitchen where I'd kicked off my boots at some point. I wasn't sure why I was skulking around like a thief in the night, but for some reason I felt like an intruder now that I'd woken up in Silas's house in the middle of the night with no sign of him anywhere around.

I pulled my boots from underneath the table and hopped around on one leg, pulling my left boot on, but when I switched to the other leg my balance let me down and I tilted precariously, knocking my hip bone into the edge of the kitchen table.

"Ow!" I whisper-cried, rubbing my hand against the spot that would undoubtedly become a bruise.

I thought I heard footsteps and paused to listen, but the sound stopped as soon as it'd started. I shook my head and resumed Operation Right Boot, this time without any additional injury.

My next mission was to find my keys. I tried to remember what I'd done with them when I walked in the door, but my brain wasn't coughing up that information. *Thanks, whiskey.*

Another footstep had me pausing again, and before I could zero in on the sound, my keys came levitating through the air toward me, flying around like they were possessed.

I rolled my eyes. "Thanks, Felix. Um. I have to go. I don't really know what the protocol is here, but I'm guessing you can let Silas know? I have to work in the morning. I…I really don't know what to even say at this point, but he knows how to get in touch with me if he wants, okay?"

I stared into the empty space in front of me like I'd miraculously be able to discern Felix's reaction to my statement if I just stared hard enough. After a moment I shook my head at my idiocy.

"Right. Okay then. I guess I'll…well, I won't *see* you later. But, you know what I mean." I was backing toward the door and somehow I thought I could hear laughter, but I was definitely imagining things.

I'd left Nelson at my house to take care of Mags when I went to meet Silas, so when I pulled into my driveway twenty minutes later, his car was still there. I saw a light come on inside as I approached the front door, and I cringed.

I hadn't felt like that since Kyle and I had been teenagers trying to sneak into our house past curfew, only to realize we weren't going to be able to pull anything past our mother.

Even knowing Nelson had registered my arrival, I gripped the doorknob and turned it slowly, trying to reduce the squeak. When the door swung open in front of me, I was greeted by the sight of Maggie sleeping on her back with her head in Nelson's lap and all four of her feet in the air. He sat with his arms crossed over his chest and the glare on his face would have made my mother proud.

I cringed again and bit my lip as we faced off. "I can explain."

As soon as the words came out of my mouth, I wanted to snatch them back. *Could* I explain? Really? That was one thing I hadn't really thought to ask the night before, but was any of the information Silas had shared with me a secret? I briefly considered shooting Silas a message to ask him, but then realized it was still the very early hours of the morning. Closer to the middle of the night, actually, and surely he wouldn't even be awake to see my message.

Guess I was on my own for this one then.

I held my hands out in front of me. "Before you yell

at me, you should know that I just had what is arguably the strangest night of my life. Of anyone's life, really."

He *harrumphed* at me but tilted his head toward the kitchen. "There's fresh coffee."

"You are an angel." I blew him a kiss on the way to the coffee pot.

"And my bottle of emotional support Baileys is in the cabinet. Make me one while you're at it."

I briefly debated. "I shouldn't have emotional support Baileys. I have to work today."

He craned his neck over the back of the couch. "Bitch, that's not for another seven hours. Pour the Baileys, and once you've told me everything, you can go have a nap. You look like shit."

"Gee, thanks, Nel. You really know how to make a girl feel good."

He snickered. "No, I don't. But I do know how to make the boys feel good."

I rolled my eyes. "Too much information this early in the morning, Nel."

I settled onto the other end of the couch and Mags rose and stretched before flipping her position and laying her head in my lap.

"Hey, sweet girl." I crooned, rubbing the velvety spot between her eyes as she snuggled into me and went back to sleep with a tail thump.

Nelson cleared his throat dramatically.

I suddenly understood how Silas had felt the night before. How did I even begin this story?

"First off, I'm going to tell you you're going to have to take my word for some of this. And it's gonna be really hard to believe. Like…really hard to believe." I took a long sip from my coffee cup, relishing the sweetness and the burn from the liberal amount of liquor I'd added and hoping it would help the words flow.

"I'm on the edge of my seat," he deadpanned. "Incredulity suspended."

"Okay. Well, I guess it all started sometime back in the 1920s," I began. "With a man named Felix."

Chapter Forty

FELIX

*A*nka crept out of Silas's house like a cat burglar. I watched her from the window as she climbed into her car and stared out of the windshield for a few minutes before cranking the engine. I wondered what was going through her mind at that moment. In all the times I'd watched her, I'd never felt as close to actually knowing her as I had for the past eight hours, and I found I suddenly wanted to know everything.

As I'd watched her interact with Silas, I'd begun to loathe the barrier preventing her from seeing or hearing me. I didn't think I'd ever experienced the emotion before but, based on what I'd read in books, my best guess was that I was jealous.

Which was ridiculous. This was what I'd set out to do. The fact that it'd gone so well that I had no doubt they would be seeing each other again, and soon, was exactly what I'd hoped for. I should be patting myself on the back for how well my plan was working. Instead,

I tasted something sour in my mouth, and I had a feeling it didn't have anything to do with the whiskey I'd sipped on a few hours before.

"Whatcha doin?"

I looked back over my shoulder at Kyle, proud I hadn't jumped this time. But maybe I'd been expecting him.

I turned and studied his face, noting that there was sadness there that he usually hid from me. "You okay?"

He snorted. "I'm dead, Felix. What kind of question is that?"

I rolled my eyes. "I'm well aware. But I didn't know how much of that you were here for last night. I didn't see you."

He stared out the window for a moment before he turned and met my eyes. "All of it."

I nodded, having suspected that.

He spoke again. "It feels different. Knowing she knows I'm here. But she still can't see me or hear me. I don't have a heart anymore, and yet somehow it feels like it's breaking all over again."

"Do you think it would be easier if she could see and hear you?" I asked, knowing the answer might not apply only to him.

He shrugged. "I don't know, Felix. Maybe it would. And maybe it wouldn't."

Chapter Forty-One

SILAS

"Felix?" I broke the silence.

I'd been puttering around in my study for hours getting absolutely nothing accomplished. He'd managed to cram himself into one of the armchairs, draping his wings over the back of it, and that's where he'd remained the whole time I'd been "working."

"Yes, Silas." He sighed.

Something was bothering him, but I didn't know how to go about broaching the question. Something told me there was a lot more going on in his brain than I'd previously given him credit for.

I opted to wait him out, pretty sure he'd get around to telling me eventually. Instead, I focused on what was on my mind. "What am I supposed to do now?"

He turned his head and met my gaze with a brow raised. "How do you mean?"

I shrugged. "Well. She knows the whole story now, or most of it, so...is that it? Am I just supposed to go on with my life knowing everything I know and not reach out to her? Should I wait for her to reach out to me? What if she never does?"

Felix offered me a half-smile. "Aw, Silas, are you asking me for dating advice?"

I snorted. "Under the circumstances, do you see anyone else I could ask? You have to admit this situation calls for a specific kind of advisor."

He chuckled. "Yeah. You're right." He turned back to study the fire again, and I thought he'd drifted back into his thoughts, opting not to answer my question, but he eventually spoke again. "Give her a little time. And then I think you should probably reach out. Check on her. That story was a lot to swallow. But she did ask me to tell you that you know how to get in touch with her if you want to."

"You saw her?" My eyebrows climbed toward my hairline.

He nodded. "Yeah. I saw her."

When he settled back in the chair I could tell I'd been dismissed and, despite still having all the questions about their interaction when she'd left, I let him be. I wondered, not for the first time, if Felix realized that his own fascination with Anka might not be limited to his promise to Kyle.

Chapter Forty-Two

ANKA

The miniature penis cakes had turned out exactly as I'd hoped, twelve perfect little penises of varying shapes and sizes, and I applauded my efforts on that front. The problem, however, was that I wanted to put them on sticks, like cake pops, but they crumbled whenever I tried to insert the stick. Apparently, I hadn't made them girthy enough, and they kept breaking when I inserted it.

"That's hurting me just watching you do that, even if it is only cake," Nelson spoke as he leaned over my shoulder.

I snorted. "Well, if you feel like eating a dick today you can have these, I'm going to have to remake them. I need them to be girthier."

"That's what he said." Nelson cackled at his own joke as he plucked one off the counter and slid it into his mouth in a lewd gesture.

I shook my head, chuckling at his antics. "Thanks for

coming in with me today. I know it's your only day off this week, but if you'd left me to my own thoughts all day I might have gone insane."

"I told you. I'm invested. And this is how we do, bitch. Don't thank me. Next time I'm having boy drama I'm gonna expect the same treatment."

I started on a new batch of cake batter, ensuring I made the penises bigger before I slid them into the oven to bake. It was a good thing I'd started earlier than I needed to on Ms. Osborne's order this week. I hadn't planned on having to make them twice, but I had time.

"Do you think I need to use bigger sticks?" I asked him without thinking.

He opened his mouth but I stopped him before he could answer me. "Shut up. I already know what's about to come out of your mouth."

"Well…" he replied. "Ask a stupid question…"

"Yeah, yeah." I laughed. "I hear ya."

"So, have you heard anything from tall, dark, and wordy today?" He popped another penis into his mouth as he passed by on the way to the drink cooler.

I shook my head. "Nope. But he was still asleep when I snuck out." A thought occurred to me and I jerked my head in Nelson's direction with a gasp. "What if I don't?"

"What if you don't what?" he asked, chugging half a carton of chocolate milk in a single go.

"Hear from him. What do I do then?" I asked, resting my butt against the edge of the counter.

"What do you want to do?" He cocked his head.

My cheeks heated. "I think…" I considered some more. "I think I want to hear from him again."

"Got a thing for the agoraphobe, huh, babe?" He winked at me.

"Nel. He's gorgeous. But it's not just that. He's kind of sweet and nurturing. He's got these weird little quirks and they're—endearing?" I could feel the dreamy look spread across my face and Nelson's snort confirmed it.

"You mean, aside from the fact he hasn't left his house in four years?"

I shook my head. "Honestly, I'm not sure I blame him for that. What he went through? Gah, Nel, I can't even imagine how he got past the guilt. But no, that's not what I'm talking about. It's like…for instance, he's got a matching china set to hold his cream and sugar for coffee. And there's a basket full of snuggly blankets in his study, just perfect for cuddling up under while you're sitting in front of the fire. And everything in his house is so pretty. It's way better decorated than my house ever thought about being."

"So, you're saying he's gay. Why didn't you say he played for my team, girl?"

I thought about all of those things for a moment, wondering if Nelson was right, but I hadn't gotten that impression from him when we'd been talking. Not that I thought you could just automatically sense when a person was gay, but the way he'd looked at me a couple of times during the night, I'd sensed interest.

"I don't think so?" I answered, unsure. "But maybe bi?"

"Oooo. Girl, if that isn't right up your damn alley, I don't know what is. Are all of your pegging dreams finally going to come true?" He giggled and ducked away from me as I whipped a hand towel in his direction.

Ms. Osborne was ogling this week's creation but I closed the lid on the box before any of our other customers could catch a glimpse.

"I hope they're what you had in mind." I placed a sticker on the top of the box and slid it across the counter to her.

"They're perfect. None of us liked the book we read this week, and when we complained, the leader told us all to eat a dick. I figured they should at least taste good if we were going to do that."

I covered my eyes, laughing at her explanation. "Oh my gosh. Ms. Osborne, you are too much. I love you. Please never change."

"My dear Anka, if I haven't changed by now, it's safe to say this is the way I'm going to be till I die," she assured me.

"Okay, well, you're all settled up. I'll see you next week?" I found I looked forward to her visits more and more each time. I'd be sad if she didn't pop in.

"Of course, darling! I'll see you soon." She blew me a kiss and left me to get back to the kitchen and clean up my mess. Nelson had left me with a kiss on my cheek and a pat on my ass an hour before, so I was on my own to close up shop.

I was tired, probably from having slept cramped into Silas's armchair most of the night, so I was ready to go home and snuggle with Maggie. I made short work of putting the kitchen back together before I wiped down all the tables in the cafe.

When the last customer waved and left, I breathed a sigh of relief and locked the door behind them.

I'd changed into comfy sweatpants and tank top the minute I cleared my front door. Once Maggie had gone outside and done her business, I fixed us both something for dinner, and ever since then I'd been curled up on the couch, rubbing her belly absently as I studied "my" book with fresh eyes.

One thing that was still bothering me, even after Silas's explanation, was the scene where the note appears on Anna's bed while she's in the bathroom.

That hadn't happened to me. And I hadn't thought to ask Silas about that scene when we were talking.

Maybe that was just something he'd added for extra suspense, but not part of the story that Felix had "fed" him. Maybe. Hopefully.

Anna had been figuratively, and literally, looking over her shoulder ever since the note had appeared on her bed that

morning. She'd whirled on someone in the grocery store, thinking they were following her, but the little old lady behind her squeezing avocados just gave her a startled look.

God, she was losing it.

"I'm sorry. I didn't mean to startle you." She smiled at me kindly.

"No, no. You're fine. I've just had a really weird day. It's not your fault." I returned her smile and took a few steps away toward the fruit.

"Does it have anything to do with the man who's been watching you?" she asked.

"What?" I widened my eyes at her.

She nodded to the end of the aisle closest to us. "He's been lurking nearby. I noticed him a little while ago and thought I'd better stick close. Us women have to watch out for one another, right?"

I carefully peered over my shoulder, just in time to see the back of a man walking away quickly. When I turned back to her I could feel that all of the blood had drained out of my face.

"Thank you," I whispered, suddenly wondering if I should just abandon my cart and get the hell out of the store before whoever that was caught up with me again.

"Of course, dear. You be careful, okay? He looked harmless enough, but you can never be too cautious." She patted me on the back as she passed by, heading for the checkout line.

"Right," I responded, feeling my knees start to shake.

I slammed the book closed again and felt a shiver climb up my spine. I needed to talk to Silas.

As soon as possible.

Chapter Forty-Three

SILAS

The ding announcing a new message had me grabbing my mouse like a man possessed. My hand shook as I clicked on my inbox, anticipation making my skin feel like it was electrified. I'd avoided human companionship for so long that all the new feelings I'd been flooded with since Anka had appeared on my doorstep were overwhelming. I forced myself to take a calming breath before I clicked on the new message from @shebakes.

@shebakes: Hi, Silas. We need to talk. I just read some more and I'm more than a little bit freaked out. Like…a whole lotta bit freaked out, if I'm being totally honest. Can I come over again?

I could imagine, without her even telling me, which part she'd read. Now that I viewed it through this new lens Felix had provided, I could understand why she was freaking out, and I kicked myself I hadn't thought to ask him about it already. I quickly typed out a reply to her before I stood and headed to the kitchen, where I'd last seen Felix.

@wordhermit Of course. You know I'm here. I'm always here.

"Felix?" I strode down the hallway, listening for him as I did, but there was no response.

I stepped into the kitchen and found it empty. My brows dropped and I spun around, heading for the stairs that led to the second floor. To my knowledge, Felix hadn't left my house since he'd touched me that first night. I couldn't be sure he hadn't gone out wandering at night while I slept, but he'd been present every waking hour for the past week.

I rounded the banister and noticed the door to my spare bedroom was shut. I stepped closer and tapped lightly on the wood, but didn't get a response there either.

I slowly turned the knob and eased the door open, eyes widening when I saw Felix sprawled out on his back in the guest bed, clad only in black boxer briefs. His wings were spread across the breadth of the bed beneath him, the tips spilling over the edges like a black waterfall. He was so tall that his feet were hanging over the end of the bed. As I watched, his skin pebbled from the draft coming in the open door, but he didn't stir. He was fast asleep.

I stepped into the room and pulled a quilt from the

closet, draping it over him carefully before I returned to the doorway, giving one last glance at his sleeping form before I pulled the door shut behind me. My questions could wait for a bit.

Anka burst through the door in a flurry of movement, her hands going a mile a minute as she spit out words but I couldn't understand a word she was saying.

"Slow down," I urged. "I'm not going anywhere."

She came to an abrupt stop and took a deep breath, closing her eyes for a moment before she began again.

"The part about the note on her bed and the man following her. Was that part of the story that Felix fed you? Or did you just add that in for…suspense, or whatever?" Her stare implored me to tell her I'd added it myself, but the truth of the matter was that I didn't know. I had no way to discern which parts of the book he'd given me from the parts I'd added.

"Anka, you have to understand that I'd answer this question if I could, but up until a week ago, as far as I knew, every part of this book had come from my imagination. I understand why you're upset, but I don't have the answers you seek." I held my hands out, expression begging her to believe me.

She stared up at me and the green of her eyes seemed deeper in that light. Nearly black. When I saw her lip tremble, I didn't think twice about my next move. I stepped forward and wrapped my arms around her tightly, pulling her to my chest.

"We'll ask Felix, okay? But, rest assured, whatever the case is, no one died in your book. I promise. I swore never to write a book like that again, and yours wasn't the exception. It's going to be okay."

I felt her release a shuddering breath before she nodded against my chest.

"Thank you, Silas. I couldn't force myself to read anything further after the scene in the grocery store. Because none of that stuff has happened to me yet, and I got so scared."

I rubbed my hands up and down her back reassuringly before I slowly released her, allowing some distance between our bodies. Her hands remained on my waist while mine were on her shoulders as I smiled at her, trying to impart whatever calm I could.

"It's completely understandable, Anka. I should have brought it up last night when we were talking. Honestly, there was so much to tell you, I think I just got bogged down in the details. I hope you can accept my apology."

She nodded, her mouth tilted up in an embarrassed half-grin. "Of course. Sorry for freaking out."

"No apologies necessary." I squeezed her shoulders once more before I released her entirely, suddenly self-conscious about how I'd just grabbed her.

I gestured to the kitchen with one hand. "How about some coffee? Or tea, if you prefer. Felix is resting, and, well, I'm not entirely sure this isn't the first time he's done that in over a week. I'd like to give him a chance to wake up on his own if that's okay with you. If not, I can go wake him."

She tilted her head at me, a question in her eyes. "No. That's fine. Tea would be great."

She followed me into the kitchen and resumed her seat from last night at the table while I pulled down my grandmother's tea pot and my favorite loose-leaf Oolong.

I put the water on to boil and began the methodical process of placing the tea into matching set of tea infusers for steeping. When I turned back to her while we waited for the water to heat I noted that same expression remained on her face.

"Is something else on your mind?" I asked.

Her cheeks turned a little pink before she cleared her throat and replied. "I was just…you've got matching china, and fuzzy blankets, and your house is beautiful. Most men wouldn't care about any of those things, I guess. You're an anomaly, Silas Wells."

I grinned at her, endeavoring to poke fun at my own idiosyncrasies. "Well, how many men do you know who are trapped, for all intents and purposes, within the same four walls every single day of their life? I've had a lot of time to try and make my prison as comfortable as possible."

At my admission she suddenly looked aghast. "Oh my god, Silas. I'm so sorry. I didn't even think." She let her head fall into her hands, groaning into them.

"Hey, hey. Anka. It's fine, really. You're right. Most men haven't taken this much interest in interior design. But I've just spent so much time pacing these floors that, eventually, it became a compulsion to make every single space as pleasing to me as I could. And, as for the china, all of this belonged to my beloved Trixie, my maternal grandmother. I inherited it when she passed away and I try to use it as much as possible. It reminds me of her."

"I really like that about you, Silas," she said, resting her chin in her hand.

"What?"

"You don't apologize for the way you are, you just… are. It's refreshing." She smiled.

I'd never really thought of it that way, but I returned her smile. "Thank you."

I came awake with a jolt, disoriented as I looked around the room before I remembered I'd passed out in Silas's guest room. I rubbed a hand over my chest, idly scratching when I realized a blanket covered me where there hadn't been one when I'd laid down. I reached down and lifted it to my face, breathing in the scent that I'd come to associate with Silas and his home. A faintly smoky, cedar aroma that reminded me of the forest just as the season was turning to fall.

It was…comforting.

I laid there for a few more minutes, basking in the feeling of being well-rested for the first time since I'd revealed myself to Silas. I'd tried to remain alert since then, on the off chance that he decided he really was insane and had himself committed. I was fairly certain that was no longer a concern, especially since Anka had come into the picture, and I'd finally hit a wall that I couldn't push past earlier that day. I'd needed rest.

Just as I was considering getting up and dressed again, I heard a laugh drift up from the kitchen and it most certainly didn't belong to Silas.

Hm. *What do we have here?*

I tread softly down the stairs and paused at the bottom, eavesdropping shamelessly on the conversation happening in the kitchen. Anka was telling Silas a story about one of her customers, but she was laughing so hard I couldn't understand much of her story from my hiding spot. It didn't matter, though. Just the sound of her laughter warmed me all over.

I leaned through the doorway, meeting Silas's gaze over her head with my eyebrows raised. Did he want me to leave them alone?

He grinned at me. "Ah, Sleeping Beauty returns to the land of the living."

Anka's head whipped around and her gaze settled uncannily close to the spot where I stood. I wondered again if she could sense me, even without being able to see me properly.

"Good evening, kids. What's going on in here?" I stepped into the room and wandered over to turn the burner back on so I could make myself a cup of tea.

Silas nodded in Anka's direction. "Anka had some more questions, but when she arrived you were sleeping. I couldn't remember seeing you sleep at all in the past week, so I lured her into staying with a cup of

Oolong and the threat of terrible conversation while we waited for you to wake."

"I'm sure she has lots of questions. Just let me find this other infuser thing..." My sentence trailed off as I opened the cabinet and slid things around, looking for it.

"It's almost comforting that you don't know where every single thing is in my kitchen, Felix." I could feel him rolling his eyes, even with my back turned.

When I sensed him behind me I turned slightly and he reached around me to the next cabinet over, pulling down another little basket and handing it to me.

"Oolong? Or that Orange Pekoe you liked last time?" he asked, turning away to grab it.

"Oolong is perfect, thanks." I studied him as he took the infuser out of my hand and began loading it for me. He looked lighter. Happier.

I couldn't help but smile at how much had changed in him in just twenty-four hours.

The water had begun to boil, so I pulled the kettle from the heat and poured it into my cup once Silas placed it on the table. While it steeped, I pulled a container of sliced lemons out of the refrigerator and set it on the table as well.

I watched Anka out of the corner of my eye, noting how her gaze followed Silas as he moved around the room, but also how she seemed to have a knack for locating the space that I occupied. There was something about her. Something beneath the surface that Kyle hadn't told me. I looked around to see if my ghostly friend was in residence. I had some questions for him.

Once I had all the things I needed for my cup of tea, I settled into the chair at the end of the table, directly between Silas and Anka.

I turned and directed my question to Anka, testing my theory, but also knowing Silas would translate if I was wrong. "So, what can I help you with this evening?"

Anka tilted her head a bit and her eyes clouded before she shook her head and turned to look at Silas. "Is he talking?"

Silas gaped at her. "Can you hear him?"

She shook her head. "Not exactly. It's just like... there's a disturbance in the force right there. I can feel his energy, but I can't actually make anything out."

Her eyes bulged before she spoke again. "Oh my god. Is that weird? Am I a witch?"

I threw my head back on a laugh. "Tell her to rest assured, my radar for witches is finely tuned these days. I'm fairly certain she isn't one."

"So, the thing about the note on Anna's bed." Anka shifted her attention between Silas and the spot where I supposed my tea cup appeared to be levitating in mid-air as I sipped it. "Is that something you 'saw,' or something Silas added to add an element of suspense to the story. Obviously, he and I have already gone over it, but there's no way for him to know which is which. Because, let me tell you, that storyline freaks me right out."

I tilted my head and thought for a moment. "Silas, can you bring me the book? I need to look at it again."

Silas nodded and hopped up from the table, jogging off down the hallway toward his study.

While we waited I studied Anka.

"I can feel you watching me," she said.

"It seems you can," I whispered.

"You watch me a lot. You've watched me a lot. Haven't you?" she asked, looking down at the table.

I knocked twice on the surface. *Yes.*

"I think I knew it then, too. But it never felt bad. Like, whatever I was sensing meant me harm." She raised her gaze to where I sat, though her eyes were focused on my shoulder rather than my face.

I knocked once on the table. *No.*

"Is my brother here now?" she asked, a tremble in her voice.

I knocked once again. *No.*

I wasn't actually certain Kyle wasn't there, but if he was, I couldn't see him.

"If he was here—could he hear me?" She looked away and swiped at the corners of her eyes.

Two knocks. *Yes.*

"Okay," she whispered. "Would you tell me when..." Her breath caught. "Would you tell me when he is here?"

Two knocks. *Yes, Anka.*

B y the time Silas returned with a copy of my book I'd wiped away my tears and straightened in my seat, like the exchange with Felix had never happened. As weird as it was, I really could feel him watching me. And I didn't hate the sensation.

"Okay, here it is." Silas held it out to Felix, his finger marking the page. "I've already read over it a couple more times today and nothing about my memory tells me if this was something you 'gave' me or something I added to the story." He shot me an apologetic look.

We both stared in silence as Felix read and flipped pages. Obviously I couldn't determine anything about his expression, so I cut my eyes back and forth between the turning pages of the book and Silas's expression as he watched Felix, trying to get a sense of what was happening.

Silas nodded, as if Felix had spoken and he turned to me. "He says he remembers this vision, but it was really foggy. His 'gift'—and he uses that term very loosely—is sketchy at times. Just showing him enough to tease what could happen without giving the full story."

My shoulders slumped. So we were no closer to an answer then.

"But," Silas continued, sounding optimistic, "he said that when something bad is coming he nearly always gets a strong sense of foreboding along with whatever vision he receives. Given his obsession"—he winced and reached down to rub his shin, glaring at Felix—"given his *oath* to Kyle to protect you, he thinks that if this were anything to truly worry about, he would have gotten a sense for that at the time. And he didn't."

I considered Silas's words and turned to look in Felix's direction, addressing him as directly as I could. "Have you ever been wrong?"

I didn't sense anything at all coming from Felix and I looked back at Silas but his face had gone entirely blank.

"Silas?" I said.

Silas looked down at the table before he met my eyes again. "He said yes. He has been wrong before. But he wanted to qualify that, in the span of a century, he's been right more times than he's been wrong."

"How many more times?" I widened my eyes.

"He isn't willing to guess at that. But he assured me that he'll keep a close eye on you in the coming weeks until we're sure you're not in danger."

I cocked a brow at Silas. "Wow. That's so comforting."

I could tell Silas was trying hard to solve the mystery of who was following Anka. I could almost hear the gears in his brain turning as he sat staring out the window in his study. Anka had left the night before and I'd followed to make sure no one was waiting for her there, but the coast had been all clear. I'd ducked inside when she opened her front door, narrowly missing a run-in with Maggie, but a quick inspection of the house while Anka let the beast out to do her business confirmed we were the only ones there. I stayed until she'd fallen asleep, just to be safe, before making sure everything was locked up tight and heading back to Silas.

"Okay, who are our suspects?" he asked, as if we'd been in the middle of a conversation.

I cocked my head. "Well, Ted is an obvious guess."

He nodded. "That's the first place the police look when something like this happens. Either the significant other, or the ex. But is that too easy? From what I gathered, Ted doesn't seem motivated enough to pull anything like this off."

I agreed with his assessment. "You're right. Ted's a tool. That level of effort would be out of character for him. But she did leave him hanging there at the last..." I chuckled at the memory.

Silas's cheeks flushed and I knew he, too, was remembering that chapter. "Well, it was what he deserved."

I agreed with that as well, wholeheartedly. "True. But, she definitely injured his pride with that move, so I don't think we can rule him out just yet."

"How accurate do you think the words on the note were?" Silas was scribbling things down on a pad of paper in front of him, and I could tell the crime writer in him had been activated, maybe without him even being aware of it. Under the circumstances, it was a skillset that came in handy.

"That part was fuzzy. I saw a note, but I think you embellished the words for the sake of suspense," I admitted.

"What about the ending of the book? Nothing bad actually ends up happening to Anna in the book, but do you think we can rely on that to be accurate?" He paused in his scribbling to shoot me a worried look.

I considered his question for a moment. "I think we can hope that whoever this is doesn't bear her any ill-intent. And I truly do think I'd have 'seen' it if she were in danger. But I won't swear to it. Not when the stakes are so high."

Silas sighed and nodded. "Okay. So, who else then? Besides Ted."

"What about someone tied to Kyle's murder?" I replied.

"Like who? A family member or something?"

I nodded. "From what I gather, nearly everyone in the community knew Kyle, and they knew he had a twin sister. If someone related to one of his murderers bore some guilt for what their family member had done, they could be checking in on her to assuage that."

"Where is Kyle anyway? We could really use his help right about now." Silas glanced around the room.

"I don't know how much control he has over where he appears, and when, but I haven't seen him in a few days," I admitted.

"You rang?" a voice whispered in my ear, and I fucking jumped. Again.

Silas's laughter rang out in the room to accompany Kyle's.

"Dammit. Stop doing that," I grumbled.

"Not until my eternal soul moves on to the next plane, Felix. It's too much fun." He giggled before using the mantelpiece as a perch for his ghostly form.

"I take it Elvis is back in the building?" Silas grinned.

"Yes," I growled, gesturing at the fireplace. "He's currently perched on your mantel like a gargoyle."

Silas considered that for a moment before he shrugged. "As long as he doesn't go poltergeist and start shoving family heirlooms onto the floor, I guess it doesn't matter where he chooses to perch, as far as I'm concerned."

"So, what hath thou summoned me for today, bird-man?" Kyle intoned in a spooky voice.

"Oh, knock it off, you idiot. We've got serious business." I looked at him pointedly before I turned to Silas. "Do you want to explain?"

Kyle had been strangely silent as Silas explained the situation. Strange because, on the one hand, Kyle was rarely silent when he made his presence known, and on the other hand because this particular situation related to Anka's well-being. Something that he took very seriously.

I watched his face as Silas repeated everything we knew, from my original vision, to what had ended up in the book, and how we were both pretty foggy on whether she was in actual danger or not. Throughout the whole of it, Kyle remained a blank slate. Completely passive in his expression. I drew a hand up to rest it on my chin, tapping a finger against my cheek as I considered his lack of reaction and filed it away as another clue.

When Silas had finished his recap, Kyle remained silent.

"What's he saying?" Silas asked me.

I tilted my head, keeping my gaze locked with Kyle's. "He's not saying anything at all, Silas."

"What?" He sounded surprised.

"You heard me. Not a peep from Casper over here

upon hearing that someone might be stalking his sister."
I raised a brow at Kyle.

Kyle flattened his lips and shook his head at me.

"Hey, Silas?" I called over my shoulder.

"Yeah?" Silas sounded confused.

"Can you think of any reason why Kyle would remain so deathly silent, pardon the pun, at the news that his beloved twin sister could be in danger?"

Silas got up from his desk and came to stand next to me. "Well. I suppose if he already knew someone was following her, but knew she wasn't in any danger, he might not be too worried. But that doesn't explain why he's not talking."

"Ah. Right you are, clever boy," I commended him. "Do you know what that tells me?"

Silas turned and looked at me, shrugging his shoulders. "No, but I have a feeling you're going to tell me."

I grinned, giving Kyle a wink before I spoke. "That tells me there are *secrets* afoot. And I love getting to the bottom of secrets."

Kyle shot me one last annoyed look and began to fade from my view. I suspected he wasn't planning on leaving the room, but whatever he was hiding, he didn't want me getting to the bottom of it.

How fun.

Chapter Forty-Seven

ANKA

I unlocked the door to the cafe, feeling like my skin was crawling. I'd been staring over my shoulder all morning, and I didn't trust anymore if it was paranoia or a real sixth sense that I was being watched.

After I'd gotten dressed in the bathroom I'd come out and stared at my rumpled bed sheets, heart thudding, half expecting a note to be waiting for me, but there was nothing but sweet Mags grinning her doggie grin as she snuggled into my pillow.

I let myself in and locked the door back behind me, something I didn't normally do when I worked the opening shift, but the idea of someone walking in while I was doing prep in the back freaked me out too much to take the chance. I'd come unlock it again when open hours began.

Pushing through the swinging door into the back, I patted around on the wall to my right for the light switch. I wished, as I had on many other occasions, that we had a motion activated light back here, it was so damn dark that finding the switch was difficult even if you knew where it was in theory. After several pats on the wall I finally hit the lights and turned to survey the kitchen. Nelson had closed the day before, and I hoped he'd had time to get everything clean before he left.

Thankfully, everything looked spotless, and I mentally gave myself a reminder to text him later thanking him. I walked over to the main cooler to pull out the croissants and get them in the oven before I began pulling the trays of muffins out to go in the other oven. All of our pastries were baked fresh every day, which was tough for one person to keep up with, but Nelson and I had a system down and it hadn't failed us yet. Whoever closed the previous day did as much dough prep as could be done, so that the next morning all that had to be done was actually bake everything. As long as I kept the right timers going, everything would be done and ready to put in the cases by the time we opened. By then, the day clerk would be in to help me get everything stocked. We were a well-oiled machine.

Once the first batch was in the oven, I stepped over to the dry-erase board we kept near our lockers, to see if Nel had left me any notes about today's orders, but there was something there that didn't belong. And it wasn't in his handwriting. A note was held to the board with a magnet.

Anka, I know things have been stressful of late, but rest assured, all will be revealed in time. Have a little faith.

All the blood drain from my face and I grabbed blindly for my phone in my back pocket, snatching my latex gloves off and tossing them on the counter as I started pacing.

"Hello? Is this an emergency? Because I know my best bitch knows I'm still asleep this time of the morning." Nelson's voice was far too chipper for me to think I'd woken him up, but I didn't have time to argue.

"Nel. Someone was in here. I don't know when, but someone was in the kitchen. Did you look at the board before you left last night?" I could hear the panic in my voice.

"Wait, what? Slow down, babe. Of course I looked at the board before I left, I left you a note. Didn't you see it?" he replied.

The air escaped my lungs in a whoosh. "This was from you?" I let out a hysterical laugh. "It doesn't look like your handwriting and I freaked out a little."

"Duh, bitch. Of course it's from me, it's about that goddamn dough sheeter breaking down again. Who else does that machine hate?" he asked.

I was right back to panicking. "Nel. That's not the note I'm talking about." I lifted my eyes back to the board and saw the message he'd left me. Directly underneath the spot where the strip of paper had been. As if whoever left it wanted to make sure I knew they'd been there after Nelson had locked up.

"Hang tight. I'm on my way." Any note of teasing had left his voice. "Stay on the phone with me until I get there."

"Thanks, Nel," I whispered, backing myself into a corner where I could see the whole of the kitchen. If someone was in there hiding, I didn't want to give them a chance to sneak up on me.

"I'm here. I'm just going to unlock the front door. But it's me, okay? Don't freak out." Nelson sounded so worried and I loved him all the more for rushing to get to me. He truly was the best friend a girl could ever ask for.

When he pushed through the swinging door he hung up his phone and slid it into his pocket just before he snatched me and pulled me into a hug. "Hey, babygirl, you're white as a damn sheet. Come here, let's get you some orange juice and you can show me that note. We'll get to the bottom of it, okay?"

He pulled me toward the front, grabbing a bottle of orange juice out of the cooler and shaking it before opening it for me. "Here, take a few sips. I don't want you passing out on me."

I did as I was told and nodded at him gratefully once the sugar had hit my system. I already felt a lot better, just having him there, but the juice helped, too.

"Thank you." I leaned up and gave him a kiss on his cheek. "I love you for this."

"Shit, girl, you scared the ever-loving hell out of me. I wouldn't be anywhere else but here. Now, can you tell me what happened?"

"I just…came in and started my day like any other. Oh shit!" I bolted back through the door into the kitchen and grabbed the neoprene holders, snatching the oven open on the croissants. "Thank fuck," I wheezed. They weren't burned.

Nelson rolled his eyes and made his way to the other oven, knocking on the glass and checking the progress on the muffins before he turned back to face me.

"Now, let's try again. What happened?"

"I came in and started my day. Got all the prepped stuff out of the cooler and into the oven, then walked over to the board to see if you'd left me any notes, and this was held to it with a magnet, directly on top of where your note was written." I held out the note to him and he studied it closely.

"I don't recognize then handwriting," he said, looking back at me.

"Me neither." I shrugged.

"It doesn't seem…threatening, though. Right?" He was re-reading it.

"I don't know. Threatening? Maybe not? Ominous? Maybe so? But whichever way you look at it, someone was in here after you locked up last night. And that's freaking me the fuck out. You did lock up last night, didn't you?" I blinked up at him.

He cringed and looked away.

"Nellll…" I warned.

"I lost my key to the back door last week. And you know I hate going out the front door when my car's parked out back. Nobody ever does anything bad in this little podunk town, and I haven't had a chance to get a new key made." He gave me a sheepish look.

I hung my head. "Nel. Dammit. Well, that solves the mystery of how they got in, at least. Now I guess I just need to figure out who the hell would want to leave me ominous notes in the first place."

I'd wrapped up the end of my shift and hung my chef's coat on the hook inside my locker, turning to watch Nelson through the window as he chatted with the girl working the counter. I knew he was probably telling her to keep an eye out for anything weird, but I hoped he wasn't scaring her.

I pushed through the door into the cafe, after having checked to make sure the back door was securely locked, and jerked my head toward the exit.

"Okay, cutie. Just call me if you see anything bizarre, okay? Have a good rest of your night." He saluted her before joining me at the door.

"Tacos and beer," I declared.

"And tequila," he added.

"Stat," we said in unison.

Three shots of tequila, one bowl of queso, two twenty-two-ounce mugs of a dark Mexican lager, and a tray full of tacos between us, we were trying to solve the mystery.

I wondered idly if Felix was around somewhere, but the low-level hum I seemed to get whenever he was close by either wasn't present, or it had been numbed by the tequila, so I couldn't tell for sure.

Nelson waved his taco in my direction. "Okay, I think we can rule out the unicorn bandit, on account of that note not making any mention of his 'self-esteem.' So, can you think of anyone else?"

I took a huge bite of my tacos al-pastor, letting the flavors burst over my tongue and chewing slowly while I considered his question.

I chased the bite with a big sip of my beer. "Well, it seems like whoever it was *thought* they were being reassuring? Maybe. So if we go with that, then who knows me that also knows what's been going on and would want me to be—less stressed?"

"Hm. Okay. That makes sense. And that should narrow down the list. Do you think this has to do with the book stuff? Or does it go back to Kyle's...um..." Nelson suddenly looked uncomfortable.

"Murder. You can say it. Kyle's murder." I reached for one of the shot glasses Miguel had left in front of us. "And I don't know. It's not like whoever left the note was super specific about what 'things' they were referring to."

"Then I think we have to assume that 'thing' with

Kyle is a possibility. So who knows about that? And knows that you're his sister?"

I shrugged. "Everyone knew Kyle, Nel. He was... magnetic. You know. And anyone who knew him for more than five minutes knew he had a twin sister."

"Okay, so what if it's someone tied to the guys that murdered him? Like...a family member. A brother, maybe?" he asked.

I shook my head. "No way. Did you see that handwriting? No way that was a dude."

"I'll have you know I have lovely penmanship," he grumbled.

"And you, my love, are the exception to the rule." I tipped my glass at him.

Nelson's face lit for a moment. "What if whoever it was got someone else to write the note for them?"

I scrunched my face up. "How would that even work? How would you ask someone else to write a mysterious and vaguely ominous note for you and them just be like 'okay, sure, and here you go!' That seems highly unlikely."

His face fell. "Right. Okay then, so we think whoever left the note was a woman. What does tall, dark and nerdy think?"

I lifted my head and grimaced at him. "Um. I don't know?"

He looked stunned. "You didn't reach out to him?"

I glanced around, again wondering if Felix was nearby. "Well, no. I don't have his number and it seemed like a really weird thing to send him a message about on social media and then what was he going to do? He never leaves his house, Nel. I didn't want to make him feel some sort of way. So, I just...didn't."

"You know you need to, though, right? I mean, he's involved in this one way or another. You should at least let him know." He crossed his arms over his chest and leaned back in his chair, giving me a reproachful look.

I rolled my eyes. "Find. I'll send him a message. Happy?"

He grinned. "Very."

Chapter Forty-Eight

SILAS

$\mathcal{I}$ 'd turned into Pavlov's dog when it came to the "ding" from my computer telling me I had a new message. When I leaped for the mouse to open up my messenger it suddenly occurred to me that I could have, should have, given Anka my phone number. I mentally smacked myself in the head. Idiot.

"What is it?" Felix came and stood over my shoulder.

"A message from Anka." I clicked it open and immediately felt utter terror all the way to my core.

"She got a note today." I turned and looked up at him.

For the first time in four years, I had a real urge to step outside my door. The thought of it made bile creep into my throat and my skin felt like it was electrified, but dammit, I felt useless. Damaged. Why the fuck would she ever want a man who couldn't even step foot outside his door to go to her when she was scared?

I read the rest of the message and only felt somewhat better when she included a picture of the note. It didn't sound threatening. Not exactly. Ominous, perhaps.

I could feel Felix leaning in closer so I waited until he'd backed away before I started typing a response.

@wordhermit: I've shown it to Felix. We'll get to the bottom of this, Anka. I promise. I'm so sorry. Are you safe right now?

A few minutes later she responded.

@shebakes: I'm having tacos and tequila with Nel. I'm safe. But um…would it be okay if I got your number? It'd be so much easier to just text you, lol.
@wordhermit: Yes! For sure! Definitely. My number. Because texting is easier. Absolutely.

I looked down at my phone and realized I didn't even know my own number. How fucking sad was that?

"Felix!" I didn't know why I was asking a being that had been around for a lifetime before cell phones were even invented, but desperate times called for desperate measures.

"Silas." He popped his head up over the top of the chair where he was slouched.

"She wants my phone number. What do I do?"

"Well, buddy, I'm gonna get really crazy here for a minute, but what if…you gave it to her?" He raised a brow at me.

"Obviously. But…I don't even know what it is. How

do I find that?" I was frantically pressing buttons, but none of them were getting me to the information I needed.

He laughed and stood, sliding a phone out of his own pocket that I had enough presence of mind to wonder about before he held it up to mine and suddenly his contact appeared on my screen.

"Press there." He pointed to the little picture of him on my screen.

When I pressed it, his phone started ringing and he grinned. I wondered how long it would be before I severely regretted that transaction, but I just stared at him expectantly until he read my number off and I added it to the message to Anka.

I flung myself back in my chair and took a deep breath. "That was really stressful."

He shook his head at me with an indulgent look on his face. "Poor little Silas. You really do need to get out more. The world outside is so stressful that what just happened would have seemed like nothing to you!"

"Wow. You're really selling it." I rolled my eyes.

Chapter Forty-Nine

FELIX

I needed to find the wayward little witch. Something about that note had triggered my memory.

As odd as it seemed, however, I didn't have any real idea of where to find her. I could have gone to Felicity and asked her if she knew how to track Serafina down, but I thought that might stir up a can of worms I didn't care to delve into. And I didn't yet want to explain to anyone what my theory was. Not until I'd spoken to Sera.

On a hunch I went to Anka's house, lingering by the large oak tree in her yard, idly observing Anka as she moved about inside her house. She was singing to Maggie, and I chuckled as I caught the lyrics to an old Rod Stewart song, wondering if that's where Maggie had gotten her name from.

I'd nearly given up on my quarry when a shoulder

brushed up against mine. I grinned, delighted I'd found her so easily.

"Felix," she said in greeting.

"Sera." I nodded at her. Wanting to fire questions at her immediately but deciding, instead, to wait and see what she would say first.

"Fallen in love yet?" She shot me a sly grin.

I shook my head slowly. "Nope. Not that I'm aware of."

"A pity. You've burned two of your chances already."

My eyes widened. "You know?"

"Of course I know, Felix. It's my curse. You don't think I'd make it so I feel it every time you touch someone?" She rolled her eyes at me like I was simple.

I leered at her. "Sera, you naughty little bird. How kinky."

She smacked me on the arm, harder than I'd have thought her capable of. "Not like that, you pig."

"Oh, so you missed that whole thing with the demon then?" I winked at her.

"You're disgusting."

"From what I recall…" I trailed off, trying to rile her.

She narrowed her eyes at me in warning. "We aren't going to revisit my brief insanity once upon a time."

I threw my head back on a laugh. "Okay, Sera. Truce?"

She turned and studied me curiously. "What do you want, Felix?"

"What makes you think I want anything, Sera?"

She put her hands on her hips. "You're being funny.

And charming. You haven't been funny and charming with me since that night."

"You mean, since the night you threw a burlap sack over my head and cursed me to hell for a century? How odd that would have changed our dynamic." I felt my own irritation beginning to rise to the surface and I shoved it back down. I needed her talking. Laughing. Spilling secrets. "Okay, fine, you caught me. I do have a question." I shrugged, giving her my most innocent expression.

She eyed me suspiciously. "Okay. Maybe I'll answer, maybe I won't, but ask your question, Felix."

I watched her face closely for any reaction at all as I spoke. "Did you ever have any kids, by chance?"

The only thing that gave me a hint I'd hit a nerve was a single twitch of her left eye. It was so fast that, had I not been paying such close attention, I'd have missed it altogether.

She laughed in my face. "Why would you ask me that? Do you see me running around with a baby strapped to my chest?"

I cocked my head at her. "Not at present." But I didn't let her off the hook, maintaining eye-contact until she cracked.

She glared at me, gritting her teeth for a moment before she looked away. "How did you know?"

I relented a little, knowing whatever her reasons for keeping her child a secret weren't mine to know. "I didn't know, not for certain, but someone has been following Anka, other than me, keeping an eye on her." I gestured toward the little bungalow in front of us.

"Taking an interest in her well-being. One might even say, taking a *maternal* interest in her well-being."

She stubbornly remained silent.

I raised my brows at her before I continued. "And that person left her a note with a pretty common phrase on it, but it jogged a memory. It was something you'd said to me a few years back. It stuck with me, as it seemed a bit out of character: you told me to 'have a little faith.'"

She closed her eyes briefly before turning to watch Anka dance with Maggie through the window.

Softly, I asked. "Who is she to you?"

She didn't turn back to me, but her whisper drifted to me on the breeze. "My granddaughter."

A sudden, very acute, terror overtook me. "Mine too?"

Sera turned to me then and snorted. "Hardly, Felix. Magical though your cock might be, even you couldn't get a woman pregnant by fucking her ass."

elix had been gone most of the day. And it wasn't like I missed his company or anything. That would be weird. But I had been wandering from room to room for the past hour, aimlessly adjusting a book on the shelf, a candle on the table, a picture frame on the wall, only to circle back to the book on the shelf a few moments later.

Okay. Fine.

Maybe I missed his company a little bit.

I picked up my phone and stared at the screen, wondering if it was normal to just text someone out of the blue to ask how their day was going. You'd be surprised how many social conventions you lost track of altogether when you'd avoided humanity for four whole years. The only person I'd spoken to on the phone in that time was my agent, the power company once when someone hit the transformer on our block, and my youngest brother, the only member of my family who was still a part of my life after it had imploded. None of those people required me to give any real thought as to when and how I reached out to them.

But now, as I wandered the house without Felix to distract me, I started thinking about texting Anka. Just —because. I didn't have any news. I hadn't solved the mystery of who had left her the note, though Felix was acting very suspicious about that, so I had a feeling he was working on a theory. I just wanted to say hi. Because I liked her.

My palms started sweating and my heartbeat took on an irregular rhythm in my chest. No way this was normal behavior for a grown man.

> Silas: I want to text Anka. What do I say?

I stared at the message until I saw the dots pop up, indicating he was typing a reply.

> Felix: I've met children better versed in how to flirt with a woman than you are. How did this happen?

> Silas: Mock me later. Help me now.

> Felix: Okay. Fine. But you're really stealing all the joy from my life at the moment.

> Felix: If you're not sure what to send, you can't go wrong with a funny GIF.

Felix: Look for something about coffee.
Or Mondays.

Silas: A GIF. Okay.

Felix: Keep it lighthearted. Funny.

Silas: Got it. Thanks.

I stared at my phone for so long that Nelson nudged me.

"Your muffins are burning." He jerked his head toward the oven closest to me.

"Shit." I grabbed a heat glove and snatched the door open, thankfully just in time. They were a little more brown than I liked, but they'd still be edible.

"What has you so enthralled, anyway? Did tall, dark, and wordy send you a dick pic, or something?"

"Nooo. He sent me a GIF." I handed him my phone.

"Are those fucking coffee beans?" Nelson looked confused too.

"I think so? What do you think it means?"

"Uh. Maybe he wants you to come over for coffee and chill?" He snickered before handing my phone back.

"That's not a thing. Right?" I asked. "I mean, nobody

does that. And anyway, I just met him. I'm not going over there for any 'chilling' yet."

Nelson cackled. "I heard that 'yet,' girl. You're so into him."

My cheeks darkened. That word had popped out without my consent, but I didn't really want to take it back. I kind of did want to "chill" with Silas, but it was definitely too soon. Definitely.

"How do I even respond to this, though?" I looked up from my phone, imploring Nelson to help me out.

"How about 'Good morning!'? That seems...safe." He was giggling to himself as he iced the cake in front of him.

I nodded. "You're right. That seems safe. Okay."

> Anka: Good morning! [smiley emoji]

I stared for a few minutes, but no response came, so I locked my screen and went back to work. Puzzled he'd reached out, but happy, nonetheless.

"**Y**ou did what now?" Felix wasn't even trying to contain his laughter at my expense.

"I did what you said!" I exclaimed.

"You sent her a GIF of two coffee beans mimicking a sex act, Silas. That's neither fun, nor lighthearted. It's just weird." He snorted.

"No, I didn't! They're dancing!" I looked at the little moving picture again with fresh eyes. "Aren't they?"

Felix was slowly shaking his head at me. "No. Buddy. They are not dancing. Unless you're referring to the horizontal mambo."

"*Fuck.*" I let my head fall to my desk, rolling it back and forth in my misery. "Now what do I do?" I groaned at the woodgrain.

Felix sighed before snatching my phone out of my hand and typing something out before he handed it back to me.

> Silas: So...I thought those coffee beans were dancing. My GIF game is rusty. [laughing face] Forgive me?

I read what he'd written and looked up at him. "Do you think that'll work?"

He shrugged. "Not sure, but a good rule of thumb with women is to always be willing to admit you're a dumbass. They find it endearing."

I breathed a sigh of relief. Okay. Maybe I hadn't ruined everything.

Thank god for Felix.

It was several hours before I got a response, and by the time I did I was pacing again while Felix watched me with an amused expression on his face.

> Anka: Haha! No worries, it was funny!

"Silas, I have to ask. Because I'm looking at you, and you're arguably an attractive guy. One might even go so far as to say devastatingly handsome. Is this the first time you've ever tried to court a woman?"

I stopped in the middle of my fortieth lap around the study, shrugging somewhat sheepishly. "Well, I mean, obviously not in the past four years."

He nodded. "I'd assumed that much. But what about before that?"

I'd started lap number forty-one at that point, if my

count was correct. "I had a girlfriend in high school, and we dated all through college. I went on a baseball scholarship and she played the part of the perfect ball player's girlfriend. We both thought I'd be going pro once I graduated." I paused, shrugging. "She had our perfect life all planned out."

"What happened?" His eyes followed me around the room.

"I got injured. Tore my rotator cuff. It wouldn't have been a career-stopping injury, but I ignored it. We were mid-season and had a shot at the college world series. I was the only left-handed pitcher on the team and it gave us an edge. I thought I could just ice it, keep getting cortisone shots, ride it out through the end of the season, and then deal with it." I shook my head at my own stupidity. "In the last game of the series I injured it again. By the time I got to a surgeon they confirmed I'd done too much damage for it to ever be fully mobile again."

I subconsciously rotated my arm, still getting a twinge from it when I did.

"So what happened to the girl?"

I stopped pacing long enough to meet his gaze. "When the possibility of a rich, pro-ball playing husband went away, so did she." I shrugged. "It was all very amicable. But the end result was the same."

"Has there been no one since her?" He sounded appalled.

"Eh. A couple here and there, but nothing serious. I've always been quiet. A little too introspective. Women are attracted to it until they realize it's not an act, that's actually how I am. And then they lose interest." I rolled my eyes. Maybe it wasn't such a stretch that I'd ended up confined in my own home. I'd always been a loner.

He studied me as I continued my path around the room but didn't say anything else on the subject.

"Where did you go today?" I changed the subject.

"To see an old…friend," he answered vaguely.

"Okay. I'm going to be honest, Felix. I didn't know you had any friends. But good for you?"

"Well, *friend* might be an exaggeration." He smirked. "But I solved the mystery of who is following Anka, so my adventure served its purpose."

I stopped dead in my tracks. "And you didn't lead with that? Who is it?"

He shrugged, looking a bit smug. "You were having a crisis. But we can both take a deep breath and rest in the knowledge that Anka is absolutely not in any danger. Probably. Mostly."

I gaped at him. "Probably. Mostly. Felix, your reassurance game is really bad. Terrible, if I'm honest. What the hell does that even mean?"

He sat forward, resting his elbows on his knees as he addressed me. "It means I know she's in no danger from the person who has been following her. That being said, when the rest of the story gets revealed, I can't swear she won't be in any danger at all. There are some big secrets being kept, Silas, and even I'm not privy to the entirety of them."

"So, what am I supposed to tell her, Felix? What are *we* supposed to tell her? Because we can't let her keep walking around looking over her shoulder, scared,

when we know she isn't being stalked by some psycho."
I was nearly yelling now, and Felix raised a brow at me.

"Yes, Silas. I'm aware. What do you think I've been sitting here trying to work out while you've been wearing a path in the hardwoods?"

I deflated. "Oh. Well. Why didn't you say so?"

Chapter Fifty-Three

ANKA

I'd gotten an extremely vague text from Silas asking if I could come over that night. After the fucking coffee beans GIF he'd sent me, pun intended, I really wasn't sure if this was a social visit or something to do with our collective "situation," but I decided to dress for something in between those two options.

I was standing in front of my closet while Maggie watched me from the bed, surrounded by discarded clothes which I'd now probably need to rewash because she'd rolled all over them. I had Nelson on speaker as I debated.

"Jeans? Or a skirt?"

Nelson snorted. "Jeans, for sure. A skirt just screams 'I thought you invited me over for sex' these days."

"What? No, it doesn't! Since when does a skirt scream that?"

"The fuck do I know, I haven't hetero-dated in ten

years, I'm just saying that skirts are for easy access," he grumbled.

I conceded. "Well, you may not be entirely wrong, but it's still messed up. Which jeans?"

"The Levi's," he stated, without any hesitation.

"Really?" I pulled out the jeans in question.

"Trust me. They make your ass look fantastic." He sounded smug.

"My ass always looks fantastic, you jerk, but fine. What else?" I shimmied into the jeans, sliding them up over my hips and buttoning the first couple of buttons before I returned to the shirts I hadn't already pulled out and thrown on the bed.

"Is that green off-the-should one clean?" he asked. "The one that matches your eyes?"

I flipped through but didn't see it. "Oh crap. Hang on. I think it's on the bed already."

"Do not wear it if it smells like Maggie," he warned.

I shuffled things around and found the shirt in question at the bottom of the pile on the bed, thankfully protected from Maggie's shenanigans. "We're good! Confirming it does not smell like dog."

"Perfect. Now, put your boots on—the brown ones with the little heel. Add that thin gold necklace I got you for Christmas last year, but that's it. You're going for understated, got it?"

I saluted him even though he couldn't see it and giggled.

"Did you just salute me?" His voice was deadpan.

"Yes, sir," I replied.

"Good girl." I could hear the smile in his voice. Nel

loved it when I did as I was told, as long as he was the one doing the telling.

"Okay, gotta run, Nel. Do you think you could swing by a little later and let Mags out?" I bit my lip, hoping he'd agree.

"You nasty bitch. Of course I will. Now go, have fun." He hung up, and I slid the phone into my pocket, grabbing the necklace he'd told me to wear on the way out of my bedroom.

Maggie followed me all the way to the front door, looking optimistic, and I hated to let her down, but I didn't actually know how Silas felt about dogs. Showing up with her in tow didn't seem like the right move.

"I'll take you for a car ride tomorrow, sweetie. I promise. We can go to the dog park and see if your friend Louie is there."

She whined a little but sat down on her haunches, resigned to being left behind again. I felt like the worst dog mom in all the land.

I leaned down and gave her a hug and a kiss on top of her head. "Love you, sweet girl, I'll be back soon."

*A*nka climbed out of her car, and I grinned, rubbing my hands together.

"What are you smiling about?" Silas asked, stepping up next to me.

"Oh, nothing."

He leaned forward to pull the curtain back, and I smacked his hand.

"Ow! What the hell was that for?" He rubbed his hand, glaring at me.

"You look pathetic, peeking out the curtain to watch her walk up. Where's your pride, man?"

He gave me a blank look. "You're literally doing the same thing."

"Yes," I agreed. "But she can't *see* me doing it."

He rolled his eyes at me but took a step back from the door, probably to avoid getting smacked again.

When she knocked on the door he shot me a look. "Is

it okay if I answer that? Or will that make me look too pathetic?"

"Well, now you're just being ridiculous. Of course you can open it." Gah. Kids these days.

Silas pulled the door open to reveal Anka standing on the other side, looking like a dream in a pair of light blue jeans, an off-the-shoulder top that matched her eyes perfectly, and a thin gold chain draped around her neck that disappeared beneath the shirt, somewhere that I suddenly wanted very badly to follow.

I swallowed, hard, and Silas cut his eyes in my direction with his brow furrowed. I must look as panicked as I felt. I just shook my head at him and gestured to Anka.

Everything was fine. Going perfectly according to plan. I was a changed man. I could do this for them and move on with my life. There was no need for my dick to get involved. None at all.

"Hey," he greeted her warmly. "Thanks for stopping by on such short notice."

She smiled back, but I saw her eyes move in my direction subconsciously, before she responded. "Oh, sure! I figured maybe you had some information for me? Or...something?"

Silas cleared his throat, his cheeks flushing, and I knew he was imagining what that "or something" might be. Damn, I was really good at this.

"Yeah, of course, um...Felix found out some stuff and we just wanted to talk. About that. The stuff. You know? That he found out."

I used one of my wings to smack his ass. "You're stammering. Take a breath, buddy."

I saw his chest rise and fall with a deep breath before his shoulders relaxed back to their normal position. "Come on in, we can go sit in the study. I've got a fire going already."

She beamed up at him. "Sounds great."

It turned out the modern world had made it relatively easy for a grown man to remain within the confines of his own house and still manage to do things we used to have to go out for. Silas had procured a couple of lovely bottles of Pinot Noir, three thick filet mignon steaks, the makings of roasted red potatoes, and a salad, all delivered right to his door in a matter of a couple of hours from the time he'd invited Anka over.

We'd all settled in the study with a glass of wine while the steaks were resting, and I could almost feel the electrical current that flowed between Anka and Silas.

And when I felt that same current flowing between us, as well?

I ignored it. Simple.

"I'll go get the steaks started in a bit," Silas began. "But I thought maybe we could get the information sharing out of the way first? That way we could just enjoy our meal?"

Anka tilted her head at him, and I enjoyed that the skin just above her cheekbones turned a subtle shade of pink before she, uncannily, turned and looked right at me where I leaned an arm on the mantel. Like she'd known I was there all along.

"The anticipation, and okay, maybe also the anxiety, is killing me, so yes, please." She let her gaze switch back and forth between the two of us. I didn't know how it was possible, but it seemed with every new exchange, her ability to find me in a room had improved.

Silas looked at me, his own eyes widened, like he too had noticed her attention on me. "I don't really know what to say then, because you never told me what you discovered earlier. Do you want to tell me, and I'll relay your words to Anka?"

I tilted my head at her, noting she was looking at me again. "Yes, that will work. But first, could you ask her a question?"

"Okay. What would you like me to ask her?" His focus was bouncing back and forth between me and Anka.

"Can you ask her if she remembers anything about her mother's parents?"

I shot Felix a perplexed look, but repeated his question, searching Anka's face for any indication that she knew where he was going with this.

She scrunched up her brow. "I never met them. My mother was adopted as a baby, but her parents, her adoptive parents, died tragically before she ever met my Dad. Why? What does that have to do with any of this?"

I turned to Felix to see him looking thoughtful. "Ah, yes, that explains why I never knew."

"Knew what?" I asked, not thinking about the fact that Anka couldn't hear Felix's reply.

"What? What's going on?" she asked.

"One second," I told her, never taking my eyes from Felix's.

"Serafina," he replied.

I could feel my eyes widen comically. "Wait…you're saying Serafina is…" I cut my eyes to Anka.

Felix nodded. "Apparently, her grandmother."

"You guys, if someone doesn't start explaining really soon, I might go insane. What is happening?"

I turned and looked at her. "I think…" I looked back at Felix, and he nodded, shrugging. "Anka, your grandmother, your biological one, is the witch who cursed Felix a century ago."

Anka just stared at me, mouth hanging open, but before she could say anything, a new voice rang out in the room.

"Well, now you've done it."

Anka's head jerked around, her hand climbing up toward her mouth. "*Kyle?*"

PART IV

AFTER

The mind, once enlightened cannot again become dark.

-Thomas Paine

I stared at the shimmering vision of my brother as he offered me a sad smile. A sob crawled up my throat, unbidden, choking me as it fought to get out. Tears sprang immediately to my eyes, clouding the image of him, and I swiped at them furiously, not wanting anything to obscure the sight in front of me.

"Hey, sis."

The voice I thought I'd never hear again broke on the second word and the image of him wavered for a moment before becoming more solid before my eyes until he looked almost...real.

There was no controlling the tears as they poured down my face. "God, I missed you."

He rolled his eyes and smirked at me. "Kyle. Not God."

I choked on a laugh before I stood and walked closer to where he...stood? "How?"

He gave me that sad smile again. "There's a lot you

don't know, sis. And honestly, I think you might have been better off not knowing any of it, but I guess the cat's out of the bag now, huh?"

He turned his attention to Felix. "You're too clever for your own good, friend."

I turned around, wondering if I'd be able to see Felix now, too, but the space by the fireplace remained empty according to my eyes. There was another sense, though, that told me he hadn't moved from that spot. I could feel him. It was a very peculiar sensation, but the air surrounding him just had a different weight to it. Like he was bending the light, even when I couldn't see his actual form.

Felix must have replied, because Kyle chuckled ruefully. "I didn't tell you it was a secret because that would have just made you more determined. Tell me I'm wrong."

When Kyle looked back at me, I asked the most important question. "Can you stay?"

He tilted his head back and forth a couple of times, like he was weighing his answer. "I don't know. But something tells me that my unresolved business isn't any closer to being resolved." He stepped closer and held a hand up to my face, not quite a touch, but I swore I could feel the barest sensation his palm against my cheek. "I'll stay as long as I can."

For once, I wasn't the only one in the room who felt lost. Silas still couldn't see Kyle, and none of us knew why he'd been able to appear to me but not Silas, but the situation led to a lot of the telephone game happening as Silas cooked our steaks in a cast iron skillet on his cooktop.

"Wait…so the two of you tried to sneak past a half-witch after curfew and you thought you wouldn't get caught?" Silas was laughing as I tried to explain the story.

"Well, it's not like we knew she was half-witch at the time." I chuckled, glancing down into my glass, suddenly struck by sadness.

When I lifted my eyes again, Kyle was giving me a concerned look. "You okay, sis?

I nodded before taking a gulp. "Yeah. I just wish things were different. If she hadn't died, then maybe Dad wouldn't have been such a dick to you, and our family wouldn't have fallen apart. Now, here we are, and I have so many questions for her. Like…did she know? Did she have any idea?"

My brain was working overtime and suddenly everything stopped. I looked up at Kyle, excited. "Wait. Have you seen her? Is she around? Can I see her? Is she like you?"

I was firing off questions so fast I couldn't have expected him to answer any of them, but he just shook his head at me with a pitying look on his face.

"No, babe. I don't think she's here anymore. But, hey, that's good right? It means she didn't have anything unresolved keeping her here. She's moved on to…I guess, Heaven? Or whatever the next step is beyond this." He gestured at his form.

My shoulders slumped. "Yeah. Yeah, of course, that's better. It'd be selfish of me to want her here when she could be floating on a cloud or something."

I sensed something from the space to my right, and I looked that way, raising a brow.

Kyle coughed. "Felix says he doesn't think that's exactly how it is and he's laughing at your...how did you put it, Felix?" He raised his brows at him. "Ah, yes, your childlike understanding of the beyond."

I narrowed my eyes in Felix's direction. "Well, it's not like we know what it's like. And I choose to stick with that vision. It's fluffy. And pure. And it makes me happy to think of our mom there. So, fuck off." I shot a bird at the empty space.

Kyle and Silas both broke into laughter at whatever Felix's response was to that.

"What did he say?" I looked back and forth between them, but Silas just shook his head, miming zipping his lips.

"Bro?" I tried Kyle.

"No fuckin' way, sis. I'm not repeating that." He shook his head adamantly.

Kyle stayed by my side until his body began growing more and more transparent.

I panicked, but he was quick to reassure me.

"It takes a lot of energy to be this present. Don't worry, I'm not going anywhere yet. Nowhere permanent, at least. I'll see you soon, sis." He blew me a kiss before he disappeared entirely and I stared at the space he'd occupied, feeling unbearably sad.

Silas cleared his throat, drawing my attention to where he stood with another bottle of wine in his hand.

"Would you like to go sit by the fire for a bit? Tonight has been—revelatory. Maybe we could just sit and soak it all in?" He offered me a boyish grin.

I nodded, grateful for the reprieve. "I think I'd like that."

*A*nka had curled up in the same chair she'd fallen asleep in just a week before, and I marveled at how much had changed in such a short period of time. As I poured her a glass of wine, I realized that my solitary existence had been indelibly altered, and I was suddenly, passionately, opposed to it ever going back to the way it had been before Felix had appeared in my life.

I paused what I was doing, soaking in the moment I knew everything had changed. I lifted my gaze and met hers, and she smiled at me, a tired smile that hinted at both the happiness and the sadness the night had been for her.

A boldness came over me I hadn't experienced in a very long time.

"Anka?" I asked, stepping closer to hand her the glass.

"Yes, Silas?" she returned playfully.

"Do you think I could kiss you?" I would have smacked myself in the forehead if I hadn't been holding a nearly full bottle of wine, but she just grinned at me, setting her glass down before she stood and stepped in front of me.

"Silas?" she asked.

"Yes, Anka," I answered playfully.

"I thought you'd never ask."

I groped around behind me until I located the surface of my desk and nearly hurled the bottle of wine onto it before I stepped closer to her. My hands were shaking and my mouth had suddenly gone very, very dry.

I cleared my throat. "It has been a very long time since I've done this."

She grinned at me. "It's just like riding a bike, Silas. But with more tongue."

I paused while her words sunk in before I tipped my head back on a laugh. "Thank you."

She tipped an imaginary hat at me. "It's my superpower."

I edged closer to her, bringing my hands up to cup her jaw and tilt her face toward mine. "Something tells me that's not your only superpower."

I kept my eyes open when my lips touched hers, despite the nearly overwhelming urge to shut them and bask in the electricity which had been humming between us finally making contact, but I wanted—no, needed—to keep my eyes locked on her face as I slowly moved my mouth over hers.

I slid one of my hands to the back of her neck,

tangling my fingers in the silky dark strands, tugging gently until she gasped. I used the opening to dart my tongue into her mouth to tangle with hers.

When she slid her hands up my chest and curled them over my shoulders, pulling me closer, I groaned into the kiss and let my eyes fall shut.

When I needed a breath, I withdrew a bit, nipping at her lips, and she followed, drawing me back in in the most delectable first kiss in the history of the world. My body was straining toward hers and the urge to let my hands fall to her hips and lift her so we aligned more fully was so strong that it was all I could do to hold back. But I knew, if I did, our embrace wasn't going to stop with a kiss.

As bizarre as it sounded, I wanted to take my time with Anka. The utter gravity of her presence in my life, the *weight* of her existence, told me that she was the one for me. I wanted to do this right.

Unfortunately, convincing my straining dick that we needed to let her go was going to be far more difficult.

I pulled my lips away from hers and tilted her chin back, leaning in and placing my lips on her neck just over her pulse point, breathing her scent deep into my lungs where I hoped it would never leave.

"Anka," I groaned against her neck.

"Hmm." She stretched against me, making my body come alive everywhere we touched.

"I want to see you again," I whispered in her ear.

"You're seeing me right now, Silas. Not to tip my hand or anything, but I'm pretty confident you could see anything you wanted to right now."

I chuckled, placing a little distance between us and meeting her confused expression.

"I want to woo you," I said.

I heard a snort come from the hallway, and I narrowed my eyes in the direction.

Anka followed the path of my glare and looked back at me with wide eyes. "Do we have an audience?"

I leaned forward and rested my forehead against hers. "It would seem so."

She seemed to consider that for a moment before she gave me a mischievous grin. "Might be a new kink I didn't know I had."

I heard a groan from the hallway, and when I started laughing I couldn't make myself stop. When I was weak-kneed from hilarity and nearly hanging onto Anka to keep me upright, she offered me another cheeky grin. "So, what exactly does this 'woo' entail?"

Chapter Fifty-Eight

FELIX

I perched at the top of the stairs like a creep as Silas walked Anka to the door, confirming that he'd be in touch soon with some "woo."

I was intruding on a private moment, but couldn't make myself turn away as they shared another kiss before she ducked out the door, giving him a little wave as she climbed into her car.

He waited until she'd pulled away before he shut the door, quietly sliding the lock into place. He turned to face me like he knew exactly where I'd been all along.

"I should thank you," he said, staring up at me with a serious look on his face.

I smirked. "Because I was right about how perfect you two are for each other?"

He tipped his head. "Well, yes, that, but something else occurred to me in there." He jerked his head toward his study.

"And what's that?" I asked.

"You've changed my whole life. I had this, admittedly, small existence...but, Felix? I don't think I would have ever changed it. The fear..." His words drifted off and he looked away.

"I know a little about fear holding you back," I admitted.

He met my gaze again. "I know."

I cocked my head. "Oh yeah? And how do you know that?"

"I understand more about what holds you back than you give me credit for, Felix. And I know you think you've wasted two of your chances to truly be happy in this life, but I don't think you see the big picture. Because you're scared, too."

I studied him for a moment before I conceded. "Okay. Then show me the big picture."

When he just grinned at me and shook his head, I knew he was about to really piss me off. "Nope. That's not for me to do. But, boy, I can't wait until you figure it out."

$\mathcal{I}$ didn't have legs anymore, I was sure of it, because I'd simply floated everywhere since Silas had kissed me and told me he wanted to "woo" me.

"If you grin any bigger, I'll be able to see your fillings," Nelson grumped.

"Aw, don't be a spoil-sport. I had an amazing night. I'm basking. And what are you so grumpy about?"

He sighed. "I had a date last night."

"Oh. I want the tea. What happened?" I leaned my hip against the prep table and gave him my full attention.

"First of all, it should be a fucking crime for someone to post a picture of themselves on the web that's at least a decade old. And second of all, he said he was an entrepreneur, but when we got to the 'what do you do' part of the evening, it turns out that 'entrepreneur' means he runs the ring-toss booth at the carnival." He leveled me with a blank stare.

"Well…" I hedged. "Everyone loves the carnival, and someone has to work those booths! He brings joy and laughter and humongous cheaply-made stuffed animals to children everywhere!"

Nelson slashed his hand through the air. "Not 'everywhere.' He doesn't travel with the carnival, so he only works the four nights they're in town every season."

I blinked at him, unable to come up with a response.

"Anka. That's like…twelve nights a year. And I saved the best part for last." He got a smug look on his face.

"No," I said.

"Yes," he said.

"But it's so cliché!" I cried.

"It is, indeed," he confirmed.

"His mother's basement?" I had to confirm.

"Yep." He let the p pop off the end of his tongue for added emphasis.

I let my head fall into my hands. "Sorry, Nel. Hey, did he at least buy you dinner?"

"With what, bitch? Monopoly money? That boy is baaaarookkee." He turned back to the cookies he was icing. "I'm done dating for a while. I'm just going to live vicariously through you for the foreseeable future." He sighed again.

"I'm really sorry, Nel. I swear, there's somebody out there for you, don't worry. Have a little faith?" I gave him an optimistic thumb's up.

"Oh, shut the hell up, Pollyanna, you're just on the love bus because you've got a guaranteed dick-down headed your way."

I grinned at him, not even trying to deny it. "I do, don't I?"

I locked up the cafe door and dropped my keys into my jacket pocket, wondering idly if Nelson had ever gotten his keys for the back door replaced. I rolled my eyes. Probably not.

When I turned toward the sidewalk I stopped in my tracks. There was a bouquet of flowers levitating in front of me, and I jerked my head around quickly to see if anyone else had noticed, but the sidewalk was blessedly empty.

I held out my hands and the bouquet floated just above them before dropping. I caught them to my chest and looked back up, noting that odd bent-light effect that meant Felix was still standing in front of me.

"Thanks, Felix," I murmured with my head tilted down so no one caught me talking to myself on the street. The note that was tucked into the flowers jiggled before it floated up in front of my face and danced around there.

"Okay, read the note, got it." I plucked it out of the air and tucked the flowers under my arm so I could open it.

Good evening, Anka. Pardon the unconventional delivery method, but I know you understand.

I've set up a "date" for us for this evening, if you're up for it? Just let the "delivery boy" know your answer. I hope to see you soon.

I looked up from the note, cocking my head. "Date? But how?" I wondered aloud before I shook my head. Obviously I wouldn't hear it even if Felix was inclined to answer me.

"So, now?" I didn't know why I asked, but I heard two knocks on the doorframe above my head and remembered the "conversation" Felix and I'd had in Silas's kitchen. Two knocks for yes.

"Well, okay then. Let him know I'm just going to run home and shower and I'll be over."

Two more knocks, then the air around me returned to normal, and I was alone again.

I shook my head. This was fucking weird, but I couldn't deny I was excited to see what Silas had come up with.

I briefly recalled Nelson's comment about skirts and easy access, but well…I decided I was okay with that, so I pulled a cute little black dress I'd bought to wear to a cocktail party last year and never ended up wearing because Ted had decided to be a dick that night. I'd made him go without me and spent the evening curled up on the couch in my sweatpants with Maggie and a good book.

Now, I grinned; I liked the idea that the first man to see me in it would be Silas. And maybe Felix?

I ignored the little thrill that thought gave me. Too much to unpack there.

"Mags?" I called, and I heard her nails clicking against the floor as she trotted into my room. "I'm going to call Nelson to come check on you in a bit, okay? Mommy might be gone for a few hours. You be a good girl, okay?"

She just yawned and hopped up into the middle of my bed, circling twice before she curled up on my comforter.

"I guess I've been dismissed then." I laughed, leaning over and placing a kiss on her head. "Love you."

I called Nelson on my way to Silas's house, and he grumbled but agreed that Maggie was the best chance he had of a good date for the night, so he'd go by in a bit and stay with her until I got home. I knew she'd actually be fine by herself for a few hours, but she'd already been home alone all day and the guilt was real.

I needed to talk to Silas and see where he stood on giant dogs that thought they were lap dogs if this was going to become a habit.

When I pulled up at his house, the porch light was the only thing breaking up the darkness, and I wondered if I'd misunderstood his note. He did mean tonight, right?

As I stood uncertainly on the sidewalk, the front door opened and he stepped out under the golden glow. "I'm so glad you came," he said without preamble.

I let out a nervous laugh. "I was starting to wonder if I'd misunderstood. It's so dark in there."

He stepped back and waved me toward the door. "You didn't misunderstand. Come on in, I'll show you."

Silas took my hand as he shut and locked the front door then tugged until I followed him through the house to the back door. Oddly enough, I'd never even realized there *was* a back door, but I realized that was ridiculous. Of course there was.

He opened it and motioned for me to go first. When I stepped onto his back deck, I gasped as I looked around his yard.

There were string lights stretched in a criss-cross pattern across the center of his tiny patch of grass, and a giant white sheet had been stretched between two trees, pulling the material taut. On the ground it looked like every single blanket he owned had been laid over the grass, with cushions and pillows strewn about. In the center, a bucket of ice had a champagne bottle poking out of it.

I heard music start and looked back at the screen as an old movie began to play, couples gliding across the dance floor were accompanied by big band music just loud enough that I could hear it without drowning out the sound of Silas stepping up behind me.

"I wanted to take you to a movie. But obviously that would be...difficult. Then Felix said movie dates are terrible, because you can't actually talk."

I turned to face him and he looked so nervous that I reached up and put my hand on his cheek, leaning up on my tiptoes so I could place a kiss on his mouth. "This is perfect. Very romantic, Silas."

His breath escaped his lungs in a whoosh. "Really? Okay, good. Do you want to..." He held his hand out toward the blankets.

"Yes, thank you. I just need to take these off." I put a hand on his shoulder for balance while I undid the ankle strap on one shoe before switching to the other. I gathered them and looked at him and he jumped to take them from me. He arranged them carefully on one of the porch steps, perfectly lined up with the edge, and I grinned. He was so odd, but I found I really liked it.

We settled down on the blankets and Silas pulled a cushion over for me to lean back against. He lifted the champagne bottle out of the ice, expertly removing the cork, and poured us each a glass.

He turned to me and cleared his throat. "I know this is weird. I'm so sorry, Anka, I want to do all the things, but..."

I shushed him with a finger on his lips. "I don't need you to do anything you don't want to do, Silas. I like you just the way you are."

His eyes widened before he ducked his head and grinned. "I like you, too."

"Well, I sure hope this isn't what you do for women you don't like, Silas. *That* would be weird." I stared at him blankly until he broke into a laugh.

"I guess you're right. That would be a little weird," he agreed.

"So, what next?" I asked, a teasing note in my voice.

"Oh. Well, I thought we could talk? And I have chocolate covered strawberries in the cooler. I made them myself. Do you like dark chocolate? I guess I should have asked. Oh my god, what if you hate dark chocolate?"

"Silas, stop. Relax. I'm a pastry chef. It's one of my job requirements to love dark chocolate. And I love chocolate covered strawberries, especially when I'm drinking champagne."

He sighed. "Okay, good. Good. So, I'm not fucking this up entirely?"

"You are not fucking this up entirely. Or at all." I smiled. "This is perfect."

Silas and I sipped on champagne and talked about our lives for the next couple of hours. We ate dark chocolate covered strawberries, which were delicious.

I told him about my job, about Ms. Osborne and her wild pastry orders, and Nelson, and Maggie.

He told me more about Trixie, and how he'd been close with his family until everything had happened four years ago, but that now the only one that kept in contact was his younger brother. It made me unimaginably sad for him, but he was quick to tell me not to worry. That he'd finally started to feel like he wasn't so alone anymore.

I was thankful for the dim light to hide my blush, because I thought maybe, at least a little, he was talking about me.

It was the perfect date. He was attentive and listened to all my stories, laughing at the right parts, asking questions when he wanted to hear more. I hated to draw any comparisons between Silas and the men I'd dated in the past, because there really wasn't any comparing them. But if I had, Silas would have dominated in every single category.

When he laid me back on the blankets and kissed me again, I thought I might spontaneously combust.

"Silas," I gasped. "Can we go inside?"

He peered down at me, his look clearly asking if I meant what he thought I meant.

I nodded. But also, I thought maybe a mosquito had just bitten my ass and that was not the kind of three-some anyone wanted.

He nodded slowly, but I could tell he was more than a little freaked out.

"It's okay. We can go slow. But I'm starting to feel like a smorgasbord for the bugs," I whispered.

"Oh! Oh my god, I'm so sorry!" He jumped up and pulled me up by my hands, ushering me up the stairs to the back door of the house.

"Slow down, Silas. I'm fine." I laughed. "Let me grab my shoes." I bent down and scooped them up and he held the door for me before he followed me into the house.

When I turned back to him, he looked wildly uncertain, and it started to make me wonder if I'd misread the situation entirely.

He cleared his throat. "Do you…" He looked up at the ceiling for a minute before he met my gaze again. "Anka, you know I didn't invite you over here thinking…or planning…I didn't have any notions…"

I decided to put him out of his misery. "Silas, do you want to take me upstairs?"

He nodded slowly, a light appearing in his eyes that told me I wasn't alone in what I was feeling.

"Why don't you lead the way?" I nodded at him encouragingly.

"Okay. Yes, let's go upstairs."

I could see his hands shaking, so I grabbed one in mine and gave it a squeeze.

He led the way up the stairs and into his bedroom. I'd probably take the time to have decorator's envy later, because it was gorgeous. Peaceful. And the bed centered on the longest wall? It was humongous. Easily the biggest bed I'd ever seen. Which, I guess, made sense. Silas was a tall guy. He'd need a bed long enough to accommodate his height.

We both stopped and stared at it before I turned to look up at him. I'd been so focused on his nerves that I hadn't noticed, until that moment, that I was nervous, too.

"I have an idea. Why don't you go get the last of that champagne? Maybe it'll help us...relax?"

He started to argue and I spoke before he could. "I'm not remotely drunk, Silas. You aren't taking advantage of me. Are you drunk?"

"No. No, definitely not." He shook his head.

"Okay then. I'll just make myself comfortable? And you go get the champagne. We'll have another glass and see what comes up to talk about?" I giggled at my terrible joke, and I was happy to see Silas roll his eyes at me, some of the nervousness already fading from his expression.

"Deal." He chuckled before he headed back out the bedroom door.

I looked around briefly before making my way over to one of the nightstands and turning on the little brass lamp there. Perfect. Just enough light, but not too much. I had dimples and such in places I hadn't had in my twenties; I didn't need a spotlight shining on them.

By the time I'd slipped my dress off and draped it over the chair in the corner, slipping under the comforter on his bed, I heard the back door slam and anticipation had me shivering. Whatever was to come, I was here for it.

Chapter Sixty

SILAS

Silas: I'm panicking. Do you know how long it's been since I've been with a woman?!

Felix: Relax. I can talk you through it.

Felix: Wait…

Felix: Does that mean you've been with a man? [eggplant emoji]

Silas: FELIX… [grimacing emoji]

Felix: Okay, okay. Not the time. I can see that now.

Felix: Where is she right now?

> Silas: She's waiting in my room for me to... I don't know. Sex her up!

> Felix: My man. Did you just say "sex her up"?

> Felix: Sigh. This is worse than I thought...

> Felix: I'm on my way. [superhero emoji]

I whirled around when I heard a noise behind me, worried that I'd been gone so long Anka had come to find me, but it was just Felix.

"Wait...how did you?" I looked at the front door then back at him where he'd just appeared in my kitchen.

"Eh. Sometimes it works, sometimes it doesn't. These things are notoriously unreliable as far as transportation goes." He hooked a thumb over his shoulder at his wings.

I shook my head, rubbing my hands over my eyes. "I can't even address that right now. What's your plan?"

Felix squinted at me like I was stupid. "What do you mean, 'what's my plan'? I came to help, so I'll help."

I tilted my head at him. "And by that, you mean..."

He shrugged. "I'll talk you through it. If you get stuck, no pun intended, I'll make suggestions. It'll be fine. I'm really good at fucking."

I blinked at him slowly. "Felix. She's going to sense

you in the room. There's no way this will work. And, anyway, why would you want to...do that for me?"

"Why would I want to watch a live-action sex act between two extremely attractive people? Gosh, Silas, I don't know...maybe you're right."

"Haha. I get that part, but...wait. You think I'm extremely attractive?"

"Focus, Silas. There's a woman in your bed waiting for you to sex her up, remember? And she'll be so distracted by your rippling abs she won't even notice I'm there. Just get...started, and I'll come in in a minute."

"Get started," I deadpanned.

"Yeah. Like...take off your shirt. Kiss her neck. Roll around a little bit. It'll be fine. I'll be there before you know it."

I rolled my eyes. "This is not how I envisioned this happening."

He gave me a wide-eyed innocent expression. "Silas, I'm scandalized. You imagined me talking you through it?"

I walked out of the room, remembering to grab the champagne at the last minute, calling back over my shoulder. "You're an idiot."

I paused in the hallway outside Silas's bedroom door, cocking my head to listen. I heard the bedsheets rustle just before Anka spoke.

"Were you talking to someone down there?"

"Oh, um, no just giving myself a pep talk. It's been…" Silas stuttered, and I shook my head. I really needed to work on his pillow talk.

I heard the fizz of champagne being poured into glasses and the *tink* of their glasses clicking together.

"Cheers," Anka said softly.

"Cheers," he echoed.

After a moment of silence, I heard some murmuring I couldn't decipher, even through the open door. I leaned closer.

"I think I wanted to take that dress off you myself," Silas whispered.

"Next time," she moaned, and I grinned. *Good boy, Silas.*

"Come here," he uttered in a low voice, nearly a growl.

I took the opportunity to step into the room, watching closely for any indication that Anka sensed my presence, but her attention was focused entirely on Silas as she climbed on top of him, straddling his hips.

I slid Anka's dress to the side as I settled into the chair in the corner of the room, leaning back to watch. I congratulated myself because they truly looked stunning together.

Anka looked perfect as she settled on top of him; her full hips gripped in Silas's hands made my own hands clench, wishing I could feel the silk of her skin against my palms.

Silas leaned up, placing his mouth against her neck, kissing and nipping at the skin there, and her back arched as she ground against him with a moan escaping her lips.

I shifted in my seat. *Focus, Felix.*

"Slide one of her bra straps down her shoulder. Follow it with your mouth."

Silas jerked a little at the sound of my voice, but I watched avidly as he moved to follow my instruction, sliding his fingers under the lacy strap of her bra and pulling it slowly off her shoulder. His fingertips grazed her there as he did, and I saw her skin pebble in response.

"Very good, Silas," I praised.

He placed his open mouth against the curve of her shoulder and I saw his teeth glint in the low light as he ran them along the curve, not truly a bite, just letting her feel the edge of them. They both moaned at the sensation, and I smiled wide. *So responsive.*

Silas repeated the action with the strap on her other shoulder and I watched, rapt, as he reached behind her to undo the clasp and removed the lacy bra entirely. She rolled her shoulders, probably glad to be free of the restriction, and I watched fascinated as the muscles in her back shifted with the motion. The twin indentions just above her panties drew my attention tempted me to run my tongue over them.

"Cup her breasts. Don't grope, *cup.* Lift them to your mouth, kiss them, lick them, whatever she responds to most, until you've gotten them nice and wet, until her nipples are drawn tight and she's writhing in your lap."

He obeyed again and the feeling of power which came over me was intoxicating. I liked this game. Very much.

When he lifted his head, continuing to run his thumbs back and forth over her peaked nipples, Anka ground down on him, sliding her hands down to where his shirt met his pants.

She lifted the hem, skimming her fingers underneath, and slid his shirt up and over his abs. I groaned at the sight of her hands against his skin, the way I knew he must have been feeling at that moment, after not having been touched like that in so long. I could nearly feel her hands on my own skin and my pants tightened over my stiffening cock.

She pushed and tugged until he released her so she could pull his shirt over his head. I raised my brows at the sight.

"You've been holding out on us, Silas. Look at you. Why would you ever cover all that up?" I teased.

He moaned and I didn't know if it was from my words, or the fact that Anka had leaned down, using her cute little teeth to tease one of his pierced nipples.

"I like these," she said, and I could hear the grin in her voice. "But I have to admit, I'm surprised."

She turned her attention to the other one, tugging on the bar, and he jerked against her.

"It was a drunken dare..." he gasped. "In college. I figured I'd just take them out if I didn't like them."

She ran her tongue around one and then the other, and his breath stuttered. "It turns out, I like them, so I kept them."

"Well, here's to drunken dares then, because these are very, *very* sexy." She followed her words with kisses leading down his abdomen, following the thin line of dark hair that led to his waistband. "Did you get anything else pierced on a dare?"

I bit my knuckle. One could only dream.

He chuckled. "Only one way to find out."

Anka and I both let out a shocked sound at his words, but I needed to slow this down a bit, or my man was going to come the minute she touched him. His hips were already jerking as he ground against her.

"Grab her hands, Silas."

His eyes flew open and briefly cut toward me.

"Do it. Now," I commanded.

Silas did as he was told, but kept his gaze on mine as he did.

Anka gasped when he bracketed her wrists, stopping her hands from moving any farther south and, when she looked up at him, she followed his gaze to where I sat. I knew she couldn't see me, but he'd given away the game. I watched as her head turned slowly from where I sat back to Silas.

"You were talking to Felix. Downstairs."

I couldn't tell from her tone if she was angry. Apparently, neither could Silas.

He nodded slowly, his eyes glued to her face.

"You asked him to...watch?" She tilted her head, but didn't try to pull her wrists free of his hold.

Silas winced a little. "I was worried...it's been so long...I didn't know if I would disappoint you..."

Anka shifted her hips against his, rocking a bit before she responded. "You don't feel disappointing, Silas."

"Are you angry?" he asked.

She looked back over her shoulder, and I swore she met my eyes before she returned her attention to him. "So what was your plan?"

The smile widened on my face.

Silas stared into her eyes. "He was going to tell me what to do...to you. To make sure you're satisfied."

Her hips rolled again, in a move I suspected was entirely subconscious. "And...you want him to watch me? Watch us? Tell you how, and where, to touch me?"

He nodded slowly, uncertainly, but he never broke eye contact.

She considered that for a moment, and I wondered if she was absolutely soaking at the thought of it. I suspected so.

"From now on, if you're going to invite your emotional support demon into the bedroom, you should let me know ahead of time." Her voice was a mock-rebuke.

Silas nodded enthusiastically. "Yes, ma'am."

He waited for her to say something else. We both did.

She looked back in my direction again before leaning over him, using her forearms for leverage to lift her hips off his, as her wrists were still restrained.

When she arched her back, giving me a clear view of just how wet her panties were, I nearly came on the spot.

"So what does he want you to do to me now?" she asked Silas.

I thought I saw Silas's eyes roll back in his head at her consent. Now we could really have some fun.

"Silas," I said, bringing his attention back to me. "Take her wrists and lift them up over her head, stretch her out on top of you, and then roll. I need those panties off. Now."

He nodded and grinned, suddenly looking far more confident than he had when we'd started. I hadn't realized he was so conflicted, but her approval seemed to have assuaged his conscience, because he didn't hesitate.

He tightened his grip on her wrists, pulling until their arms were extended above their heads and she was stretched out flat on top of him. He rolled so their positions were flipped, and her legs immediately came up to wrap around him. The sight of her thighs wrapped around his hips was glorious, but I needed him to back away and pull those wet panties off her. Slowly.

"Press her hands to the mattress and tell her not to move them when you let go. And if she's a good girl, she'll be rewarded," I told him.

He ground against her once, a full-body caress that had all three of us moaning, before he pressed her hands into the mattress. "Keep these here. Don't move them. If you're a good girl, you'll be rewarded." His voice was husky as he repeated my command and desire flooded through my veins.

"Now, slide down her body until your mouth is between her thighs."

He did as he was told and, when his mouth hovered over her pussy, I gave him another instruction. "Bite down on her mound. Gently, Silas. Just enough to let her feel you. Your want. Your desperation."

He lowered his head, pressing his face between her legs, and inhaled. "You smell like heaven," he groaned.

When he gently bit at her mound, her hips jerked toward his mouth and a moan escaped from between her lips. I saw her hands twitch where she had them clenched above her head, and I knew the need to grab at him was likely killing her.

"Now, slowly ease back onto your knees and meet her eyes while you slide your fingers under the edges of her panties, right at her hip bones. Those are usually quite sensitive on a woman. Find out if they are for her."

I watched as he pushed himself up, leaning back a bit before he placed his hands on her knees, encouraging her legs to fall away from his hips, before he ran them slowly up the insides of her thighs. We both watched in fascination as her muscles jumped under his fingers.

When he reached her hips, he slid his hands under her panties and gripped her hip bones, applying enough pressure that I could see the indentations his fingers created. She rolled her head against the pillow and whimpered but didn't move her hands from their spot.

Such a good girl.

"Now, slide her panties down slowly, letting your fingertips trace the length of her legs as you do."

Silas tugged gently and Anka lifted her hips, helping him slide them over her ass; as he moved down her body, dragging his fingers all the way, her hips began to shift again. Her legs parted once he'd freed her from her panties, and her glistening core was revealed to us both.

"Do you want to lick that gorgeous cunt, Silas? Taste what you've done to her? What *we've* done to her?" I asked him.

He turned to look at me over his shoulder. His gaze had turned feral. "More than anything."

I smiled at him. "Good. Put your hands on the insides of her thighs. She'll want to close her legs, clamp them around your head, but I want to see. Keep her open for me."

He grinned before turning back to her, giving her another warning. "Remember, don't move those hands."

She nodded, eyes darting between him and where I sat.

"Start at her center. Lap up her juices, sliding your tongue all over her before you dip your tongue inside.

But don't touch her clit. Not yet." I reached down and unbuttoned the top button on my pants.

He leaned forward, wrapping his hands around her thighs, pressing them open further before he lowered his mouth to her, placing an open-mouthed kiss against her cunt. Her body jolted at the contact and another moan exploded from her mouth.

"Go slowly, Silas. You're making love to her with your mouth. Savor her taste. The feel of her soft skin beneath your tongue. The sounds you're drawing from her as you feast."

I rose from my chair, taking a step closer to the bed.

I watched as his tongue circled her entrance, lapping up her juices, and I had to know.

"How does she taste, Silas?" I leaned in.

He lifted his head but didn't take his eyes off her as he replied, "Like honey, Felix. So sweet." He turned to me. "I could eat her all night."

Anka and I groaned in unison and her head jerked in my direction like she'd heard me. She knew I'd moved. Her ability to sense me was growing stronger.

"Do you want a taste?" He got a wicked glint in his eye, and I was honestly shocked. Silas was just full of surprises.

I tilted my head at him. "How does she feel about that?"

He turned back to Anka. "Do you mind if I let Felix see how good you taste?"

I watched as her pupils blew out entirely, and I grinned. Oh, she certainly did not mind.

She shook her head, watching him intently. I myself was a little curious about his plan.

He dipped his head back down, licking at her entrance, and I could see another surge of wetness drip out of her. She'd be making quite the mess of Silas's bed if he wasn't doing such a wonderful job of cleaning it all up.

He pulled his head away from her and turned toward me, a brow cocked. "Don't look so shocked, it's not like it's our first time, Felix."

Anka moaned at his words.

I caught his meaning and grinned. "Oh, but I am shocked, Silas, I didn't think you liked it when I kissed you before."

"You just...surprised me, that's all." He lifted one side of his mouth and then beckoned me closer. "Come here."

I leaned in and pressed my lips to his. He parted his lips, letting his tongue come out to tangle with mine, sharing the delicious taste he'd just licked from her. My cock leaped in my pants, aching for more, but I forced myself to pull back.

"You're right, she does taste like honey." I leaned in for one more taste before I withdrew.

Anka was staring at the space where our mouths had met with a dazed expression and I nudged Silas's head back down.

"Now, work your way up to her clit. Circle it slowly with the tip of your tongue and look up at her while you do it. Make sure she knows you are exactly where you want to be." I undid the next button on my pants, desperate to touch myself.

"God, Silas, your mouth." She rotated her hips, trying to gain more friction.

"Ask her if she'd like you to fill her, give her something to grip as you drive her to madness with your tongue." My voice had turned to a growl and I'd stepped back to the edge of the bed before I realized it.

"Anka," he breathed against her. "Do you want my fingers inside of you? Do you want something to fill you while I make you come on my tongue?"

"Please, Silas, I need to come. I feel like I'm going to combust," she panted, shifting beneath him.

He gave me a quick look over his shoulder, taking in my partially undone fly, and grinned wide before he turned back to her. He released her left thigh, dragging his fingers from her clit down to her core. She was so close to coming that her pussy gushed as his fingers got closer to her entrance and he used her juices to coat them before sliding two inside her. When he slowly rotated them she writhed at the sensation.

He lowered his head back down, wrapping that gorgeous mouth around her clit as he thrust his fingers slowly in and out of her, the wet sounds of her body trying to pull them back in each time he retreated had my hands moving of their own accord, releasing my cock from my pants. I groaned as I gripped it tight, and Silas paused his movement.

"Don't stop, Silas. She's close," I barked, starting to stroke myself from root to tip, gathering the precum from the head and using it to slide my hand up and down in time with the thrust of his fingers into her.

"Rotate your hand, find her G-spot, Silas. Stroke it as you wrap your lips around that gorgeous little nub of hers and suck, hard. Watch how she comes apart so beautifully."

He twisted his wrist, curling his fingers against her inner wall like a good boy, and she started chanting unintelligibly. When he parted his lips and wrapped them around her clit, sucking hard as he rubbed against her G-spot, she came on a low moan that was nearly a sob.

She was so fucking beautiful with her head tilted back against the pillow, hands clenched into fists as her back bowed, lifting her off the bed. Her heels dug into the mattress and I watched, fascinated as her body moved with the pleasure that he'd brought her.

That *we* had brought her.

I paused my hand, my cock jutting out in front of me, as Silas lapped at her gently, drawing out her pleasure. She finally moved her arms and tangled her hands in his hair, pulling him away from her sensitive pussy.

When he met her gaze again, she laughed. "You were worried?"

She looked my way, and I nearly wished she could have seen the affect watching them had on me. I wanted her to know how incredibly sexy she was coming apart for him. How perfect they looked together. How hard I was from what I'd just watched, and what was yet to come.

My dick was so hard I was worried it might start trying to force its way out of my jeans if I didn't get them off.

I watched Anka as she writhed and curled her body, riding out her orgasm, and I couldn't resist lapping at her slowly as she did, wanting more of her taste on my tongue. She was so beautiful when she came, so uninhibited. Her back bowed up off the bed, and I let my tongue trace the full length of her, ending my stroke on her tight little asshole.

She jerked and dropped her hands, wrapping them in my hair, pulling my mouth away from her sensitive flesh.

"You were worried?" She laughed.

I grinned up at her. "Guess it is kind of like riding a bike, huh?"

She nodded sagely. "Just with more tongue."

I threw my head back on a laugh. "You're amazing."

Her eyes widened. "I'm amazing? You're the one who just destroyed me."

I gave her my best leer. "We're not done with you quite yet."

I turned and looked over my shoulder to see Felix gripping his cock like it owed him money, and I knew *my* plan was coming along perfectly. He thought he was the only one who could be sneaky, but he'd underestimated me.

I rose from the bed to unbutton my jeans, and Anka followed, climbing to her knees in front of me. "Let me."

I nodded, threading my hands through her hair and cupping the back of her head, loving the way the silky strands wrapped around my hands.

She bit her lip and started slowly working the buttons through the holes, looking up at me every time she got one free, a grin hovering around the edges of her lips.

"It's time for show and tell, Silas. I wonder what I'll find, hmm?" she teased.

I shook my head at her. "I'm really good at keeping secrets, Anka. You're going to have to find out for yourself."

She chuckled. "Okay then." She slipped the last button free and slid her hands into the waist of my jeans, pushing them past my ass, before gravity took over and they fell to the floor.

She licked her lips and dipped a finger into the band of my briefs, giving me one more look before she pulled it away from my stomach and looked down. She stared for a beat before she released the elastic with a pop that had me grunting.

"Oh my god." She took a deep breath.

"I know it's not that she's never seen a cock before," Felix chimed in.

I grinned over at him until I felt both of her hands dip into my underwear, grabbing them and tugging until they fell to the floor with my jeans. She stared at me long enough that Felix stepped closer and looked down at my rigid cock.

"Well, well, well. Silas is just full of surprises, isn't he?" He gave me another appraising look before he met my gaze. "Who are you?"

I winked at him. "There's more to me than meets the eye."

He looked back down before he answered. "It would seem so."

Anka was watching, likely getting the gist of our conversation from my half of it, and she raised her hand.

Felix snorted.

I nodded at her. "Yes, Anka, you had a question?"

She giggled. "I do! Um. Is that what they call a Jacob's Ladder?"

I nodded. "It is."

She continued. "And...does it...feel good? Um. You know."

I tilted her chin up so she met my eyes. "It's my understanding that, done correctly, it can be quite pleasurable."

She tilted her head, staring at my dick again. "Okay then. Let's do it."

Felix laughed out loud, and she jerked her head in his direction. She really was getting much more sensitive to his reactions. Very interesting. I wondered how much that had to do with her lineage. Something to think about, but later. Much later.

I reached into the nightstand next to the bed and pulled out a bottle of lubricant and her eyes widened comically.

"When I said 'let's do it,' I didn't mean..."

"Relax." I chuckled. "Sometimes the entry and exit can offer mild discomfort. This will help."

"Ohhhhh." She made a face, and I laughed again.

"I can take them out if you don't like it," I assured her.

"Well, I want to at least try. I mean...how many times in a woman's life does she get a chance to experience that?" She was back to staring at my dick, and it grew impossibly harder with her attention.

Felix and I growled simultaneously, and I turned to look at him with raised brows.

He shrugged.

I turned back to Anka. "Why don't you lie back. I'm going to slide this pillow under your hips, and you tell me if I hurt you."

"In a good way? Or a bad way?" She grinned as she reclined on the bed, lifting her hips to accommodate the pillow I placed there.

"Either." I winked before I opened the cap on the bottle and poured some out into my hand.

She watched, rapt, as I gripped my cock with that hand, slowly gliding it up and down, careful to get everything nice and slick.

As I put a knee on the bed she looked up at me, her mouth in the shape of an O. "What about protection?"

I paused. "Well, I haven't been with anyone in over a decade, and I've had a physical since then, so I'm clean. I'm sorry, I don't have any condoms. I honestly didn't think that's where this night would lead, or I would have been prepared. If I have any, I guarantee they're expired."

I started to back away but she shook her head adamantly. "I have an IUD. And I got tested after the unicorn horn situation. I'm clean too."

I turned to look at Felix and he looked nonplussed. "I don't need a condom to jack my own dick, Silas. Plus, unless you can get an STD from a demon, it's been, oh, say…at least a century since I've been at risk."

Okay. Fair enough.

I reached down and grabbed the pillow beneath Anka's hips, dragging it, and her along with it, to the edge of the bed.

"Is this okay?" I asked her.

"Somehow, I feel like I've lost control of this situation," Felix grumbled, but his dick was back in his hand.

I grinned at him. "Control is an illusion, Felix."

I lifted one of Anka's legs, hooking it around my hip and holding it tight before I slicked my other hand over my dick again. "Are you ready?"

She nodded, her face equal parts excitement and nervous.

"Relax. I'll never hurt you," I reassured her.

Her face fell.

"Unless you ask," I amended.

She beamed up at me, but before she could reply, I ran the head of my dick over her pussy. Letting her get accustomed to the feel of the metal against her.

"Oh. Oh, that's...that's different," she groaned. "More."

I grinned as I fed the first rung into her, watching her mouth pop open. I pushed forward, feeling the next one slide in and her eyes closed, a low hum escaping from her throat.

The third rung had her wriggling around, and I smacked the side of her ass. "Be still. Let me get it all the way in before you start moving around. I want to make sure you're okay."

Her eyes popped open and she gaped at me as I felt Felix's stare from my right.

"What?" I asked them both.

"Who are you?" they said in unison, and I shook my head as I pushed forward until the fourth rung had disappeared inside her. I knew this was the point where it would start to stimulate her G-spot once I was moving, so I rocked back and forth a bit, making sure she could take more.

"Oh my god, Silas. That's so good." She was staring up at me in shock and a delicious blush had crept over her chest, her nipples peaked, and I knew I didn't have to be quite so gentle.

"You feel so good wrapped around me," I grunted. I lowered her leg and put both of her heels at the edge of the bed. "More?" I panted, honestly trying not to come on the spot. She was gripping me so tight, so wet and warm, no amount of jerking my own dick could ever compare to the feeling of sinking inside her.

"More," she moaned, and I felt Felix brush up against me as he stepped next to me.

"The view from here is too good to resist." He watched as I rocked in and out of Anka, her thighs spread so wide that nothing was hidden from our view.

"What happens if you come," I asked him, using two fingers to bracket her clit, applying pressure, as I pressed forward. One rung to go.

"What do you mean what happens?" he grunted, stroking his cock as he stared at the place where Anka and I were connected.

"Well, I know where I'm planning on coming, Felix. I just wondered what would happen if you came somewhere other than in your hand." I spoke slowly so he wouldn't miss my meaning.

Anka moaned, her eyes wide as she looked back and forth between me and the space Felix took up immediately to my right.

I met her gaze. "How do you feel about that, baby? Do you want Felix to come on you while I'm pumping your gorgeous cunt full? He could come on your clit, or your stomach, or your beautiful breasts." With every option I gave her I could feel her clamp down on me tighter, so I knew she wanted him to, but I wasn't sure if she would be brave enough to say the words.

"My clit," she panted with absolutely zero shame,

and it was at that moment that I thought, just maybe, I might love Anka Kelly for the rest of my life. "I want you to use it to make me come."

"*Fuck*," Felix panted, his hand blurring as he stroked himself.

"That I can do. One more to go. Can you take it?" I grinned down at her and she nodded vigorously.

"I need you to move, please, Silas."

I eased my hips back and then pushed back in, seating myself fully inside her tight cunt. "Oh, fuck, Anka. You feel so fucking good."

"Move, Silas. Now," she growled at me, lifting her hips and glaring at me.

"Yes, ma'am." I laughed.

I pulled halfway out and slid home again with no resistance now that we were both thoroughly soaked between the lube and her own juices. I returned my fingers back to her clit, alternating pressure and a circular pattern that had her eyes rolling back into her head as I fucked her slow and intently.

"Silas," Felix groaned. "I thought for sure I'd outlast you."

I chuckled, pulling my cock out of her almost to the tip. "Do it."

I was so fucking turned on that I didn't know how much longer I could hold out, but I wanted to make every single one of Anka's wishes come true. She wanted me to use Felix's cum to get her off while I filled her up, and I'd always been an overachiever.

"Do it, Felix," I grunted again as I looked over at

him, watching with great fascination as he choked up on his cock before he stroked one more time and groaned, long and low as we both watched the ropes of cum explode from his cock, every drop landing on Anka's pussy and my mostly exposed cock.

"Oh my god," she moaned as she tried to slide a hand down, but I grabbed it, placing it on her chest instead.

"Play with those gorgeous nipples for me, baby. I've got this."

While Felix panted next to me, trying to recover, I rubbed my fingers through the mess he'd made, slicking it over my cock and her clit before I slammed back into her. She let out a scream, and I resumed my pattern on her clit with increased urgency and the added slickness courtesy of Felix.

"Oh god, Silas, faster. I'm about to come." Her head was thrown back, both hands gripping her breasts.

I increased my pace, hips snapping as I pounded into her, my fingers blurring over her clit. The filthy sound of me fucking his cum and mine into her at the same time, combined with her walls clamping down on my cock, pushed me over the edge.

I jerked, feeling my balls pour everything I had into her as she writhed in front of us, the aftershocks causing her to squeeze every last drop out of me until I was a panting mess, leaned over her on the bed.

When she opened her eyes, she stared up at me in wonder. "Why do I feel like I didn't know the real you until tonight?" She grinned. "Not that I'm complaining."

I laughed. "It's all the real me. I've got layers, Anka. I'm complicated."

"I'll say," Felix quipped from where he'd flopped back into the chair. "Layers," he snorted.

Never fry bacon shirtless. That was the lesson I'd learned that morning. When Felix came into the kitchen, I'd grabbed one of Trixie's cute little aprons and thrown it on over my pajama pants to prevent further injury.

"Well, aren't you adorable," he said, leaning against the doorframe.

I tossed him a grin over my shoulder. "Morning, dear! Hungry?"

He didn't answer, and once I'd pulled the bacon out of the pan I turned toward him. "Everything okay?

"You played me." He crossed his arms over his chest.

I put my hand to my heart. "Felix, whatever do you mean?"

He dropped his arms and began stalking closer to me as I backed slowly around the table, evading capture. Or consequences. I wasn't entirely sure which he had in mind.

"You took advantage of my kind nature." He followed me step for step.

I snorted, continuing to back away.

"You knew I would try to help you if you were 'nervous' and 'panicked,' and you suckered me into your night last night."

I rolled my eyes, grabbing a piece of crispy bacon from the plate as we'd come full circle.

"What exactly were you hoping to accomplish with that?" He stopped chasing me, but he held me in place with his expression.

I chewed slowly, giving myself plenty of time to consider my answer. There was the "answer" and then there was "the answer he was willing to hear," and I wasn't sure which I should go with.

I studied him thoughtfully. "Well, Felix. I guess I got tired of waiting for you to see the big picture."

He took a step closer to me and stopped again. "And what exactly is the big picture, as you see it?"

I held up a finger. "The first person you touched, in over a century, was Kyle."

"Pre-sent."

I jerked my head around and my eyes bulged as I took in the shimmering form of who could only be Anka's twin brother.

"Please, continue. I can't wait to hear the rest of this." He grinned, and I looked at Felix in astonishment.

Felix just shrugged. "I don't think I'm capable of being surprised anymore."

"Okay then." I took a deep breath, trying to avoid

eye contact with Kyle after all the ways I'd defiled his twin sister the night before.

"No need to be embarrassed, Loverboy." Kyle snickered. "I'm not here to turn poltergeist and kick your ass."

I widened my eyes and looked at Felix again. For his part, he only looked a little flushed in the cheeks about his part in last night's activities.

Kyle waved a hand at me. "No, really. We are *not* talking about any of that. But I am positively enthralled to hear the rest of your 'big picture' theory."

I heard bare feet padding down the stairs, and I looked up at the ceiling, not sure which deity I should ask for help in this situation, but I smiled warmly when Anka stepped into the kitchen.

"Do I smell bacon?"

"Morning, sis," Kyle called from where he'd perched on top of the refrigerator.

Anka gaped up at him. "Um. Morning. And why are you sitting on top of the refrigerator like a kitchen gargoyle?"

He shrugged at her and grinned. "It's a thing. Just roll with it. It's story time, get your coffee and let Loverboy there tell us his theory."

Anka turned to look at me with a puzzled expression. "What theory? And since when can you see Kyle?"

Kyle cackled from his perch before I could respond. "We're practically family now, it only seemed right. And Silas was just about to tell Felix all about how he thinks that we're all"—he circled his hand to include all the occupants of the room—"the keys to breaking Felix's curse."

Chapter Sixty-Four

FELIX

I turned my head from Kyle to Silas. "What? How did you come to that conclusion?"

Silas shrugged. "It's simple, really. All this time, you thought you were self-sabotaging, or whatever you call it, but look at the chain of events. And how it all comes together to make this"—he gestured at Anka and Kyle and me—"weird little...family. None of that would have happened if you hadn't been the catalyst, Felix. You brought us together. You saved us."

I took a breath to speak, but Kyle interjected. "Technically, he didn't save me."

I shot him a look. "Not helping."

He threw his hands up. "Just...if we're speaking literally."

Anka even rolled her eyes at that. "Yes, I think we all knew what you meant, bro."

"Anyway," Silas continued, "so you're wandering through the library and pick up one of my books and get curious about the author—knowing now how much time you have on your hands, that makes so much more sense." Silas held up one finger in the air.

"Then, you try to save Kyle, and end up being too late, but you still risk your eternal happiness to touch him so he doesn't have to die alone."

Kyle made a heart out of his hands, and I rolled my eyes.

"Then..." Silas raised his voice to get my attention again. "Kyle tells you about his twin sister and asks you to watch over her, as a personal favor to him—his dying wish."

I leaned back against the counter and crossed my arms over my chest.

"So you come up with this wacky plan," Silas continued.

"Still full of plot holes," Kyle muttered.

"Kyle, shush." Anka gave him a look.

"So, you came up with this wacky plan, that may or may not have been full of plot holes, to draw me and Anka together so we would meet and fall in love." Silas stopped short, and I raised my brows at him, smirking.

"Too soon, man, way too soon." Kyle snickered.

"So that we would meet and hopefully live happily ever after."

I nodded. "So far you haven't told me anything I didn't already know. I was there, Silas."

"You're still not seeing it, Felix!" he growled, throwing his hands up in the air.

Anka sat down hard in one of the kitchen chairs, staring up at Silas.

He gestured at her. "See! She gets it. Why can't you see it, Felix?"

"What, Silas? What am I not seeing?" I was starting to get frustrated.

He went to stand behind Anka, resting his hands on her shoulders. "It's us." He looked up at Kyle, who met his pleased smile with one of his own. "All of us."

He stepped around the table, coming toward me slowly, like he was afraid I was going to bolt.

"Felix. You didn't need three chances to break your curse. You needed three *people*."

EPILOGUE 1. FELIX

I didn't know where to go, but I suddenly felt claustrophobic in a way that I hadn't in a very long time. I could actually feel the beating of my heart in my chest, reverberating like a drum through my sternum.

"Felix, wait," Silas said, lifting a hand toward me.

I backed away, shaking my head. "I just need...a minute. Just give me a minute, Silas." I shook my head and turned on my heel, feeling my wings twitch on my back, and before I knew it they'd transported me to the alleyway where I'd watched Kyle die, as if I ever wanted to revisit that place.

I didn't know what I was doing there, but as soon as the world had righted itself, I felt a presence there with me.

"Did you know?" I said, my voice low, but knew she would hear me.

When I turned to face her, she gave me a wry smile.

"Yes. Of course I knew, Felix. It was my curse."

"But...you never said anything." I widened my eyes, exasperated.

"What would have been the fun in that? No, Felix, you had to figure this out for yourself. But look at you now? Well on your way to your happily ever after. And such a well-adjusted made-demon after all these years." She winked at me, and I growled in response.

"Don't patronize me, Sera, I've been misled by everyone in my life in the past few days. I don't have the patience for it from you as well."

"Felix, I cursed you. There wasn't an implied 'honesty' clause in there." She lifted a brow and leaned against the wall behind her.

"How do I know if this is the right path?" I asked, hoping she'd be straight with me for once.

"Don't trust me, Felix?"

"Not any farther than I can throw you." I griped.

She chuckled before shaking her head and leveling me with a direct stare. The silver outline of her irises more pronounced at that moment than I thought I'd ever seen them. "As much as it pains me to offer you reassurance, I've known for quite some time that you were on the right track. Now, was it my intention that your redemption involve my descendants?" She shook her head ruefully. "Not in a million years. But we don't get to control destiny, Felix."

"So...is this really my happily ever after, Sera? Truly? I'm terrified I'll touch her and this...family that we've created...will disappear in a blink, leaving me to wander alone for the rest of my years. Because this situation looks nothing like I ever imagined." I implored her with my gaze, begging for candor.

Sera screwed her face up at me. "Did you suddenly develop some traditional values? Who the fuck cares what it looks like, Felix. Does your soul feel complete? When you're with them?"

I considered her question for a moment.

"In a way I didn't think possible." I could hear the wonder in my own voice, but the fear wouldn't release me from its cage.

"Then you have to leap." She gave me a kinder smile than any I'd seen on her face in a century, briefly reminding me of the girl she'd been so long ago. "Have a little faith." She patted me on the shoulder, running her hand through the feathers there. "You know? I think I'm actually going to miss these."

Have a little faith.

I shook my head, staring up at the front of Silas's house. Of all the things I'd ever claimed to have in my long life, the only thing I'd truly placed my faith in was my own inability to break this curse. I'd begun to come to terms with the fact that I would eventually wind up wandering the mortal plane alone until I eventually succumbed to old age or disease or a freak logging truck accident.

It was much harder to put faith in the idea that I'd somehow redeemed myself enough to deserve another chance to live my human life with someone, more than one someone, that I loved and who loved me back. But the alternative left me with a hole in my chest that I couldn't quite reconcile.

I was scared to risk it. But I was more scared not to.

And that was what ultimately had me walking through the front door and approaching Silas's study. Treading softly across the hall to where Silas and Anka were huddled up together in front of the fire, wrapped in a blanket and sipping on hot cocoa. The picture they made together was exactly as I'd hoped it would be. They were beautiful.

Silas was staring down at her with a half-smile on his face, listening intently as she told him a story, her face animated as she spoke, and the fear crept right back up into my throat. What if I took a leap of faith and ruined it for us all?

I must have made some noise because Silas's head jerked up, and he met my gaze where I stood just beyond the doorway. He stared at me for a moment without speaking, raising his brows as if to say "well?"

I shrugged, letting him see the vulnerability in my expression, the fear. And the longing.

He nodded. I knew he understood. He jerked his head, urging me to step into the room. Take the leap.

When I crossed the threshold, he grinned and nudged Anka. "Babe. There's someone here to see you."

Anka whipped her head around, uncannily pinning me with her gaze, and I marveled again at how good she'd gotten at finding me in a room even when she couldn't see me.

She widened her eyes and looked back at Silas. "Is he? What's happening?"

He watched me step closer, sinking to my knees in front of the chair they shared. I tugged my gloves from my hands one at a time. He was kind enough to ignore the tremor I couldn't control, even though I knew he hadn't missed it.

"Welcome home, Felix," he said softly.

I lifted my hand slowly, bringing it closer and closer to Anka's face as Silas watched with a rapt expression on his face.

I wasn't sure what I expected would happen when I cupped her jaw in my hand, but when I touched her silken skin, when I felt her warmth seep into my palm and watched her eyes close on a sigh as she felt that first touch, I offered up a fervent hope to whichever deity might be paying attention that what came next wouldn't ruin everything.

"Anka…" I exhaled on a breath, the feel of her skin against mine immediately making me feel as if I'd been launched into orbit while simultaneously grounded, tied to her forever, in this life and the next.

She opened her eyes and the crystalline green looked brighter, more vivid, as if I'd been seeing her through a window all this time, and now she was right in front of me in perfect clarity. That thump in my chest sounded again, my heart realigning itself to beat in time with hers forevermore.

"Felix," she gasped. Her eyes crawled all over my face, taking in everything she could in her first glimpse, her eyes widening as she caught sight of my wings. "You're beautiful," she whispered.

"Told you." Silas smirked.

"But what's with the wings? I thought you'd lose those when you broke the curse?" Silas looked at me, worried, and I felt his worry echo in my own mind. Hadn't it worked?

I turned my head, catching sight of them in my peripheral vision. "I don't know...I—" My sentence was cut off by a searing pain in my shoulders, and I was forced to release Anka for fear of hurting her as I writhed.

"What's happening to him?" Anka cried.

"I don't know, babe, but I think...I think he's broken the curse," Silas said reverently as he eased out of the chair, dropping to his knees with me, sliding his hands to my face.

I could feel all the blood leave my face as the pain consumed every thought I had, my vision fading in and out, and it took everything I had not to scream as I felt the curse breaking, the wings feeling as if they were being ripped from my back. Of course, Sera would make sure breaking the curse would be ten times more painful than receiving it.

"Felix, can you hear me?" Silas held my head up, staring into my eyes urgently.

I could see Anka's hand creep up to cover her mouth as she watched in horror.

"Get me out of here," I gasped to Silas. "Don't let her see this."

And then everything went black.

EPILOGUE 2. FELIX

"*H*ow long has it been?" the voice whispered from close by.

"Two days." Silas's voice sounded gravelly, tired.

"Damn. Are you sure he isn't dead?"

I felt my chest jerk with a laugh.

"Kyle!" Anka's voice barked from my other side.

"I'm kidding, sis. Gah. But I think your boy is waking up now, so you can thank me later. I'm sure it was the sound of his best friend's voice that brought him back from the void."

I tried to open my mouth to speak, but it was like my lips were glued together, my tongue so dry that I couldn't force it from the roof of my mouth. I felt something press up against my lips, and I sighed gratefully when a cool trickle of water slid into my mouth. I tried to gulp it, pursing my lips around the straw to draw more, but it disappeared, and I opened my eyes to see

Anka holding a large cup of ice water just out of my reach.

"Take it slow. You've been out for a long time; I don't want you to make yourself sick." She was staring at me with a worried expression, though I could tell she was relieved to see my eyes open.

I nodded and looked to my left where Silas was perched on the edge of the bed. He gave me a wink and a grin. "Well, that was one hell of an entrance you made."

I coughed, trying to make my vocal cords do their job. "You know how much I love a big entrance."

Silas tipped his head back on a laugh. "That you do, friend."

Anka was hovering. She'd gone home at some point while I'd been "out," and I knew that because there was now a large mound of fur that had taken up permanent residence in Silas's bed with me.

"Do you need anything?" she asked for the millionth time.

I raised a brow at her. "Anka. Love. I'm fine. I was fine twenty minutes ago when you asked, and again five minutes ago. Though I love your Florence Nightingale impression, I have to admit that this is not how I envisioned our first time in a bedroom together would go. Please relax," I implored her in a soothing voice.

She fluttered her hands around, but I noted the way

her cheeks pinked at my words. "Well, technically, it's not our first time in a bedroom together."

I leered at her. "Indeed, but this time you can see me. Even more importantly"—I lifted the covers that were draped across my lower half—"you can touch me." I wagged my brows at her suggestively.

"You were essentially in a magically induced coma up until three hours ago, Felix. Now is hardly the time for us to...consummate our relationship." She propped a hand on her hip and gave me a disapproving glare, but I saw her eyes cut toward my lower half despite her words.

"I don't know, he looks pretty healthy to me," Silas chimed in from the doorway. He raised a brow at me and grinned.

"See? Silas says I look fine. Don't you think I look fine, Anka? What if I really need to touch you to fully break the curse. What if I need to touch all of you?" I grinned at her, and she rolled her eyes.

She looked over her shoulder at Silas. "You're really not helping."

He laughed and stepped into the room, clicking his tongue at Mags as he did. "Hey, pretty girl, I made you a snack."

Mags lifted her head and cocked it at Silas before she turned to look at Anka like, *did he just say snacks?*

Anka chuckled. "You're going to spoil her," she admonished Silas.

"I have every intention of doing exactly that. Plus, I think it's probably best that she's not present for what he has in mind." He gave Anka a lecherous look.

Anka whipped her gaze back toward me and started shaking her head emphatically. "No way. Felix! I thought you were dying! You need to rest more, drink fluids, recover. There's plenty of time for"—she gestured at my rapidly hardening cock—"us to get acquainted after you're fully recovered."

I cut my eyes to Silas, nodding at him, before I replied. "I feel quite hale and hearty..." Silas stepped up behind Anka and rested his hands on her hips, his thumbs toying with the exposed skin between her jeans and her sweater. "One might even say I'm thriving."

I sat up at the edge of the bed, insinuating my body between the bed and where Anka stood with Silas pressed against her back. I reached up, sliding my hands under her sweater, running my fingers up her sides, and marveled at the chill bumps my touch created as I went. I looked up and met her gaze, imploring her with my eyes, but letting her see some of the real intent behind my teasing.

"Please, Anka. I need you." I lifted my gaze to include Silas. "I need you both."

She stared at me, her bottom lip gripped between her teeth, before she nodded. "But if you feel faint..." she admonished.

I nodded my head solicitously. "Yes, ma'am. I promise I will stop worshiping your body if I begin to feel peaked." I held up three fingers. "Scout's honor."

Her eyebrows shot up. "Were you a scout, Felix?"

I pressed my open mouth to her stomach, dipping my tongue into her naval, before I grinned up at her.

"No, love, but if I could have gotten badges for this, I think I might have considered it."

Silas gripped the edges of her sweater and nudged her to lift her arms so he could pull it up and over her head before he began stripping off his own clothes, as if he were attempting to win an Olympic medal for speed-stripping. I leaned around her with my eyebrows raised. "Impressive."

He grinned back at me with a shrug. "Time is of the essence."

I laughed. "Truer words, my friend, truer words."

Silas resumed his position behind Anka, and I returned my attention to the beautiful woman in front of me, drawing one of her nipples into my mouth through the lace of her bra as her head tilted back against Silas's shoulder on a gasp.

He moved his hands to the button of her jeans. "I need to see all of you," he growled into her ear, and I felt the shudder that passed through her body at his words.

When she nodded, he slipped the button loose, easing his hands into her jeans and sliding them down over her full hips, pressing kisses along her spine as he dropped to his knees behind her, dragging the denim all the way to her feet before he helped her step out of them.

I placed my hands on her hips and pushed until she took a step away from the bed, forcing Silas to move back with her, so I could rise to my full height in front of her.

She watched with hooded eyes as I looped my thumbs into the pajama pants that Silas had lent me, the elastic catching on my stiffened cock. Her attention was rapt on that bit of fabric, and I tipped a finger under her chin.

"My eyes are up here, love."

She lifted a brow. "Oh, I know exactly where your eyes are, Felix, I spent two days staring at your face when I thought you were dying. It's your cock that's undiscovered territory at the moment. Are you holding out on me now that you've convinced me you're well enough for this?"

"Saucy." I reached my hand into the pants and palmed my cock, giving it a squeeze before I slid the pajamas past the head and let them drop to the floor. I watched her face for her reaction.

Anka stared down, raking her eyes from the tips of my toes all the way back up, until she met my gaze again. "Not bad, bird-man."

Silas snorted from where he stood behind her, and I shot them both a glare. "Very funny."

Anka was shaking, trying to control her laughter and Silas wrapped his arms around her, joining her in the hilarity. "Good one, babe."

"Laugh it up while you can, kids." I gave them both a wicked grin before I dropped to my knees in front of her. "Silas, I need you to lift her," I directed, waiting until he'd slid his hands under her thighs and picked her up.

"Good boy." I grinned up at him. "Now, let her rest her heels on the edge of the bed. I'm going to see if she's ready for what I've been dying to do since the other night."

Anka's eyes rounded as she stared down at me, but she obediently placed her the heels of her feet on the edge of the bed to steady herself while I lined my mouth up with her pussy, now at the perfect height for me to worship it.

"I've been dreaming of this since the other night, love. The taste Silas granted me was amazing, but not nearly enough." I placed my hands on the insides of her thighs, pressing them wider and forcing Silas to adjust his stance behind her. In this position, not only did I have perfect access to her gorgeous cunt, but also his very hard cock which was nudging against her entrance as if it had a mind of its own.

She was completely exposed in that position and the access I had to both of them had me licking my lips before I flattened my tongue, running it from the base of his cock until my tongue slid off the head of him to tease her entrance, dipping inside briefly, before I continued until I'd circled the tip around her clit, making them both moan.

"You little minx," I admonished her. "You were playing hard to get, but you're positively soaked." I lapped at her again, groaning at her taste on my tongue. "You taste so fucking good, love."

Anka moaned and shifted her ass against Silas. "Just because I was wet at the thought of both of you doesn't mean I couldn't control myself, Felix. I'm not an animal."

I gripped Silas's cock, running the head of it between her folds and making them both jerk at the sensation. I slid him back and forth between her clit and her entrance, watching as she dripped all over him. When I stopped, she growled at me.

"Hm. Not an animal, love?" I laughed. "Sounds pretty animalistic to me. What do you think, Silas?"

He chuckled. "I'd be a little scared if I were you, Felix. She sounds ferocious." He shifted his hands again, spreading her legs farther apart, giving me even better access to them both.

I slid my hand up the inside of his leg, nudging until he widened his stance as well, and then I got to work.

I was between his legs, nearly underneath her at that point, and took the head of his cock between my lips, making him jerk again.

"Jesus, Felix," he groaned. "That mouth."

Anka moaned. "I'm so mad I can't see what's happening right now."

I lifted the hand not holding onto Silas and ran my fingers through her slit before I slid them inside her, sliding them languidly against her walls. When another gush of liquid rushed from between her legs, I backed up, releasing Silas's cock with a pop. I fisted him again, directing him to her opening, feeding his cock into her, little by little, watching as she stretched to take him, loving the sight of his piercings disappearing into her.

Anka had her head thrown back against Silas's chest, moaning incoherently as I fed his cock to her.

"You're taking him so well, love. Do you like Silas's jewelry, Anka? What does it feel like sliding inside you?" I lapped at them both with the flat of my tongue, licking at her opening and his cock where they were joined, adding to the moisture, easing his way inside her.

"Felix," Anka gasped. "I need more. Please. I need all of it."

Her begging unlocked the feral beast in me that had lain dormant for too long. I slid back up until I was sitting on the edge of the bed between her splayed legs and leaned forward, wrapping my lips around her clit and sucking before I rolled my tongue into a point and tapped it against her.

"You're gushing, love. If I torture this beautiful little nub with my tongue and teeth and slide my fingers inside your pussy alongside Silas's cock, are you going to come all over my face like a good girl?"

Her only response was a keening moan, but I took that as a yes.

I met Silas's gaze over her shoulder and gave him a wicked grin before I lowered my head back to her and slid my hand between her legs, cupping his balls and making him jump again before I slid my fingers through the mess we'd made of her pussy, getting them slick, sliding one in beside his cock where he was filling her, stretching her beautifully as I licked and sucked her clit, alternating suction and motion.

"Oh god, Silas, more," she panted, and he obliged by bouncing her in his hands, forcing more of his cock inside her and drawing a wail from her throat.

"Are you okay, baby?" Silas buried his head in her throat, and I lifted my head to watch the perfect line of his teeth bared against the tendon in her neck, leaving little indentations as they strained against one another, chasing their peaks.

He bounced her one more time and that had her fully impaled on his cock, and I couldn't help but lower my mouth again to where they were joined, running the tip of my tongue all around the stretch, running my tongue over his lowest piercing, all while slicking my thumb around and around her clit until I heard him grunt.

"Fill her up like the good boy you are, Silas, just like that."

I stroked them both as they came in a rush until they were both panting and gasping.

"My legs are Jell-O," Silas grunted, and I laughed.

He lowered Anka to the bed so she straddled me, resting her head on my shoulder as she tried to catch her breath.

I leaned in close. "You did so good, Anka. You take our boy so well."

She shivered at my words and rubbed against me.

"But you're not done taking us for the night, are you, love?" I encouraged, sliding my hands up and down her spine, rubbing the muscles there and making her shift and groan.

When she lifted her head to meet my gaze, the fire there had most definitely not been extinguished, and I grinned. "Good girl."

I stood with her in my arms and turned, laying her gently on the bed before I looked over my shoulder to see Silas splayed out in the chair I'd occupied last time. I raised a brow at him and he just grinned. "You're not the only one who likes to watch."

Anka groaned and squirmed against the sheets at his words.

"Fair enough." I winked at him before I climbed back onto the bed, running the tips of my fingers from the arches of Anka's feet, all the way up her legs, bypassing her still very sensitive spots and trailing them up and over her stomach, her rib cage, the place between her breasts where I could feel her heart pounding against my hand as it rested there.

I leaned over her on one arm, using the other hand to trace the line of her jaw, the slope of her nose, the bow of her lips, all while she stared up at me in wonder.

I leaned in and placed my lips against her neck, breathing in her scent, reveling in the silky feel of her skin.

"Anka," I breathed. "I've lived in hell for a hundred years and I've never felt so close to burning as I do just from the feel of your velvet skin beneath my lips."

She blinked up at me. "That's beautiful, Felix. How long have you been practicing that one?"

Silas snorted from his corner, and I rolled my eyes at both of them. "I'm trying to be romantic here," I groused.

"That's not our vibe, Felix." Anka laughed.

"Fine then. You asked for it." I laughed evilly and raised up on all fours before flipping her over and pulling her ass into the air in front of me.

Her laughter died on a gasp, and I gripped the head of my cock. "I hope you're ready for this, love. You might want grip those sheets there and hold on for dear life."

I teased her entrance, and she ground back against me. I smacked her ass in response, and she and Silas moaned in unison.

I looked over my shoulder to see him splayed in the chair, legs spread wide and his dick in his hand, already hard as a stone. I motioned him over, but he shook his head at me, and I conceded that I wouldn't mind having Anka to myself for that moment.

I returned my attention to the beautiful, round ass propped up in front of me, running my hand from one end of her to the other before I teased her entrance with the head of my cock. I tapped her asshole with my pointer finger.

"Have you had anyone back here yet, love?" I asked.

"Yes," she moaned.

"And you liked it?" I asked.

"Some of it," she admitted. "Some, not so much."

"Not enough prep then, hmm?" I raised a brow despite the fact she couldn't see it.

"Felix, are you going to fuck me or fill out a questionnaire?" she groaned, rubbing herself against me.

I chuckled low. "Just wanted to know what your limits were before I did this."

I slid my cock inside her warm, wet pussy, groaning at the sensation, Silas's cum easing the way so that I could sink all the way in until my hips were flush against her ass. When I withdrew, I dipped my thumb inside her before I slammed back in and slid my thumb into her ass, working it past the tight ring of muscle, drawing another animalistic growl out of her as I did.

"Fuck, Anka, having you wrapped around me like this is heaven." I pulled out, nearly to the tip, before I slammed back in, making us both moan. "And this tight little ass is fighting to keep my thumb. We'll have to work you up so you can take us here, I promise I'll make sure you love it. Look at this pretty little asshole gaping as I pull my thumb out and dip it back in—so sexy, Anka."

"Jesus, Felix, your dirty talk game is gonna drive me over the edge." Silas was pumping fast and faster, and I could hear the slick of his hand as he abused his cock while I fucked our girl within an inch of her life. It was utter debauchery and the thrill of it was towing me ever closer to the edge.

"How are you, baby?" Silas called out to her. "Are you gonna come all over Felix's cock? I want to hear you scream when you do."

Anka moaned again but raised up on all fours and looked over her shoulder at him. "Come here."

It wasn't a request, and Silas wasn't a stupid man, so he rose from his chair and stepped closer to the bed, waiting for her to direct him.

"I want you, too." She blinked up at him, a sublime smile on her face as I pounded into her pussy.

He groaned and climbed onto the bed in front of her, feeding his cock into her mouth when she opened it wide. When he was seated fully he groaned long and low. "Fuck, Anka."

I felt the moan she let out as it reverberated

throughout her body. I looked up at Silas and marveled at the sight of him kneeling before her, a sheen of sweat covering his body, his strong neck corded as he struggled to hold himself in check, so he didn't impale our girl on his cock by accident, his dark eyes almost black as he met my gaze over her. I tipped my head at him with a grin.

"Silas," I gasped out, driving into her and forcing her onto his cock with each thrust.

"Felix," he responded.

"You were right." I grinned at him just as Anka clamped down so hard on my cock as she came that she dragged me right over the cliff with her. I pumped into her until every single drop of my cum was inside her, along with Silas's, so that as I withdrew I watched in fascination as the combination of us both began to leak from her.

Silas was still working toward his orgasm, so I leaned down. "Ass up, love. I'm going to eat this pussy again."

She moaned around Silas's cock, and he cried out, "Fuck, baby. You're going to make me come down this beautiful throat."

I lapped at her, cleaning her up from all we'd pumped into her, drinking the combination of all our pleasure down and reveling in our combined taste. I slid my tongue deep inside her, thrusting with it and feeling her tremble as I ate at her like a man starved. When I had her all cleaned up. I lifted my head and met Silas's eyes, winking at him before I lifted my hands and pulled her pert round cheeks apart, baring her to both our view.

"Are you going to eat that like the dirty boy you are?" Silas grinned at me.

"Absolutely." I lowered my mouth and teased her tight ring of muscle with the tip of my tongue before forcing it inside, dipping it in rhythmically to the sound of her moans and Silas's rapidly deteriorating control.

"Fuck, Felix, if you keep making her moan like that around my cock, I'm going to come down her throat before I'm ready to." He thrust a little harder, and I saw her hands tighten around the sheets.

I lifted my head long enough to grin at him before I returned to the absolute pleasure of giving Anka pleasure. When I slid two fingers into her pussy and my tongue back into her ass I felt her convulse, the orgasm ripped from her and a fresh gush of liquid coated my hand, making me grin proudly as I lifted my head.

"Love, you can squirt?"

"Oh fuck, goddammit..." Silas threw his head back and snapped his hips twice more before he unloaded into her throat, moaning and praising her the whole time.

"You know, for a man who was mostly dead for the past two days, you really outdid yourself there." Anka giggled as she stretched out in the middle of the bed like a cat, arching her back as she grinned up at me.

I leaned down and grabbed the pajama pants I'd

discarded earlier and allowed my eyes to soak in the sight of the both of them utterly blissed out as they snuggled into one another. "I've been waiting a century to make love to you, it would have been poor form to phone it in, don't you think?" I raised a brow at her.

Silas snorted. "He's got a point, babe."

She rolled her eyes and curled into his side, draping an arm over his stomach as she watched me. "Where are you going?"

"Well, someone promised that sweet pup of yours a snack and never delivered. So, I'm going to take care of that and then I'm going to come back to bed." I gave them both a leer.

"Nope." Anka shook her head. "Closed for business for at least twelve hours."

I grinned at her. "We'll see about that."

I padded down the stairs listening to Silas's laughter drifting down from the bedroom, and I couldn't contain the goofy grin that spread across my face.

I wasn't sure this was what anyone else's happily ever after looked like, but I was finally certain that it was what mine looked like, and a sigh of relief crept out of my chest at the thought.

As I rounded the banister headed to the kitchen I saw Mags posted in the doorway staring into the room with her head cocked to the side.

"What is it, girl?" I called, stepping closer.

Maggie wagged her tail but looked up at me like she wasn't sure about what she was seeing.

I stepped into the kitchen and stopped short at the sight of Kyle perched in one of the kitchen chairs instead of his usual refrigerator gargoyle position and I lifted a brow.

"First of all, no, I didn't hear any of that. But *ew*," he stated dryly.

I laughed under my breath. "And second of all?" I asked.

He leveled me with a solemn look. "We have a problem."

To be continued...

Want more of Felix, Silas and Anka and the naughty pastries?

Click here to get the bonus chapter.

AUTHOR'S NOTE:

All I can say is that ONCE AGAIN I planned on this being a one and done and R.A. Hunter ruined my life by telling me this needed to be a duet. At least this time she pointed it out at the beginning instead of after I'd already finished book 1. Trust me though, you'll want to thank her as much as I do for it. I am not a huge fan of cliffhangers, so I tried to be as gentle as I could with this one, please don't send me hate mail. I promise to get the next one to you as fast as is humanly possible, all things considered.

Spoiler alert: you are going to LOVE the story of Felicity and Serafina. I promise it will be worth the wait!

Thank you's:

I'd like to send out a special thank you to my ALPHA readers, Nat and Shelby, you ladies give me life on the daily and I don't have words for how much I love you! To Stacey, the best dev editor a girl could hope for, your love for this book (and ME) has kept me going more than you know! And we cannot forget my incomparable editor, Caroline, who really knows her way around a comma AND is a literal laugh riot. I'm so flipping glad I found you and I'm keeping you forever. I'd be remiss not to mention Mauve Murphy, who stared at me through my computer screen for days on end while I gnashed my teeth until this thing became a real book. I adore you and I cannot WAIT for our beer and taco date.

This thank you section wouldn't be complete without mentioning the beautiful Destiny, who conjured a magically delicious blurb out of the hot-mess unedited manuscript I sent her, and it is fantastic! Thank you, thank you, thank you for saving me from the utter hell of writing my own blurb!

And last, but never least, thank you to Mr. Loren Lee, who makes sure I eat at least once a day while I'm huddled in the writing cave and occasionally reminds me to go outside and breathe in the fresh air. He listens to an unlimited number of unhinged plot ideas without batting an eye and has been known, on occasion, to solve a plot hole that I thought I'd never be able to fix. You're one of the good ones, baby!

ALSO BY LOREN LEE:

Standalone:

Tumble

Series:

The Burn Duet:

Burn

Sate

The Killer & The Siren (novella - tbd)

The Cursed Duet:

Inevitable

Untouchable (2026)

ABOUT THE AUTHOR

Loren currently lives just outside of Atlanta with her husband, the cutest pup known to man, and ~~four~~ *three* succulent plants that she's managed not to kill yet. The thing about the plants could change before the printing of this book, however, so don't hold her to that. She's quite possibly the most awkward person you'll ever meet and she will 100% blurt out something inappropriate if given half a chance. You've been warned.

By day she crunches numbers for her big girl job and by night she crafts stories that are equal parts plot and spice; for when you want your brain *and* your panties involved.

www.authorlorenlee.com/contact